FOREVER

Kozy

MARILYN BORGA

Carpenter's Son Publishing

Forever Kozy

Published by Carpenter's Son Publishing, Franklin, Tennessee

Published in association with Larry Carpenter of Christian Book Services, LLC

www.christianbookservices.com

Scripture taken from THE HOLY BIBLE, NEW INTERNATIONAL VERSION®, NIV® Copyright © 1973, 1978, 1984, 2011 by Biblica, Inc.™ Used by permission. All rights reserved worldwide.

Scripture is used from the New King James Version, © 1982 by Thomas Nelson, Inc. All rights reserved. Used by permission.

Scripture quotations are from the Revised Standard Version of the Bible, copyright © 1946, 1952, and 1971 the Division of Christian Education of the National Council of the Churches of Christ in the United States of America. Used by permission. All rights reserved.

Cover Design by Suzanne Lawing

Interior Design by Adept Content Solutions

Edited by Tammy Kling

Printed in the United States of America

978-1-946889-31-7

Contents

Preface .... *v*

Chapter 1 1

Chapter 2 9

Chapter 3 17

Chapter 4 29

Chapter 5 37

Chapter 6 43

Chapter 7 57

Chapter 8 67

Chapter 9 73

Chapter 10 83

Chapter 11 89

Chapter 12 95

Chapter 13 99

Chapter 14 109

Chapter 15 121

Chapter 16 129

Chapter 17 135

Chapter 18 149

Chapter 19 155

Chapter 20 157

Chapter 21 161

Chapter 25 171

Chapter 23 179

Chapter 24 189

Chapter 25 201

Chapter 26 211

Chapter 27 217

Chapter 28 223

Chapter 29 229

Chapter 30 243

Preface

You will not find Shelby Falls, Ohio on a map. It is solely the product of my imagination. But I hope that the essence of small town America can be seen in these pages. We all need a place to call home; where family and friends, both old and new, can come together often and with joyful acceptance.

All four of my grandparents immigrated to America from Hungary in the late 1800s and early 1900s. This was long before the fictional character in this book, Maria Kozma, escaped from Hungary following the short-lived Hungarian Revolution in 1956. But Maria's hardworking, courageous, faith-filled, and family-oriented life is a reflection of what I have observed in the lives of my Hungarian-American family and friends.

The people in this story are fictional, with the exception of Cardinal Jozsef Mindszenty, Premier Imre Nagy, and Janos Kadar. Each of these men played their roles, both good and bad, in the 1956 Revolution. There is one other exception. There really is a Carrieanne, though some of the details have been changed, and she is no longer on this earth. She was truly an inspiration, and a model of personal strength and faith to all who had the pleasure to know her.

One doesn't have to live long to realize that this world is full of sorrow and struggle. Christians are not immune. We know the way things ought to be, but oftentimes things don't work out as we wish. Perfection won't come until Christ returns in His glory. But meanwhile, our God is all about redemption and hope. He has given us friends as well as biological and church families to help us along the way. As we travel through this life we would do well to reach out to one another. My prayer for you is that the redemptive themes in this story might bring you hope and buoy you up in your journey.

Chapter 1

Shelby Falls, Ohio—2016

Kozy Hanner's head buzzed with a rat-a-tat rhythm as she let herself in the kitchen door and kicked off her shoes. Words bounced through her mind. *Late, late; it's already time for my date … oh!* In the bathroom she inspected her face in the mirror and pinched her freshly washed cheeks. Then she grabbed a brush and ran it through her mop of disheveled, honey-blond locks. Within moments she heard a chirp from her phone and huffed out a frustrated breath. Her friends were already waiting in the driveway. The voice in her head continued as she slipped her shoes back on and rushed out the door. *Run and run and run …* She plastered a bright smile on her face before opening the car door and tumbling into the backseat.

"Hope we didn't rush you too much," her friend Nikki said from the front passenger seat, "but the concert starts in a half hour." She faced Kozy with a slight smirk. "I wanted to make sure you have a few minutes to get acquainted with Nolan." She turned her attention back to the huge purse on her lap and began rummaging through it. "Now where are you hiding, little tickets? Oh—there you are!"

Nikki's husband Ben turned to face Kozy with a benign look and gave her a quick wink. After two years of marriage he had resigned himself to the fact that his wife was a hopeless romantic. She was not going to be satisfied until she had found a perfect match for all of her single friends. "Humor her, *please*," he mouthed silently to Kozy.

Kozy lifted her hands in mock defeat and mildly asked, "How've you been feeling, Nikki?"

"Now that the morning sickness is over, I've never felt better!" she enthused as she shoved her purse to the floor and rubbed her palms over her gently rounded middle. Not to be deterred, she continued. "I don't know why it never occurred to me to get you two together before this. You are going to *love* Nolan! He's perfect for you."

"Hmmm" was Kozy's noncommittal reply. *As were each of the other three guys you set me up with*, she was tempted to say. But Nikki meant well, so why not be a good sport? At least she wouldn't be spending Friday night alone. She wiggled her back to ease the tension, determined to enjoy the coming evening as Ben backed out of the driveway and headed the car toward the Performing Arts Center. As the couple chatted together in the front seat, Kozy's thoughts returned to the parent-teacher conference that had made her late getting home. She had almost given up by the time Shaina's mother finally made her appearance. From the very first day of classes three weeks ago, Kozy had sensed that the little third grader was struggling. The meeting today had only intensified her concern. Something was not right in the little girl's home; she was sure of it. If only she had the power to help. She closed her eyes. *My precious heavenly Father.* "Abba," she whispered faintly. *I ask you to protect each of my little ones, especially Shaina. I don't know all that's going on with her but you do. Watch over her. Show me how to be a blessing to her. Give me the wisdom I need to show her your love for her.*

Nolan Calderon straightened his tie and bent to check his hair in the side mirror as he waited in the parking lot. He promised himself that this would be *the* final time he would agree to be set up for a blind date. It was only his long-term friendship with Ben that had made him give in to Nikki's persistent wheedling. It made him feel foolish, as though at twenty-six he wasn't fully capable of finding a date of his own choosing. He hated the idea of making small talk with someone he felt must be sizing him up as a potential mate. Pushing the annoying feelings aside, he forced himself to think of other things.

He contemplated the good fortune that had landed him a decent job back in Shelby Falls after having worked out of state for several years. He fully appreciated the good life to be had in the small Ohio city that had been his hometown since childhood. Living within a mile of his father, stepmother, and younger brother and sister was a blessing he never failed to be grateful for. He enjoyed nearly every aspect of his job in the accounting office of Marley Financial Services. Working for the small company gave him the chance to learn more aspects of the business than his former job at a large corporation had allowed. He was providing a much-needed service to his clients. It gave him a sense of satisfaction when he knew he was using his God-given talents to help people. In spite of his pep talk Nolan frowned.

Life is never perfect. Just handle it.

Soon Ben's dusty red Ford Escape SUV pulled into the spot next to Nolan with a slight squeal of tires. Ben helped his wife out of the vehicle and Nolan stepped over to open the back door for his date. While waiting the few moments for introductions to be made he focused his attention on her face and away from the clothing of the petite young woman who stood before him smiling. Surely they hadn't failed to mention to her what kind of event they were attending. His eyes involuntarily made another lightning-quick sweep of the outfit: hot pink slacks and powder blue shirt on which iridescent sequins framed the cartoon image of a girl with blond braided hair. He managed a weak grin.

After the uncomfortable introductions Nolan began sorting it out. *All right. Granted, she's a third grade teacher; that may have something to do with it. Have things changed that much since I was in grade school? Nikki, you may have pushed the limit this time. Kozy? Even her name seems kind of silly.*

Yet, Kozy Hanner *was* pleasant enough to look at once he could draw his attention away from the outlandish-looking outfit. Her delicate face with its clean, natural complexion was framed by soft golden curls that glowed in the late afternoon sunlight. She looked steadily at him with deep-set brown eyes as Nikki chatted away, oblivious to any awkwardness. Nolan forced himself to concentrate and pretend that he was merely greeting a visitor at church. A friendly smile, a few well-chosen, polite questions—he could do that much. He cast a sideways glance at Ben. Though his best childhood friend wore a sober expression, the slight twitch at the corner of his mouth gave away the fact that he was getting a kick out of Nolan's discomfort. Nolan mentally growled as the four headed for the main entrance. *I'll make the best of this, old buddy, but you'll owe me one after tonight.*

Later that evening, Kozy sat cross-legged on her bed, her prayer journal in her lap. She ran a hand through her hair and selected a purple gel pen from the collection of writing utensils on her nightstand. She closed her eyes, softly tapping the side of the pen against the slight cleft of her chin, before writing in her round, distinctive script.

> *OK, so tonight was a little awkward, but I did enjoy meeting Nolan Calderon. It took me awhile to realize who he is and the fact that our paths are likely to cross once more even if we never officially go out again. He seemed as wary of the blind date as I was. Sweet Nikki—I do appreciate her friendship; she means well with her matchmaking aspirations. If only I wouldn't get so tongue-tied when I'm one-on-one with a stranger—especially a good-looking man! I seem to have no trouble in the classroom or in front of a crowd, but this dating stuff!*

She shut her eyes and winced in her frustration. Nolan had been polite; perfect almost. But the reserve in his demeanor had ruffled her feelings, transporting her back to the part of her childhood she didn't like to think about.

> *Sometimes I feel like I'm right back on the playground and the kids are pointing at me, ready to taunt me.*

She frowned as she wrote.

> *I know I should be so over this—I'm your child! But the feelings crop up sometimes. Help me (again!) to give the past to you.*

Did I sense a little sadness in Nolan? If so, I ask that you might heal his hurts and bring him joy. And if I happen to have any part in that healing process, then I will be grateful for the chance to serve you. I love you forever, Your Kozy.

A mile away, Nolan Calderon lay on his back, elbows out, head resting on his hands. He stared into the inky darkness above his bed. He had enjoyed the evening, in spite of everything. Perhaps he had needed to do something outside of his ordinary routine with the comfort of old friends. He shook his head and almost chuckled at the remembrance of the most awkward moments of the evening. The concert had been a combination of local bands with an eclectic mix of styles: a little country, some gospel, soft and hard rock. When intermission started he had invited his date to join him for a stroll to the lobby. Once they realized the music could be heard from there, they sat at a table and sipped cups of the herbal tea that the venue was famous for. The conversation seemed a bit more relaxed without their friends hovering over them.

Things were going well until someone accidentally bumped into their table and Nolan's napkin went sailing to the floor. Reaching to pick it up he chanced to glance at his date's feet. Too late, he tried to mask his expression, but she had been watching his face and was quick to notice. She looked down. Her mouth gaped and her cheeks blushed pink as she wiggled her feet. Then she *giggled.* Her feet were clad in powder blue glittery slippers—noticeably *mismatched* slippers. How many women would own not one, but *two* pairs of shoes that color? And as if that were not enough, she had managed to don both left feet.

Nolan felt his face flush all over again as he rehashed the moment. The worst of it was the realization that the fashion gaffe had bothered him more than it had her. She had handled the situation with humor. If a similar thing had happened to him … *fat chance of that* … he would have felt utterly *mortified.* That's what was most disturbing. When had he become so uptight—so unable to laugh at himself? Not really *uptight,* he reasoned, but *serious.* He had always been serious-minded in his responsibilities, his relationships, and his faith. Just as well that he had not asked for her number. He was under no obligation to see her again. They were about as mismatched as those silly-looking slippers.

***

Kozy hurried into the teacher's lounge on Monday morning and deposited her lunch bag in the refrigerator. She turned to greet her team teacher, Cathy Dawson, who was relaxing in an armchair, feet propped on a shabby, but sturdy looking coffee table. Kozy smiled at the older woman who, in the last three years, had quickly evolved from being merely a new co-worker to becoming a mentor and a best friend.

"All right, all right," Kozy said with a chuckle, "I can tell by the look on your face that you are dying to know about my date, and I can guess exactly what you will ask! I'll answer the questions you are about to ask with a 'yes,' 'yes,' and another 'yes.'"

"Well then," Cathy responded as she ran her fingers through her short-cropped salt-and-pepper hair. "I will take the challenge and try to guess the appropriate questions! Number one: Did you have an enjoyable evening? I assume the answer to that is 'yes'?"

With a twisted smile Kozy nodded.

"Second question: Is he good looking?"

"Actually, yes," Kozy answered emphatically, "I think he's wildly handsome, but in a stiff sort of way."

"I can tell that is going to be a topic of discussion for later. Question number three: Will you be seeing him again?"

"Well," she answered with a sigh, "I am pretty sure I'll see him again. Though whether he will ever actually ask me out again is up for grabs. And that is all that I will say for now because our third-graders will be arriving soon and I have some work to go over before they arrive."

"Talk about leaving a person in suspense," laughed Cathy. "How about we resume this topic after school at my house? I have stew in the crock pot that I'd be happy to share. Five-thirty?"

"Make it six o'clock to give me time to make some brownies to share and it's a deal."

***

At quarter of six that evening, Cathy set two plates on her dining room table and placed utensils and napkins beside them. Walking back into the kitchen, she contemplated the bond that she had formed with her co-worker at Central Elementary.

Cathy was grateful for the teaching job that had allowed her to support her two teen-agers after the illness and death of her husband ten years ago. A veteran teacher for over twenty years, she had had mixed feelings when, three years ago, she found that she would be sharing teaching duties with a new and inexperienced teacher. When she first caught sight of Miss Kozy Hanner, she was surprised by, and a little wary of, the fresh-faced girl dressed in a frilly pink shirt and slacks outfit that looked like it could have come directly from the children's department at the local department store. Her matching pink shoes had been accented with powder blue laces, her hair rather unsuccessfully held at bay by several sparkly hair barrettes. Cathy had been somewhat shocked at what she considered an unprofessional manner of dress, but she wisely held her tongue and decided to give the young woman the benefit of the doubt. In the days to come, she was glad that she had reserved judgment as she saw the immediate rapport Kozy held with the third-grade girls. It was as though the young woman remembered exactly what it felt like to be eight years old. Even the young boys in the class seemed to be drawn to this person who seemed to be one of them, only bigger.

While Cathy taught math and science for the two classrooms, Kozy handled the language arts courses. She quickly found out that Kozy, in spite of her sometimes-unorthodox manner of dress, was a serious teacher, eager to guide her students to be the best that they could be. Cathy saw in her an energy and enthusiasm that was inspiring, and she soon felt her own passion for teaching being rejuvenated. They found that by respecting one another's individual teaching methods their team teaching could be both effective and enjoyable.

Cathy's youngest child had recently finished college, moved away, and had begun a career that left her little time to spend with her mother. Rather than mope about and becoming the very definition of an empty-nester, Cathy instead decided to look upon the opportunity of teaching with a new teacher as an unexpected gift. She was also pleased that Kozy looked to her for guidance, rather than considering her an outdated relic. Kozy seemed confident in her own ability to relate to her students, but she also had the wisdom to know the value of experience. She often asked Cathy her opinion on things when she needed advice.

As Kozy's first weeks of teaching had progressed, she and Cathy had acclimated to working as a team. It hadn't taken long for a true friendship to bloom. In the teachers' lounge in those first days, while other teachers commented about their various family situations and relationships, Kozy was friendly but had remained reserved. Cathy decided to invite Kozy to breakfast one Saturday. As the two of them sat across from each other over their meal, Cathy chatted about her own family and then casually questioned Kozy, "So, you know a little about me and my life outside the classroom. You've not said much to any of us about your home life. I hope I'm not being too forward in asking about your family. I've just been curious."

She waited uncomfortably as Kozy hesitated. "I'm sorry if I seem to be prying," Cathy said quickly. "Please don't feel you have to answer. I was just trying to be friendly."

"Oh, Cathy, I'm not offended or anything—please, never think that. I hesitate only because I feel a little shy, and sometimes I don't quite know what to say. The reason I don't say much when the others are talking about their families is that, you see—I don't have any family. My last living relative, my grandmother, died around the time I was finishing my degree." She flicked at a tear that formed at the corner of her eye. "Sorry. I still feel a little tender, you know?"

Cathy nodded. "That's understandable. No need to apologize."

That breakfast was the first of many meals the two women had shared over the past three years. As their friendship progressed, Kozy had, little by little, revealed more to Cathy about her troubled childhood. Many times she shared about how she came to be raised, and nurtured into adulthood, by her grandmother, who happened to be a Hungarian immigrant.

Chapter 2

Cleveland, Ohio, March 7, 1997

Maria Kozma shuffled her way to the back of the stuffy Greyhound bus. She smiled shyly at the couple to her right and excused herself as she inadvertently bumped her suitcase on their seat. As she settled herself into the window seat in the empty row behind them she prayed that she would not be called upon to make small talk with anyone. She didn't feel capable of carrying on a conversation today. She glanced at the distorted image of herself in the security mirror on the bus. The straight graying hair that framed her oval face still showed a good portion of brown. Her hazel eyes, deep set and sad, looked back at her. The mirror played with her face as she moved, pulling at first one feature and then another. Like her emotions this week, she thought, pulling her in all directions until she felt utterly drained.

A week before, she had received word from the police in San Diego that her only child, her precious Betsy, had been found dead of a drug overdose. She had to force herself to keep breathing while she had talked with an officer on the phone. Her heart threatened to beat out of her chest and then, as she realized that her worst fear had come to pass, she thought her heart might stop altogether.

She had been asked to identify her daughter's body and claim her personal possessions. More importantly, a social worker asked her if she was willing to take custody of her daughter's only child, who had been in protective foster care for the past four years. The news that she had a grandchild was not a total surprise to Maria. The last time she had seen her daughter nearly nine years ago, Betsy had admitted that she was carrying Ted Hanner's child. Maria had begged Betsy to leave her boyfriend and come home with her. But Betsy had been determined to follow Ted to California. Maria wondered if she should have tried harder to see some good in the restless young man her daughter had fallen in love with. In the end, Betsy had been angry and determined to go her own way. She left and cut off all contact with her mother, which had nearly broken Maria's heart. And now Betsy was dead. Now, the granddaughter she had never seen was her last link to Betsy.

Willing to take custody? How could I not?

Stranger or not, this child was family and Maria would do everything within her power to take care of her.

Last week, when she sought the solace of her friends, the ladies at the Hungarian Reformed Church on Kossuth Street had rallied around her. They quickly took an offering and raised enough money for bus fare. There was even a generous amount left over for the necessary food and shelter she would require for her trip. Maria wouldn't have to dig too deeply into her savings, at least not yet. Those funds would be needed in the near future for her granddaughter's care. One of her closest friends had offered to make the journey with her. She was sorely tempted to accept the offer of companionship; the very idea of making such a long journey alone was terrifying to her. But in the end she had decided that the circumstances were too personal and her feelings too raw for her to lay that burden on even her dearest friend. She appreciated their love and prayers, but she decided that this trial she must face on her own. God would be her companion. She knew from past experience that He would carry her through.

This journey from Cleveland to San Diego would be the longest trip she had taken since the one that had brought her to America. Her mind traveled back in time; to the days before she and her brother began making the plans that would take them on a perilous journey to escape Hungary.

***

The Hegedus family had lived through the Second World War. They had faced terror and starvation, yet had managed to somehow survive. Twice they had to flee their home as German and Soviet forces began a vicious tug-of-war over possession of Hungary. Finally, in 1945, Germany was defeated, and with that victory came the hope of peace. But jubilation over the war's end was soon replaced with foreboding when the people realized that life under the Soviets was going to be every bit as oppressive as when they were under Nazi rule.

Nearly every aspect of life had been affected by the new Soviet regime. The Communist coat of arms was added to the red, white, and green Hungarian flag. Churches were intimidated by the authorities and soon purged of the original leaders. Cardinal Jozsef Mindszenty, beloved head of the Catholic Church, was arrested, tortured, and sentenced to life in prison. Names of holidays were changed; even streets named after Hungarian heroes were renamed to honor Russian Communists. Communist propaganda newspapers were delivered to every household, assuring the people that a new utopia was on the horizon. Even the children recognized the lie. If things were so good, why were they still hungry? Why was everyone afraid?

Parents dared not speak freely in front of their children because the AVH, the Hungarian Secret Police, were everywhere. Any neighbor might prove to be an informant. A careless remark, even an innocent one repeated by a child, could be misconstrued and might result in one being labeled a kulak, an enemy of the state. Any person who resisted signing over his own personal property to the state was considered to be the very worst kulak. Maria's parents had suffered so much loss during and after the war that they could see little reason to risk imprisonment or deportation to a Russian slave labor camp by refusing to give up their meager property to the state. The government would win, one way or another, regardless of how they resisted. Instead, they took the advice of a distant relative who had a good standing in the Communist party and sought and received permission to move from their home village to a small city just north of Budapest. There, Maria's father was able to find work, thanks to that same relative. Life wasn't easy, but it was at least tolerable.

Maria's brother, Miklos, was bright and ambitious. He admired and revered a great uncle, who had lived for a while in America before coming back to live in his small village. The stories Miklos heard at the knee of this old man had awakened in him a longing to study history, and to travel and see the world. But Miklos's teenage years were spent under communist rule with the government dictating where he could go and what he could learn. When he was chosen to attend university in Budapest, he was first elated but then sorely disappointed when he was forced to study chemical engineering instead of his beloved history. As time passed, the lack of freedom became like a festering sore to Miklos. Each new injustice he experienced brought with it more bitterness. He began to listen quietly whenever he heard whispers of resistance.

Then came the day that held the promise of change: October 23, 1956. Thousands of students marched through central Budapest protesting the deplorable conditions in Soviet-controlled Hungary. Maria could remember sitting with her parents as they huddled together over their tiny radio, listening to the student demands on the Radio Free Europe broadcast. The students were asking for withdrawal of Soviet troops, freedom of speech, press, radio, and other simple rights. Maria remembered the looks of concern and fear on her parents' faces. They suspected their son was involved in the protests, though they dared not ask him about it. It was best to not know details, in case they were ever questioned by the authorities.

In the chaos of the demonstrations that day, a student was shot by the AVH and the Hungarian Revolution began in earnest. Disorder and violence broke out in Budapest and quickly spread to other cities across the country. Protestors, mostly unarmed, marched through the streets of Budapest, tearing down symbols of communism and freeing political prisoners from the notorious 60 Andrassy Street Prison. The AVH opened fire and eight more students were killed. Newly elected Premier Imre Nagy negotiated with Moscow and on October 30, Russian troops withdrew from Budapest. For a few short days, from October 29 until November 3, it appeared that Hungary might actually experience freedom. Premier Nagy appealed to the United Nations for protection, but the world was silent. On November 4, a thousand Soviet tanks rolled into Budapest. By November 10, the Freedom Fighters, as they came to be called, were crushed. The Hungarian Revolution was over.

By mid-November, the renewed Soviet control over Hungary was nearly complete. The newly appointed Hungarian leader, Janos Kadar, was eager to take revenge on the rebellious students. Anyone suspected of having been involved in the uprising, no matter how remotely, was being sought and faced imprisonment, deportation, torture, or death. Miklos made his way back to his parents' home, but it was evident that he was in great danger because of his involvement in the protests. It was only a matter of time before the news would leak to the authorities. In secret, his family did all they could to prepare him for his flight out of the country, providing warm clothing, money, and food.

Maria had made two trips to the university to visit Miklos in the early part of October. Listening to her older brother and his friends as they debated the possibility of resistance, Maria had been caught up in the students' heady dream of freedom. Although Maria had had no direct involvement in the student protests, Miklos feared that she could face interrogation from the authorities because of her visits to the university. News was already leaking of the torture and execution of some of his friends. Maria's parents were terrified at what might happen to her if she were suspected to have had anything to do with the revolutionaries. They had seen firsthand the brutality the soldiers had demonstrated during the war years. Maria was now a pretty and shapely young woman, and they feared that she had already caught the lustful eyes of some of the Soviet soldiers. They gave their tearful consent when Miklos begged his sister to make her escape with him. It was urgent that they act quickly. Within a week, Miklos and Maria Hegedus had become two of the nearly 200,000 Hungarians who fled the country in the months following the Revolution.

She often wondered if she would have made the same decision had she had more time to think about the sacrifice she was making. She never again saw her parents face to face. The letters they had exchanged were precious to Maria but still a poor substitute when she longed to hold her loved ones in her arms. And not being there for them in their final days; it still hurt her to think about it. Yes, the cost of freedom was great.

It had been so long ago, nearly forty years. She remembered the details, but the emotions were no longer raw. As Maria stared out the bus window at the passing countryside, she pondered how she could now look back on those events with an odd sense of detachment. It was as though she were watching a film of someone else's life. But it was not a movie; it had been her life. It was she and Miklos who boarded a crowded train that cold day in late November, the day that had changed her destiny.

The radio announced that the trains would be resuming limited runs to the western cities that morning. Their safety had been in the masses of people who, like them, were headed for the trains. The streets were teeming with Russian troops, but there were not enough guards to check everyone's identification and keep order. Maria and her brother were able to push their way into a crowded car in the middle of the train. They stood packed tight against the other passengers as the train made its way toward Gyor. A small number of people got off at each stop, but they were immediately replaced by newcomers. The fact that Miklos and Maria had neither tickets nor travel documents did not pose a problem since the conductor was unable to make his way through the chaos of the crowded cars. The town of Csorna was the closest the train would come to the Austrian border, and there they got off, along with hundreds of other passengers. The security guards only managed to check a handful of identifications while the rest of the people ran helter-skelter away from the railway station and into the surrounding countryside.

For the next two days they traveled only at night. They moved over frozen fields and marshlands, occasionally fording small creeks. During the day they hid in barns or haystacks. Maria remembered a time, early in the first day of travel, when she had been completely terrified. They heard the sound of heavy boots approaching their hiding place; her heart had pounded so heavily it felt as if it would explode. She nearly sobbed with relief when it turned out to be a sympathetic farmer who quietly offered them a loaf of brown bread and a cup of warm milk fresh from his cow's udder. In the early morning hours of what was to be their last day in Hungary, they managed to commandeer a makeshift raft and cross the border canal near the village of Andau in Austria. They found out later that at least twenty Hungarians had been shot that night trying to cross the Austrian-Hungarian border. It was a miracle that they had survived.

During the winter months that followed, Maria and Miklos were relocated from one crowded refugee camp to another. They separated when Miklos made the decision to go to Canada, specifically Toronto, under the sponsorship of a distant relative there. Maria instead chose to hold onto her dream of going to the United States.

Maria eventually made her way to the Buckeye Road community in Cleveland in the spring of 1957. Thanks to her sponsors at the Kossuth Street Church, she soon found a job in a small factory. She studied English in the evenings. After a year and a half, her hard study and practice paid off. Although she retained her strong Hungarian accent, she felt confident in her ability to understand English. She lived frugally, and saved enough money to enroll in a nearby community college to learn the history of America. The next item on her agenda was to apply for citizenship in her adopted country.

Shortly after attaining her citizenship, Maria met John Kozma, a man who had journeyed from Hungary to America in 1945 after having been displaced by the war. When he let her know he was interested in courting her, she paused to take a good look at the man. He was a widower, had no children, and was nearly fourteen years older than her. He was certainly not a young and dashing prince who would sweep her off her feet with promises he could not keep. Instead, he was a modest, gentle, and hardworking man. Once they were married, he proved to be a steady and honest husband with a ready laugh. He showed his love by coming home each evening, eating her home-cooked meals with appreciation, and listening to the accounts of her day with respect and interest. When they were eventually blessed with a child, John proved to be a patient and loving father. Maria missed his quiet presence still, though it had been ten years since his passing.

The Greyhound bus rolled on into the night, silent except for the drone of its tires on the highway, and an occasional snore from one of the passengers. Maria smiled wistfully, remembering those early years of her marriage. Cushioned by her rolled up sweater, she rested her head against the window and tried to imagine what the future would hold for her.

Late the next day, ignoring her stiff joints and swollen ankles, Maria stepped off the bus and found a cab to take her to the modest hotel that the policeman had arranged for her. She checked herself in, took a hot shower, and fell into the bed, dropping off immediately into a merciful dreamless sleep.

Chapter 3

Cathy had her hands in the dishwater when she heard the doorbell shortly after six o'clock.

"Come on in, Kozy," she called through the kitchen door. "You can take your brownies right into the dining room. Everything else is ready."

Once they sat down to the simple beef stew dinner, it didn't take much prompting for Kozy to telling Cathy all about her recent blind date. After stabbing a piece of the tender beef with her fork and tasting it, she closed her eyes and sighed.

"Mmmm, this is absolutely awesome, Cathy! Thanks so much for inviting me. Besides having a scrumptious meal, I'm really glad to have a chance to talk over my impressions of Friday night."

Cathy nodded expectantly, smiling at her friend. "I'm all ears, kiddo. Give me some details!"

Kozy took a sip of water. "Well, the evening began in kind of a rush. Wouldn't you know, the first date I've had in who knows how long and I happened to have scheduled a parent-teacher conference after school that night—with Shaina's mother." She sighed in frustration.

"Shaina's not doing too well in my classes either," Cathy admitted.

"I waited over an hour. When she finally showed up, she didn't even seem to pay attention to what I was saying, but at least I tried. Anyway, once I got home and saw how late I was, I realized that I didn't even have time to change my clothes. Just a quick face wash and I was slipping my shoes back on and was out the door."

Cathy tried to hide her grimace with a smile, but Kozy was quick to see.

"Yeah, I know," Kozy wrinkled her nose. "Wearing my 'Friday frills' wasn't the ideal choice for a first date." She shrugged. "Of course, I realized that once we arrived at the parking lot of the concert hall, but it was too late to do anything about it. My date, Nolan Calderon, was dressed impeccably for the evening in a sport coat and tie. Not overly formal, but appropriate for the venue. It made me realize how silly I must look to him, which made me feel kind of inadequate, which in turn made me chatter on about nothing. I tend to do that when I'm nervous and first meet someone. Either that or I clam up because I can't think of a single thing to talk about."

Cathy thought it ironic that her friend should think herself inadequate in any way. Besides being exceptionally pretty, Kozy was an excellent teacher. She was intelligent, sensible, kind, and fun to be with. She was a girl any decent young man should love to date. Cathy could understand why her friend's childhood traumas had a negative effect on her self-esteem, but she hated to see Kozy carry those burdens into adulthood. She and Kozy had talked about it before, so Cathy decided to let it go for the time being. Instead she commented, "Calderon—that sounds familiar. Does your date happen to be related to the pastor at Grace Community Church?"

Kozy nodded. "Nolan is the pastor's son. As soon as our mutual friends introduced us, I realized why he looked familiar to me. I had recently met with Pastor Tom Calderon about my speaking at their special series of youth meetings at Grace next week. Besides noticing the family resemblance, I also recalled seeing Nolan in Pastor Tom's family portrait in his office. The evening of our date, I was so flustered that I failed to mention that I recognized him from the picture. It was time for the concert so we just hurried on in."

"Ah," Cathy said. "So that's why you believe you'll likely be seeing your blind date again!"

"I've committed to helping out for the entire series of events at the church, so I figure I'm bound to run into him again sometime." Kozy stared at her plate awhile, seemingly lost in thought.

Cathy waited a few moments before asking gently, "A little nervous about the speaking commitment?"

"No. Well, yes, of course I am a little nervous," she admitted. "I know it won't be easy. But it's another plunge I feel God is urging me to take." She smiled at the question in her friend's eyes.

"Plunge?"

Her smile twisted a little as she explained. "It's like getting into an icy-cold swimming pool. By nature, I'm more inclined to be the timid person who wants to ease into the water inch by inch, even though doing so just draws out the misery. You know better than anybody the baggage I still carry about my childhood, and how it's hard for me to open up with people, especially those my own age. I never wanted to talk about my past life, even with my grandma. After I became a Christian, I gave my testimony at our church and finally faced my feelings. It felt like that plunge into the cold water. But after the initial shock and discomfort, I was relieved of a burden I barely realized I had. Even though my grandmother's friends already knew my background, it was a relief to have it out in the open. I found it easier to relate to my friends in the youth group. Moving here, though, I was starting over and I kind of retreated back into my old habits. A few weeks ago when I heard about the planned youth series and the need for volunteers, I just couldn't get the idea out of my head that God wanted me to jump right in. I do truly want to help the youth in the community."

"Good for you, my friend," she said. "I have total confidence that you will be an encouragement to all involved. But I'm afraid I've diverted us from the subject of the blind date! You made the statement this morning that—how did you put it? 'Nolan is wildly handsome in a stiff sort of way.' Whatever did you mean by that?"

Kozy took the time to butter her roll before answering, "I definitely find Nolan attractive. He's about five foot ten. He has a trim build. I'd bet he runs or plays sports to stay fit, and he's got a sweet smile and blue-gray eyes. He's clean shaven and has thick dark brown hair, neatly cut with not a hair out of place." She chuckled with a pat of her own curls, which often seemed as though they had a mind of their own. "I saw lots of women turn an appreciative eye his way, though he was too polite to appear to notice. The stiffness I refer to wasn't as much in the way he looked, but more something I perceived in his personality. While being perfectly polite and cordial, he seemed at the same time to be, well, a little stand-offish as if afraid of opening up too much."

"But you said you had a good time." Cathy responded.

"I did. Nikki and Ben are fun to be with. They're in my small group at the church I've been attending. I guess Ben has been friends with Nolan since childhood. Nikki just had to have one more try at setting me up." Kozy smiled ruefully. "At the concert Nolan invited me to go out to the lobby during the intermission for a cup of tea."

"So, you talked then?" Cathy prompted.

"Yes, he kept the conversation focused on our careers mostly. He's an accountant and works for Marley Financial Services. He told me the basics about college, how he came to get the job a couple years ago in his hometown after several years working in another state. And he gave me the gist of what his job now involves. He asked about my experiences in the classroom. He was a perfect gentleman, smiling and nodding in all the right places; then he bent down to pick something up from the floor and got a look at my feet." Kozy blushed as she continued her story.

"When I saw the change in his expression, I looked down. In my rush to leave my house for the concert, I had accidently donned two mismatched shoes! Both were blue, but they were different enough to be pretty noticeable. To add insult to injury, I had also managed to put on both left feet! I realized then why my toes had been feeling so cramped. My blind date jitters did me in. I started laughing and couldn't stop for the longest time. Have you ever had that happen? But Nolan just sat there looking more and more uncomfortable. Once I was finally able to talk, the only thing I could think of to say was the corny joke, 'I have another pair of shoes exactly like this at home!'"

Cathy delighted in the story. "Do you mean to tell me," she hooted as she swiped at tears, "that this guy couldn't find *any* humor in the situation?"

"Oh, he managed to let out a chuckle at my comment, but it seemed to be rather forced. I think he was just embarrassed for me, and he only laughed because he felt it would be the proper thing to do. By then, I just didn't worry anymore whether Nolan Calderon liked me or not. I decided I was going to have fun the rest of the evening, and I did!"

"Seems to me that your date needs to learn to lighten up and enjoy life more."

"Well Cathy, if I ever get the chance to be his friend, I'm determined to do all I can to help him with that!"

***

Tom Calderon put the finishing touches on his outline before forwarding it to the church secretary's computer. "Helen," he wrote, "would you mind looking this over to see if I've forgotten anything? Thanks so much!" He prayed a silent prayer of gratitude for the woman who had worked with him the past sixteen years. He knew that she considered her position as much more than a mere job. The job was Helen's ministry. Her cheerful disposition, efficiency, and diplomacy were true assets. Tom could count on the fact that anything said in confidence in the church office would remain right there.

An email quickly popped up from Helen. "Will do!" she said. "And Pastor, do you have a scripture in mind yet for this week's bulletin?"

"I'd like 2 Corinthians 10: 4–5," he answered. "Use the Living Bible version please, Helen."

"Good one, Pastor!" she responded after a few minutes. "That ought to prompt us to be praying for the teens."

Helen could be counted on to have a heart for the teens in the church. She had been extremely helpful in planning the upcoming fall youth event series and wanted it to be a success as much as he. Tom, along with the youth pastor, Dan Kollar, and the crew of adult volunteers had spent months in prayer about what could be done to impact the lives of their teens. They faced many temptations and problems that could easily overwhelm them and draw them away from the church. The churches in the Shelby Falls community did not have as heavy a burden as churches in the inner cities. Still, they were not immune from the problems that drugs, alcohol, depression, sexual temptations, divorce, and abandonment brought on for the teens.

"More Than Conquerors" was the name chosen for the planned six-week series. The idea came from the verses in Romans 8:35 and 37: "*Who shall separate us from the love of Christ? Shall tribulation, or distress, or persecution, or famine, or nakedness, or peril or sword? Yet in all these things we are more than conquerors through Him who loved us.*"

Although the words may seem old-fashioned in modern times, Tom easily translated the core meanings to the problems facing the young people of today: the tribulation of drug and alcohol addiction, the distress in feelings of loneliness and alienation, and the persecution of peer pressure. Tom could picture the famine and nakedness in the yearnings of those who longed for purpose and meaning in life. And peril and sword? One need only watch a few moments of the evening news to know the horrors of the ever-increasing violence in the world. Tom knew that the only real solution to overcoming these things was a lasting faith in Jesus Christ.

The plan for the first three weeks was to have speakers from the community give their testimonies to the youth group; one speaker per Sunday. During the successive Sunday evening meetings there would be question/answer sessions giving the youth opportunities to ask questions. The Wednesday meetings would be reserved for small groups with the guest speakers and the youth volunteer leaders forming small groups with the teens.

They had sought local Christians in their mid-twenties who had overcome various obstacles and gone on to become successful and model citizens in the community. The age of the speakers was a key aspect because the "twenty-somethings" were old enough to have come to maturity, yet not so old as to have their stories seem like ancient history to the audience. Tom himself had recently turned fifty-four and he remembered ruefully how, as a sixteen-year-old, he had thought that fifty was "over the hill." He was confident that each of the featured speakers who had been recommended to him would be able relate to the youth, and especially to ones who may be at risk. The hope was that in the small group Bible studies, the teens would be open to sharing about any problems they were facing. Volunteers would be available to help where needed.

After meeting with Kozy Hanner a few weeks ago, Tom was convinced that she would be an excellent choice for the opening night speaker. An attractive and personable young woman with a compelling story to tell, she also demonstrated a sincere concern for children and teens. Her faith in Christ appeared to be genuine and solid and, Tom hoped, would prove to be infectious with her audience.

The success of the program was especially important to Tom this year since his twin son and daughter, Zane and Kelsey, were nearing their thirteenth birthdays. The twins were the blessings of his middle age, born to him and his wife Marcy when his firstborn, Nolan, was fourteen. Tom's first wife, Nolan's mother, Sharon, had died when Nolan was only ten. Tom was amazed at how fast the world had changed from the time Nolan was a child to the present day. Most of the changes he found alarming as a father, and as a pastor. But he took hope in one of his favorite verses from the Bible, *"In this world, you will have trouble. But take heart! I have overcome the world."*

***

The next Sunday evening at Grace Community Church, Kozy peeked out at the noisy crowd of teens seated in the small auditorium. Smiling shyly, she told Pastor Calderon, "Give me just a few moments please," as she slipped into the quiet of the hallway. She lowered herself into a folding chair, hugging her arms around the queasiness in her stomach. She took a deep breath and closed her eyes.

Give me the courage to do this, Lord. Help me set aside my fears and just tell these kids what you have done for me and what you long to do for them. I ask that your Spirit would speak through me tonight. Help their ears to hear and their minds to understand what you would have them learn from my testimony tonight.

As she stood she felt a gentle peace settle over her. *I can do this.* She stepped back into the room and, nodding to Pastor Tom, waited while he introduced her as Miss Hanner, a teacher at Central Elementary School. The teens quieted somewhat, gave her mild applause, and most, but not all, turned their attention her way.

One boy in the crowd, an African-American boy with long dreadlocks dyed a bright purple, called out, "Hey, Lady! I know who you are! My little sister has you for a teacher!"

"And who would that be?" asked Kozy.

"Jasmine Taylor," the boy answered. "And my name is Michael."

Kozy was momentarily confused, remembering that Jasmine was of Chinese descent. Then she recalled talking with Jasmine's mother, a distinctly Caucasian woman and recalled her telling that she had several adopted children. "Ah, yes!" Kozy said with a nod, "I should have known! You both have such beautiful smiles. It's nice to meet you, Michael." The boy grinned and stood to high-five his friends before sitting back down. With that, the room erupted in laughter. As the room grew quiet, Kozy began to speak.

"I'd like you to imagine with me a little girl, about four years old, a girl with tousled hair and smudges of dirt on her face. She's sleeping peacefully in her bed in a shabby rented ranch house in rural southern California. It's stifling hot and quiet except for the occasional buzzing of a fly in the room. The silence is shattered by a loud and frantic shout. The child's mother grabs her from her bed and carries her into the kitchen. She struggles as her mother holds her in a firm grip. She hears more shouting and the sound of breaking glass as bullets shatter windows and ping into the adobe walls. She tries to understand what is happening as her mother, arms trembling, sinks to the floor and holds her even tighter. Then a BOOM drowns out the other sounds. The little girl begins to scream."

The room was still now; all eyes were focused on her. "I was that little girl," Kozy confessed before taking a deep breath and continuing.

"My father had been running illegal drugs for a cartel. He had tried to quit, but that's not an easy thing to do when you know too much about violent people. They had found where we were hiding and had the house surrounded. My father shot at the refrigerator to let them know that he was armed. This was probably the thing that saved us. When the men outside heard the shotgun blast, they hesitated. And in the moments that they waited, sirens began to wail in the distance. This created chaos with men shouting and running to their cars. But the police sting was very well organized, and every man was rounded up and taken away in police cars, including my father. I never saw him again."

She paced back and forth across the platform for a few moments. "I was too young to understand it at the time, but my mother had become a drug addict. Mrs. Gonzales from the child protective services took me away." Kozy paused and scanned the faces of the young people before her. *I've got their attention now.* She forced herself to continue with her carefully rehearsed narrative.

"A foster family took me in that night and I stayed with them for quite a while, maybe close to a year. I don't remember much about that place except that I felt scared for a long time." Kozy went on to describe her emotions as she was moved to three more foster homes in as many years. "About the time I would start feeling like I belonged, I'd have to get used to a new family and new rules. And I never got over the longing to truly belong to someone who would love me forever and not leave me. When I was eight years old, my caseworker came to tell me that my grandmother, a woman I had never met, had come to get me."

Kozy spoke then with gentle humor of her life with her grandmother. "It was quite an adjustment to go from multiple foster homes in San Diego, California to being the only grandchild of a sixty-year-old widowed Hungarian immigrant on the east side of Cleveland, Ohio. But I finally belonged to someone! I was loved; I had a *real* family, small as it was. Slowly, I was able to leave the anger and the fear of abandonment behind. I was happy. Life was good, at least for a while."

She paused, recalling the past. "It was the beginning of my senior year in high school that we got the diagnosis. Gramma had cancer. The doctors estimated she had from one to two years left to live. She told me, 'I will try my best to stay here for you, for as long as you need me. We will trust in God's timing. Everything will be all right.'

"*'Everything will be all right?'* I thought to myself. '*One to two years? I won't even be out of college and I will be alone again!*' I did not want to be alone again. First, God took away my parents, and now he was going to take my grandma away. I was furious at the God who would do this to me." Kozy stood with her arms crossed and her body tense as she looked up at the ceiling, remembering. "Early in my grandmother's illness, I drove her to her appointments at the Cleveland Clinic. While I waited for her to undergo her treatments, I took long walks down the corridors of the hospital. I alternated between ranting at God in my mind and feeling sorry for myself.

"It was in that hospital where God placed a young woman named Carrieanne in my path. Due to severe birth defects, this woman had undergone countless operations and procedures in her thirty years, but was still left with a twisted, frail body. Carrieanne had been at the clinic for a few weeks of treatments. She couldn't walk or eat or use the toilet the way most people can, and she never would. Yet when I looked into her gaunt face, her smile was radiant, and her eyes reflected peace and joy. She never showed a trace of bitterness but instead spoke of how blessed she was. Her concern always seemed to be for others rather than for herself. She could rejoice in the smallest things, like feeling the breeze through her hair or enjoying the aroma of food that she couldn't even eat herself. I couldn't get her out of my mind, wondering how she could be so peaceful and so grateful when it looked like she lacked so very much."

Kozy shut her eyes and smiled as she remembered. "Carrieanne was never without a large tattered Bible." Kozy laughed. "Her parents told me she had actually worn out over a dozen Bibles at that point in her life. Carrieanne asked me if she could read to me and asked to pray for me and Gram. My Gram had raised me in the church. I was used to reading the Bible some and praying wasn't new to me. 'Sure,' I said. Every time we met, it was the same; she was able to lift me up with her joy. Finally I had to ask Carrieanne, 'What is it that makes the difference with you? Why do you have this peace that I'm lacking?' Then she told me in her gentle way: 'It's not enough to know who Jesus is and to believe that the Bible is true. You have to trust completely. You have to trust that the one who died for you on that cross loves you enough to want the best for you. Complete surrender is what God asks of us.'

"I went home that night thinking hard about what Carrieanne had said. My grandma had told me, 'God has no grandchildren.' I had never understood, or I never tried to understand, what she meant by that. But now I suddenly got it. God doesn't have grandchildren. You are either a child of God or you are not. It wasn't enough for me to live on my grandma's faith. I had to claim Jesus as my own and put my trust in him. I did that in September of my senior year in high school. Carrieanne, that beautiful wisp of a woman with the gigantic soul, was at my side. She had shown me by the way she lived her life that God is bigger than any problem that I might have, and that the power of his love for me is greater than all my fears.

"Philippians 4:7 says: '*And the peace of God, which passes all understanding, will keep your hearts and your minds in Christ Jesus.*' My grandma lived another four and a half years. She died the year I was finishing my teaching degree. I've missed her terribly. Yet I don't feel alone like I feared I would. I have peace. Once I surrendered my life and my future to God, I had a daddy, Abba, who would never fail me and would never leave me."

Kozy looked out at the teenagers whose eyes were now fixed on her. "I can't promise that God will take away all of your problems. I can't promise that you will have perfect understanding. But I can say with certainty that, if you let him into your heart, if you trust him with your future, he will walk with you. You'll never be alone. He will give you the strength to overcome. If you haven't already trusted Jesus as your own, I hope you'll consider it."

Nolan Calderon sat in the back of the auditorium and watched as Kozy fielded questions from the teens. She answered with poise, honesty, and good humor. As he had often done in the past, he had filled in tonight as an extra chaperone. He had felt it surreal when he realized that the guest speaker was none other than the girl who had been his blind date the weekend before. He noted that she was dressed appropriately, wearing ordinary jeans and a tasteful t-shirt, fitting in with the similarly dressed teens she was addressing. Her blond curls were the same as he remembered, bouncing uninhibited as she talked with the crowd. He was mesmerized by the candidness of her story. There was much more substance to this young woman than he had expected after their first meeting. He never would have suspected that her background deviated so much from those of the average young women he knew. He suddenly was very curious to hear more details about Kozy Hanner.

As the meeting ended and the group headed to the adjoining room for pizza and soft drinks, Nolan made his way over to where Kozy stood. She was chatting with Nolan's dad and Dan, the youth leader. Pastor Tom paused in the conversation to introduce his son and was surprised to learn that the two already knew one another. He decided that should be his cue to leave them alone, and he rejoined the youth group with Dan.

***

Kozy's pen glided across the paper.

Thank you for helping me through tonight, Abba. Thank you for giving me the courage to relive those times for the sake of the teens. Everyone at the church, including Nolan Calderon, made me feel welcome and accepted. I am trying to release all of my fears to you, but I'm not quite there yet, am I? Thank you for being so patient with me! I am so grateful to have you beside me in my struggles. You are faithful!

Revisiting the past had drained her. With heavy eyes she closed her journal and placed it on the nightstand. As she lay in the darkness, vague memories of her mother and father seeped to the edges of her consciousness before she snuffed them out with a shake of her head. "*No!*" she told herself for the thousandth time. Instead she comforted herself with memories of her grandmother's face.

Chapter 4

San Diego, California, March 9, 1997

Maria felt awkward and confused as she walked into the bustling police station. The building was teeming with people, ringing phones, and loud voices. She stopped at the first desk she came to and identified herself. With trembling lips, she explained her business there and asked to see Sergeant Cady, the officer who had spoken to her on the phone the week before. She was soon escorted into a private office, where she sat fighting tears until the officer appeared several minutes later.

Sergeant Cady was a slender, pleasant-faced man in his late thirties, with thinning brown hair. He walked into the room carrying a small cardboard box and deposited it onto an old, run-down oak table. He stole a glance at the elderly woman who was obviously in distress. He turned to face her. His heart was heavy, and he searched for the right words to say, as if there were any. She reminded him of his own mother. He had hated making that call to her about her daughter's death, but it came with the job. Someone had to do it, after all, but he would never get used to it.

He offered his hand to Maria and introduced himself. "Thank you for coming so promptly, Mrs. Kozma," he said softly.

Maria felt the kindness in his voice and it gave her a small dose of courage.

"I had to come." She looked earnestly at the man. "My grandchild, you know—she needs to be with family. I would have been here long ago, if I had only known."

He nodded in sympathy and then got down to business. Within minutes he was helping Maria into a squad car and driving her to the nearby hospital. He chatted quietly to Maria as they walked down a long corridor. Her stomach lurched as the elevator came to an abrupt stop, the doors opening to the basement of the hospital. Maria's lips moved in silent prayer as she shuffled down the hallway, but she was still unprepared for the feelings that overtook her as she entered the cold, harshly-lit room. She couldn't bear to think of her Betsy lying there in that horrible place. *How can this be happening?* In spite of the cold, she felt herself beginning to sweat. The pungent smell of antiseptic burned her nostrils and made her feel queasy. She trembled as the drawer was pulled out, and the white sheet was drawn away. Her vision clouded and suddenly her knees gave out.

The next thing she remembered she was sitting in a wheelchair. "Do you think you can stand now, Mrs. Kozma?" Sergeant Cady was asking. She nodded and stood, though she was barely aware of the ride back to the station. Once they returned to the private office, Sergeant Cady rubbed her hands and talked softly to her as a woman officer stood by. Maria took several deep breaths and tried to clear her head. *This won't do,* she thought. *They will think me unfit to take care of the child!*

"I'm sorry, so sorry," she cried. "It was just the thought of my poor Betsy …." She attempted to sit up straight to convince them that she was over her weakness.

The female officer put a mug of coffee in her hands and whispered, "Here, ma'am. Maybe this will help."

Maria took a sip of the hot coffee, her heart warmed by the woman's kindness as much as her icy hands were warmed by the steaming mug. "Please," she said after a few more minutes. "I am ready. What else must be done so that I can see my granddaughter?"

Sergeant Cady motioned toward the cardboard box on the table. "We should probably go through your daughter's personal effects," he said. He broke the seal with a small box cutter and the meager contents were taken out. One by one Maria examined the items that had come from Betsy's apartment: an expired driver's license, social security card, marriage certificate, the baby's birth certificate, and a few photographs. She noted with relief that the child had been born several months after the date of Betsy and Ted's wedding. She gazed with curiosity at the baby's pictures and couldn't help but smile. *Such a pretty little thing!* Maria was surprised to find a picture of herself and of her husband among the others. In a notebook was Maria's name and address, with a clearly written and signed statement, dated nearly a year ago, that Maria was Betsy's only other living relative. If anything were to happen to Betsy, she asked that Maria would take custody of her daughter, Kozy Maria Hanner. Tears once again flooded her eyes. "Kozy" had been the nickname that her husband's friends had called him. *Betsy trusted me with her child. And the name! She must have still cared about us!*

Sergeant Cady's voice interrupted her thoughts. "A juvenile judge has already examined these papers, Mrs. Kozma, and we did a background check on you last week. Just standard procedure, you see. Since you indicated to me that you are willing to take your granddaughter, we've been in touch with her caseworker, and if you wish, we'll set up an appointment for you."

Maria nodded and thanked the officer, her mind whirling. Everything was happening so fast. Seeing Betsy's documents somehow made it seem so final. And then the sergeant asked about burial. "What are your plans for your daughter's remains?"

Maria sighed. She knew that to have her Betsy's body transported across the country was more than she could afford. "What are my choices?" she asked timidly.

"Your daughter can be buried in an unmarked pauper's grave, paid for by the county." But when he saw the hurt in Maria's eyes, he quickly went on. "Or you can choose cremation and then you can bury her ashes in a family plot. The ashes could be shipped directly to the cemetery."

"Yes," Maria said emphatically, "Her ashes will rest in the grave with her father. I will have her name engraved on the stone."

***

The afternoon in the office of San Diego Child Protective Services seemed as though it would never end. There were multiple interviews with various people, lists of instructions, and then a pile of documents to sign. Maria massaged the fingers of her right hand before signing what she hoped was the final paper. She wiped the sweat from her brow with a tissue as Mrs. Gonzales, Kozy's caseworker, placed two thick folders onto the table in front of her.

"Don't worry," she said as she pointed to the smaller file. "You don't need to read every page right now unless you want to. I've summarized the relevant information in the first several pages. Most of the rest is just documentation from our office, her teachers, and foster parents. Just legal mumbo-jumbo."

"And the other?" Maria asked, indicating the larger file.

Mrs. Gonzales' voice softened. "Those are the records of the court proceedings starting from when the state took custody of Kozy. It's none of my business of course, but I was thinking that you might want to be in the comfort of your own home before you go through those."

The women's eyes locked for a long moment; Maria understood and was grateful for the compassion. "Thank you," she whispered. It was true; she didn't have the heart to uncover all the details of Betsy's life right now. It might be best to wait until she was home and surrounded by friends who could comfort her. For now, she needed all of her emotional strength so she could prepare to meet her grandchild. "I'll just look over the files from your office for now," she said as she took a deep breath. "There will be plenty of time later for the other."

Maria adjusted her reading glasses and shooed away a fly that buzzed around her head. After a few seconds of reading, she caught her breath and cried out in dismay, "Four different foster homes in four years! Oh my!" She instantly regretted her outcry, not wanting to appear critical. Looking quickly at the middle-aged woman in front of her, she was relieved to see that she hadn't seemed to take offense.

"Yes, she has had some tough breaks, poor thing." She explained further, "You must understand, Mrs. Kozma, the foster families do the best they can. Things happen: a job loss, a move, an unexpected pregnancy, illness or crisis in the family, new responsibilities. All of a sudden there's no room or time for an extra child. We try to keep each of our wards in a stable home as long as possible. In your granddaughter's case, things never seemed to work out for long. Just the luck of the draw, you know?" She paused and watched as Maria got back to the file and skimmed through the next page.

She continued, "You see that she's done well in school, considering everything. Caught up just fine every time she had to change. She really took off this past year; tested well beyond her grade level in reading. She's a bright child."

Once again Maria looked up with distress. "But it says she's been reprimanded for fighting. She hit other children!"

Mrs. Gonzales focused her attention on a patch of sky that could be seen outside the small window. She waited as Maria continued reading through the pages, knowing what she would find would break her heart. When she heard Maria's soft moan, she turned and looked at her pale face, her own eyes filled with tears. "Perhaps a blessing she learned to fight, Mrs. Kozma," she whispered.

Maria's eyes closed. After a moment she gave a deep sigh, lifted her chin and met the woman's eyes with resignation.

Mrs. Gonzales continued. "Once you have time to study the teachers' reports, you'll see that she's not a bad kid. She's teased; she reacts. But she's not a bully. You're getting her at a good age to break her of the fighting. She just needs to feel she belongs somewhere. I have a gut feeling that you are the very person who can do that for her."

Maria replied with conviction, "I intend to do everything in my power to see that my granddaughter feels loved and wanted."

"That's just what we like to hear!" Mrs. Gonzales' grin lit up her brown eyes. "I'll be delivering Kozy to your hotel room tomorrow afternoon, Mrs. Kozma. I believe you two are going to do just fine. It's been a pleasure meeting with you!"

***

Late the next day, the caseworker brought Kozy to Maria's hotel room. Maria felt an irrational sense of shame that the first meeting with her grandchild should be under such circumstances, and in front of a stranger. She immediately recognized the resemblance to her daughter Betsy. She could see the little girl was wary, so she resisted the urge to wrap her arms around her. Instead, she made herself wait patiently while Mrs. Gonzales introduced them, and then she smiled and patted her granddaughter gently on the shoulder.

"I am so happy to finally get to meet you, Kozy!" she said, noting with gratitude that the woman had seen to it that the girl was clean and wearing a new pair of tan shorts, a navy t-shirt, and white tennis shoes. She carried a small backpack on her shoulders.

The girl responded with a nod. She looked past Maria, taking in the details of the room. She feigned disinterest as Mrs. Gonzales went over the details of what would be required of Maria once she got back to Ohio. The woman tried to set Maria at ease, assuring her again that she had confidence that Maria was well suited to the job of taking care of Kozy. Handing Maria a large envelope of copies of the forms Maria had filled out the day before, she now turned her attention to Kozy, explaining briefly what would be happening. Kozy accepted all that was said with neither questions nor obvious emotion.

"What do I call you?" she asked Maria finally.

"My name is Maria Kozma. But I am your grandmother. You may call me 'Grandma', if you want."

The girl took in the information without response. As the caseworker prepared to leave, Kozy asked to watch the television in the room. "Of course," Maria said, busying herself with finding a suitable show for the child. She finally came across a station that was playing a marathon of Andy Griffith reruns. Kozy nodded her consent and hopped onto the bed to watch. Mrs. Gonzales walked out the door with a wave, and just like that, eight year old Kozy Maria Hanner was no longer the responsibility of San Diego County.

While Kozy sat with her brown eyes glued to the television, Maria opened the tiny refrigerator in the corner of the room and took out a container of macaroni and cheese that she had picked up earlier at a nearby deli. She divided the contents equally onto two paper plates and heated them in the microwave. She opened a small bottle of orange juice and poured some for each of them into Styrofoam cups. The little girl thanked Maria for the food and continued to watch the show while she ate. She offered no other comments and spoke only when Maria asked her a direct question. Once they were finished eating, Maria handed Kozy a new child-sized pink toothbrush and a soft pair of bright yellow pajamas, and sent her off to the bathroom to get ready for bed. Maria thought she detected a glint of satisfaction on the girl's face as she clutched the toothbrush.

A few minutes later Kozy returned from the bathroom and crawled into her bed. Before long, she was fast asleep. Maria studied the child who was lying on her back with a riot of yellow curls tumbling over her brow.

Curlier than Betsy's hair. More like my father's.

Maria noted that Kozy's delicate, heart-shaped face and fair skin resembled Betsy's when she was that age, though she was not sure about the charming cleft in the child's chin.

Perhaps that came from the Hanner side.

Her thoughts wandered as the child slept peacefully.

The child has not yet complained. That's a good thing, but neither has she cried or laughed. A child should feel free to cry if she is hurting and children should know how to laugh. She is clever. I will have to stay on my toes with this little one, huh?

Maria looked up from the child toward the ceiling. *I will give up the past to you, Father. Please let me honor my Betsy by raising her child to adulthood, if you are willing. I am broken and grieving, my Father, but this little girl has lost even more than I have. Please fill our home with laughter. Is better to laugh than to cry. And please, I am sixty years old. I will need you to give me strength!*

She rubbed both hands over her face and stifled a huge yawn. The tension from the past few days had caught up with her. Feeling exhausted, she hurried to the bathroom and prepared for bed.

Maria was up early the next morning. She tiptoed to the bathroom, taking care not to awaken Kozy. When she came out a few minutes later, she was surprised to find the child awake and dressed. All of her meager belongings had been gathered into her backpack, and she sat waiting on the side of the bed.

Like a little refugee, ready to move on at a moment's notice.

Maria had thought things over the night before while struggling to fall asleep. On the trip west, she had taken the most direct route in order to arrive as soon as possible. Now she was considering taking a little more time to get back home.

I will never get back to this part of the country, and Kozy has likely never been more than a few miles from this city. I can't afford to do much, but maybe I should try to find a route that would show us some of the country. It will give us some time to get to know each other.

Chapter 5

Early Friday evening Kozy and Cathy arrived at the concession stand for the Central Elementary annual Fall Festival. They quickly loaded the hot dog machine with wieners, arranged condiments on the counter, and started brewing coffee. Cathy turned on the popcorn machine and waited for it to heat before pouring in the first batch of oil and popcorn kernels. As she waited, she checked the supply of napkins and lined the adjoining countertop with candy bars and cookies. Kozy checked off the opening crew's to-do list as they worked.

"That's about it," she said as she placed the pen and list back on the bulletin board. "We are ready for the hungry hordes!"

"Yes," Cathy sighed, "and with time to spare. Let's sit and relax a bit."

They pulled up a couple of folding chairs and watched the activity in the wide hallway just outside the cafeteria doors. Some of the other teachers were putting the finishing touches on the wall decorations. Booths had been set up for games, and several of the parent helpers were already at their stations. The hall was a kaleidoscope of orange, red, brown, yellow, and green. Sounds of cheerful chatter and shrills of laughter bounced off the walls. Kozy and Cathy smiled as they anticipated the fun and excitement that awaited their young scholars in the next couple of hours.

"So how did things go for your first small group meeting with the teens at Grace Church on Wednesday?" Cathy asked.

Kozy smiled. "You'll never guess who I was paired with for my group!" she said.

"Your blind date, the young Mr. Calderon?"

"Yep! I don't know if it was a random thing or not, but when I looked at the list of names for my group, there was Nolan's name next to mine as co-leader."

"So, how did it go?" Cathy probed.

"The teens were great," Kozy hedged. "That first night was mostly spent getting to know one another. I'm eager to start on the Bible study the pastor prepared for us. I think they're going to find it interesting and relevant."

Cathy stared at her expressionless. "But how did it go with Nolan?"

Kozy grinned. "Maybe it's too early to tell, but he seemed almost friendly."

Cathy's eyes widened and she nodded her head knowingly, but decided to let it rest when Kozy chose to change the subject.

"How are things going with your kids, Cathy? I mean your own kids, not your third graders."

Cathy hesitated. "Oh, okay as far as I know. I don't hear much from them. I know so many parents who say the same thing. It's a busy time in their lives. They're getting established in their careers and finding new friends. Sometimes I think they forget that they ever had parents."

Kozy looked at her with sympathy. "I'm sure they think of you more often than you realize, Cathy," she said softly. "I see it with other people my age, too. Life is just happening so fast for them. They don't realize how much time has passed. Be patient. They'll get more aware eventually."

"Thanks, Kozy." She shifted in her chair and sighed. "I wish they would just get settled in life, you know? Find spouses, get married, give me grandchildren, and live happily ever after so I never need to worry again." She laughed. "They're fine, really. They *are* busy with their jobs, and they never ask for money, so I have no reason to complain. Still, I do get impatient waiting for God to give me a sign, you know, that they are *really* all right, that they are on the right track. Yes, I definitely need a dose of patience."

She looked thoughtfully at her young friend. "What's your secret, Kozy? You seem to have a lot of patience."

"Patience? Me?" she chuckled. "I probably struggle as much as anybody. But any success I do have with being patient, I believe I learned from my grandma."

"Oh, I love hearing about your grandma, Kozy! We have time before the crowd gets here. Tell me your story."

Kozy sat up straighter in her chair as she contemplated. "Well, I've explained how my grandma gained custody of me after I had been shuffled in the foster care system for four years. I had a lot of anger. Once I was living with Gram, and I realized that it was for real, and that she wasn't going to give me away, I started to relax a little. I wish I could say that I became an ideal child, and was full of gratitude. But I didn't. Gram did everything in her power to make me feel loved and wanted." Kozy chuckled and shook her head. "But as I slowly accepted the truth of the love she had for me, instead of acting grateful, I became a brat.

"One night Gram promised she'd make me a delicious treat the next morning. She said she'd make me *palacsinta*, which is the Hungarian name for something much like French crepes—a thin, sweet pancake that is rolled and filled with delicious things. In this case it was to be filled with sweetened whipped cream and sour cherries. The next morning as she was getting started, she got a series of calls from friends. She ended the calls as quickly as she was able, and continued her preparation. I was getting hungrier and hungrier. I started whining and pouting, making sure she saw how angry I was. I had suffered all those years in foster care and had been hungry sometimes so I wasn't going to put up with it! I gave her an ultimatum. I insisted that she feed me immediately!

"Poor Gramma, she was trying so hard to do right by me. She was nice, but she was only human. I think that morning she was finally frazzled enough to realize that it was time for a little discipline along with the love. 'All right my little Kozy, you want to eat now? You can eat now!' She grabbed a plate from the cupboard and set it very firmly in front of me. Then she proceeded to pour the raw batter that she had mixed onto my plate. She looked at me with a stormy face and handed me a spoon. 'Go ahead and eat the *palacsinta* that you must have *right now!*' she dared me.

"I glared at Gram and she glared right back! Well, I was just stubborn enough to take the dare. I dipped my spoon into that batter and stuffed the whole thing in my mouth. Yuk! It was pretty disgusting; I spit it back onto my plate. I tried to stare her down until the tears started. Mine and hers. I didn't want to make her cry, so I cried all the harder. Then she started to giggle through her tears and soon she had me laughing, too. She set down her mixing bowl and took me in her arms and rocked me for a long time before getting back to work.

"She poured a little oil into the iron skillet and then added a couple tablespoons of batter. It takes skill to quickly swirl the pan so that the batter spreads out thin and even. Then at the right moment, after it's bubbled for a while, the pancake is flipped to brown a little on the other side. Eventually she had turned all the batter into a neat pile of round, thin sweet crepes. We spooned the whipped cream and cherries onto the centers and rolled them up. I had never tasted anything so heavenly. That day was a turning point. I truly began to believe that I was loved." Kozy paused, remembering. "That was the first time I ever cried with my grandma. Sometime during my years in foster care, I had just stopped crying. I made myself be tough and not care."

Cathy shook her head. "It's hard for me to imagine an eight-year-old girl not crying. It's a rare week that we don't have at least one meltdown in the classroom. But do go on with your story."

Kozy nodded in agreement and continued. "Gram liked to make a lesson out of everyday happenings. That evening when she was putting me to bed, she reminded me, 'Remember how icky the batter was? And remember how much better it tasted once you waited for me to cook it? My little Kozy, there will be lots of times when you will need to be patient. When you grow up, long after I'm gone, God may ask you to wait for some things. I hope you remember not to settle for the batter, when God wants you to wait for the treat. It will be worth it.'"

Tears blurred Kozy's vision as she looked at Cathy. "Gramma reminded me every so often of the batter in the next few weeks, every time I started to get impatient and demanding and mean with her. Eventually she forgot about it and stopped mentioning it, but I never forgot. I think about that loving lesson now when I feel impatience trying to take over my life. I think of her telling me, 'Don't settle for the batter.' I'm not always successful, but it helps me to remember that."

"What a great word picture and a beautiful story! I will remember that when I feel myself being overwhelmed with impatience. Thanks for sharing that, Kozy."

Cathy stood as several children noisily headed toward the concession stand and a couple of parent volunteers joined them to help. "What can I get for you, Tyler?" she asked the youngster who stood at the head of the line. "A hot dog? Sure thing. One hot dog coming up!"

Chapter 6

Kozy enjoyed the evening at the Fall Festival, but it had been a long day, and she was relieved to get home. A relaxing soak in the bathtub was the first item on her agenda. Afterward she intended to curl up in bed with a new book she had recently started. But once she was settled in, she found it hard to concentrate. Her conversation with Cathy had jogged memories about her early childhood. She finally tossed the book aside and let her thoughts journey back in time to those first days with the ordinary, yet incredible, woman who had been her "Gramma."

San Diego, March 10, 1997

Kozy awakened the moment she heard Maria ease herself out of the bed and quietly tiptoe into the hotel bathroom. Within seconds Kozy had slipped out of the yellow pajamas she had slept in and dressed in the clothes she had worn the day before. She grabbed her backpack and made sure the pajamas and pink toothbrush were safely tucked inside. She noted a small package of crackers that she had overlooked the night before and stowed it as well. She zipped the backpack closed and slipped it onto her shoulders. The lady seemed nice enough last night, but you never knew. Kozy wasn't going to give her the chance to ditch her here with no resources. She wished that she had gotten Mrs. Gonzales' phone number.

Her anxiety lessened gradually as the morning progressed. As soon as they checked out of the hotel, they immediately stopped for breakfast sandwiches at the McDonald's next door. Two doors from there was a Goodwill store where Maria purchased several extra pairs of socks and underwear for Kozy. She then allowed her to pick out some snacks for the bus trip. When Kozy pointed to a box of granola bars, Maria nodded her approval and then added a second box to her cart, along with some nuts and dried fruit. Kozy, who hadn't spoken more than a word or two that morning, breathed a grateful "thank you" when Maria walked to the book area and allowed her to select two paperbacks from the children's section.

They then boarded a city bus that took them to the Greyhound terminal. Inside the busy station Kozy sat waiting on a bench as Maria studied a map. She kept her book in front of her face all the while furtively spying on the woman who was supposed to be her "real" grandmother. Maria was nothing close to how Kozy imagined she might be. She not only looked old to Kozy, but old-fashioned. She wore no jewelry or any other type of adornment to compensate for the drabness of her plain brown slacks and beige cardigan sweater set. Her round face was devoid of any makeup, not even a dab of lipstick. Kozy had hoped she would be more colorful. She also took note of the odd way she spoke. Hispanic and Asian accents were commonplace in Kozy's world, but Maria's accent and the peculiar cadence of her speech were completely unfamiliar. She continued to pretend to be absorbed in her reading as she kept a close eye on what was happening around her.

***

The morning Maria and Kozy were to leave San Diego, Maria was still undecided about what route they should take back to Cleveland. Now she sat in the bus terminal, murmuring to herself and frowning at the map she had brought with her. She was unfamiliar with the western part of the country and was not sure what to do or where to go. As soon as the man selling tickets had some free time, she would walk over and ask his advice.

To pass the time, she looked around the busy terminal and made a game of wondering about her fellow travelers. Despite having the child right next to her, Maria had never felt so alone. Her thoughts were interrupted when she saw an elderly couple enter the station. They were followed closely by a man who looked to be a younger version of the old man. She watched with interest as the young man set down two suitcases, then reached to give the elderly couple tender hugs. Maria's ears perked up when she overheard the woman speak to the younger man.

"*Doboson koszonom*! Thank you so much, Billy, for everything! We had a wonderful time."

Hungarians! Maria thought with surprise. *All the way out here in California!* She strained to hear the rest of the conversation, feeling only a tiny bit guilty for eavesdropping.

"I'm so glad you and Dad came out here to visit this time, Ma," the younger man said as he patted her cheek. Turning, he continued, "Now Pop, I'm putting the mobile phone here in your zippered pocket. I have the instructions written on this index card. Once you get settled on the bus, how about you look it over so you know how to work it when Steve or I call? Now if you need to call us, remember, the little bars at the top will tell you if you're in a service area."

"Sure, sure, we'll figure it out!" He put his arm protectively around his wife who was looking teary-eyed. "You go on now, Billy. We don't want to make you late for your job." With another hug and a peck on his mother's pink cheek, the man hurried out of the terminal.

The couple watched until their son was out of sight before they turned to scan the room. Maria quickly shoved her suitcase to the side. She waved and motioned to the woman, patting the seat beside her. In a moment the short, plump lady gratefully sat down while the man found a seat across from them.

"*Te magyar vagy?*" Maria asked quietly and then smiled with delight at the surprised expression on the woman's face.

"*Igen!*" she answered. Her blue-gray eyes scanned Maria's friendly face. "*Isten hozta!*" she cried. "God sent you to me! I felt so sad leaving my son and God has sent you to cheer me up!"

"*Isten hozta!*" Maria repeated the greeting. "And I was feeling so lonely; God must have sent you to comfort me."

"So you are traveling alone, honey?" the woman asked sympathetically.

"Well, no, I have my granddaughter here, but …." She nodded toward Kozy, who appeared to have her nose buried in the paperback copy of *Little House on the Prairie*. Then, before the women had even properly introduced themselves, Maria felt compelled to explain to the older woman. She whispered her story quickly in Hungarian, confessing in just a few terse sentences how she came to be here with this little girl who was still a stranger to her. The woman covered Maria's hand with her own and gave it a gentle squeeze. Maria was amazed at the instant relief she felt to let go of her shameful secret.

"Life is hard," said the woman simply, with compassion. "But it has its blessings as well." She turned to study the little girl who was now watching them out of the corner of her eye. "What a beautiful granddaughter you have to fill the rest of your days with happiness!"

A ghost of a smile showed on Kozy's face before she lowered her face once more to read.

"My name is Bertha Szabo, by the way, and this is my husband Joe." Joe Szabo, who had been silently listening to the exchange, stood and offered his hand in greeting as his wife continued, "I hope we are going on the same bus so we can sit together and get to know each other better!"

Shaking the man's hand Maria answered, "*Hogy vagy?* How are you?" She looked into his dark eyes. The man had a full head of bushy white hair that contrasted with his olive toned skin. Maria guessed that he must be in his mid-eighties, yet he still stood tall and straight. "I am Maria Kozma and this is my granddaughter Kozy." She hesitated before asking, "And what is the town you are traveling to, Bertha?"

"Henderson, Nevada we go to," Bertha smiled. "Our older son Stephen will pick us up there."

"Kozy and I will be taking that bus as well," Maria decided impulsively. "But you must excuse me for just a moment while I run over and buy our tickets." She hurried off with a prayer of thanks, keeping one eye on Kozy as she talked with the man at the ticket counter. With tickets in hand, Maria came back to her seat and sat next to her new friend. In the half hour or so they had to wait, the women kept up a steady stream of conversation, a cheerful mix of a few Hungarian words mixed with heavily accented English. Bertha peppered Maria with questions: When had she come to America? What town had she come from? Where did she live now?

As the women talked, the tension that Maria had been carrying during her journey began to subside. She spoke candidly of her flight for freedom with Miklos, her finding her way to Cleveland, and her marriage to John Kozma. She shifted her position on the hard seat as Bertha commented.

"So your brother was a Freedom Fighter, eh? I remember how Joe and I waited and waited, as the United States and the UN talked about coming to the rescue. But it was just a bunch of hot air. Nobody helped. I guess after the war, everybody was too tired of fighting." She sighed. "Some things are not meant to be."

"*Nem,*" Maria agreed.

Joe Szabo spoke up. "It was not meant to be in '56 maybe, but Hungary's courage; it gave hope to the rest: Poland, East Germany, Romania, Bulgaria, Czechoslovakia. The Freedom Fighters' sacrifice was not for nothing. It was just the beginning. It took a long time, but they are finally out from under the evil thumb of communism!"

Maria nodded. Miklos, by then unable to travel, had called her often in 1989 and 1990 when the Communist regimes were collapsing one by one in Europe. She was grateful that her brother had lived long enough to see his dream of freedom for his homeland fulfilled.

"Well," Bertha continued, "we have been in America since '43. Joe's mother was a Christian Jew, you see. She died when he was a young child. All the terrible things Hitler was doing! We saw what was written on the wall for us if people would remember and turn him in because of his Jewish blood. He had to think of me and our children. I was expecting our second son. We had to leave. Joe had an uncle in New Jersey who sponsored us. We were able to settle and raise our boys there."

"Good boys we have!" Joe interjected proudly. "Smart. Work hard. They got good jobs, nice families."

"Every summer they take turns and come visit us," Bertha added. "This year they ask us to come to them so they can show us the West. Joe didn't want to drive so far, and I was nervous to fly, so we said we would let the Greyhound take us."

Joe continued, "And Stephen is going to pick us up at the bus station in Henderson, and then he and his wife will take us for a few days to see some national parks. He has just retired and he wants to show off his new RV!"

"RV?" Maria asked. "You mean a camper?"

"*Igen!*" said Bertha, "A camper! Six people can sleep!"

"What a wonderful thing!" exclaimed Maria. "To see our beautiful country and travel with your family in a camper! You are very fortunate, Bertha."

***

Kozy smiled, recalling the party-like atmosphere when they had boarded the bus with Bertha and Joe Szabo that day.

Mr. Szabo seemed to have an unending supply of jokes and riddles and soon brought out a small bag of miniature candy bars and passed it around. Maria was quick to share the snacks they had bought. Kozy remembered how she had listened to the animated conversation lobbing back and forth. She was marveling at the fact that she was suddenly surrounded by, not one but three people, who used the same odd—and to her, humorous—manner of speech. The Szabos had a way of drawing Kozy into the conversation, and she reveled in being included.

A couple of hours into the trip, Maria and Bertha were discussing the various methods for making stuffed cabbage, while Kozy resumed her reading. A sudden muffled ringing noise startled Joe, who had been nodding off to sleep in his window seat.

"What is that?" Bertha asked.

"What?" Joe looked around in confusion. "It must be that mobile phone Billy gave us," he decided, as he wrestled it out of his pocket. "Now, how do I answer?" He sat staring at the device with a frown while the ringing persisted.

Fortunately, Maria had a friend who owned one of the new phones. and she had watched her using it. "I think maybe if you pull out that little wire thing," she suggested hesitantly. She pointed to the top of the phone. Joe clumsily pulled until he had extended the small antenna.

"Now what?" he muttered to himself.

Maria reached across Bertha's lap and pointed. "Maybe try pushing that button there, the one that says, 'send.'"

Joe scowled, pushed the button, and blinked.

"Now, speak," Maria prompted reassuringly.

"Hello?" Joe held the phone to his ear and soon smiled with relief. "Yes, Billy. No, no trouble at all. Is easy as can be."

Bertha and Maria looked at each other and burst into a fit of giggles. Kozy, who had looked up from her book at the sound of the phone, stared curiously at the two women. Her mouth worked into a smile. The smile soon widened into a grin, and she began to laugh. Maria thought it one of the most delightful sounds she had ever heard.

When their laughter finally subsided, Bertha shook her head. "What would we have done without you, Maria?"

***

"Billy thinks these phones will become so popular that some day everybody will have one." Joe was studying the index card of instructions that his son Bill had given him at the station. He dismissed the thought with a wave of his hand. "A crazy idea! Sure, they might be all right for emergencies and for traveling, but how many people would buy them? They are way too complicated!"

"And," Bertha added, "Billy says that they'll start making the phones do other jobs, like take pictures or do arithmetic! Maybe even do the work of a computer!"

"Imagine! Billy is a smart boy, but sometimes I think he watches too much of the television!" Joe mused with a shake of his head.

But by the time the Szabos' older son Stephen called a couple of hours later, Joe knew just what to do and answered the phone with pride and confidence. His cheerful look soon changed to disappointment as he listened to his son. "Wait a moment, Stephen; let me explain to your mother." He set the phone on his lap and looked at Bertha somberly. "Stephen will pick us up as planned, but there has been a slight change. He is very sorry, but Dana won't be able to go along with us to the parks. Somebody got sick at work and she can't get off after all." Bertha's countenace immediately changed. Her brows formed a *V* shape as she frowned and her lower lip pushed out into a pout. If Bertha hadn't looked so forlorn, Maria would have been tempted to laugh, because, in spite of her wrinkled face and white hair, Bertha looked a little like a spoiled child.

"Oh, your mama's pretty disappointed, Stephen." Joe was back speaking into the phone. To Bertha he whispered, "It can't be helped, sweetheart. Dana wasn't able to get off work. What can we do?"

Bertha's stormy face stared down into her lap. She suddenly brightened . "Maybe Maria and her Kozy could come with us!" she suggested as she looked over at the two.

Kozy stared with hopeful eyes but Maria said quickly, "Oh, no, Bertha! I could never impose!"

"But it wouldn't be imposing! If you don't go, I will have to ride in the back of the RV all by myself. Either that or sit like a sardine between Joe and Stephen in the cab of the camper and listen to them talk of nothing but baseball! I wouldn't have any fun at all." Tears welled in her eyes. "Please?" she begged. "Is only for three or four days."

Maria was breathless with the thought of such an opportunity. Kozy watched, her eyes silently pleading. Maria pushed away the thought. "No," she said finally. "No. We couldn't expect your son to take two complete strangers on a family vacation."

Joe held his hand up and motioned for quiet as he quickly conferred with his son. "Your mother wants to know if she can bring two of her friends along in the RV. Yes, nice people. A woman and her young grandaughter. *Magyars.* She met them at the bus station. The lady and your mama haven't quit talking in four hours."

Maria thought she could hear the faint sound of laughter coming from the phone. Joe listened for a few moments longer and nodded. "Stephen says that whatever his mama wants to do is all right with him. He trusts our judgement."

The pout on Bertha's round face disappeared immediately, and she beamed at Maria and Kozy. "So, will you come?"

Kozy had been certain that her grandmother would refuse the invitation. To this day she marveled that in the end Maria had given in to Bertha's plea. It was spontaneous and perhaps a little reckless. Kozy was convinced that the only reason her otherwise cautious grandmother had gone through with it was the fact that she was sure that the opportunity was a gift from God.

**

Maria had insisted on paying for the food they would eat and a share of the fuel cost. It was the least she could do for such generosity. Stephen Szabo proved to be every bit as friendly and fun loving as his parents. Tall and erect like his father, but with light brown hair, he had inherited his mother's fair complexion and rosy cheeks. He proudly showed off his new RV. Maria silently placed her hands on Kozy's shoulders to keep her from jumping up and down in her excitement. They all inspected the shiny, compact vehicle, tested the comfort of the beds, and exclaimed over the tiny but well-equipped kitchen. Later, at a Walmart, Maria and Bertha discussed the food they should buy.

"Just get the easiest things, Mama," Joe warned. "Remember, you are on vacation!"

Bertha and Maria looked at one another and finally shrugged. "Okay." Bertha agreed reluctantly. "But why have that nice little kitchen if we can't even have a little fun in it?"

The ladies found they didn't need the distraction of cooking once they started on the road. Stephen, a retired teacher, already had his RV equipped with a variety of board games, cards, and magazines. At the Walmart he purchased a set of cardboard puzzles of the United States and of the world.

"I started my career in elementary education," he said to Maria in explanation. "I hate to pass up a good teaching opportunity." He looked at Kozy and smiled, "If you ask these ladies, I'll bet they can show you where you are on these maps."

Once they were back on the road, Kozy removed the cellephane packaging from the United States puzzle, and spread the pieces out on the tabletop. Whispering to herself, she surveyed the base of the puzzle with the shapes indented in the cardboard.

"I know the shape of California. I'll start there." Her nose wrinkled as she searched for the piece. "Yay! Got it!" She popped the piece into its place and sounded out the name by the little red star that denoted the capital: "Sac-ra-men-to."

Maria and Bertha momentarily abandoned their conversation to watch as Kozy continued to immerse herself in completing the puzzle. She worked in an orderly fashion moving from the west to the east.

"Such a clever way to do it," Bertha exclaimed. "You will remember so much better that way."

By the end of the trip she had memorized all of the states and their capitals. She even had a good grasp of the continents and oceans as well. As a bonus she received private history lessons from Maria and Bertha who pointed out on the colorful maps where they had been born and how they had each traveled to America, and why. As they pored over the United States puzzle, Maria traced the route that they would be taking to get to Ohio. Kozy could no longer suppress her curiosity about her new home and asked Maria question after question. The idea that she might finally have a real and permanent place in a family began to sink in.

The first stop Stephen Szabo had planned for their trip was Hoover Dam. They stood on the observation deck, six hundred feet above the Colorado River, and marveled at the massive structure that had made possible the irrigation of a million and a half acres of crop lands.

"Think of it," Stephen told them. "Those fresh fruits and vegetables we bought a while ago were made possible because of this dam. It was this project that made the desert bloom. Every day, twenty million people depend on it for water. The Southwest wouldn't be what it is today without the Hoover Dam."

Joe agreed, "It was such a big deal when it was built. We even heard about it in Hungary when I was just a young boy. It seemed to be an impossible job. No one thought it could be done. But here it is in front of us!"

Afterward, they left Nevada and headed toward Zion National Park in Utah. They settled in the park campground so that they could have an early start in the morning. After a simple meal of toasted cheese sandwiches, tomato soup, and fresh fruit, they sat inside the camper around the table talking, laughing, and playing games. Kozy recited the states and capitals she had learned that day. Bertha explained to the men the organized way that Kozy had chosen to learn the the states and their locations.

Stephen commended her for her cleverness. "You seem to appreciate learning, Kozy. You might consider being a teacher yourself when you grow up."

She cocked her head to the side and looked solemnly at Stephen. The concept of being a grown up had not yet occurred to Kozy. In the mirror of her mind, she pictured herself looking as she had in her most recent school picture, only much bigger. Then she saw herself seated at a desk, reading books to a group of children. She liked that vision. School had been a constant for Kozy in an otherwise unstable world. She had had several good teachers who were appreciative of her cleverness and willingness to learn. The other children had been mean at times, but she trusted her teachers. A small seed was planted in Kozy that day: the idea that she would someday have the freedom to choose what she would do with the rest of her life.

The next morning Kozy's mouth fell open in awe at the sight of the steep cliffs and narrow canyons surrounding them. They were comfortably seated on the shuttle bus that took them through Zion National Park. The sun shown brightly, making the massive red and white sandstone walls glow. Maria, too, had never seen anything so spectacular. Later, they all departed the shuttle to hike on one of the easier trails.

Maria was torn between staying beside the slow-walking Bertha, or hurrying to keep up with Kozy, who was running up the trail. "I had forgotten how much energy children have," she whispered breathlessly as they struggled to make their way over the sandy, rocky path.

But almost as though she had heard the remark, Kozy suddenly raced back and took Maria by the hand.

"Come on, Gramma," she encouraged. "You can make it. I'll help you!"

Gramma! Maria's heart sang to hear herself called "Gramma" for the first time. She suddenly felt a new burst of energy. "We will wait for you at the end of the trail," she called to her smiling friends as she grasped Kozy's hand.

Maria had secretly thought that nothing could compare with the grandeur of Zion Park, until the next day when they visited Bryce Canyon. They stood marveling at the fiery colors and infinite variations in the castle-like rock formations and the breathtaking mountain vistas. She felt humbled when she realized that if she were to travel for the rest of her days she could never begin to see all the sights in this rugged, immense land. She was nearly overcome with a sense of the power of God that could create such a place.

Over the next two days they traveled east on the National Scenic Byway and on to Arches National Park, drinking in the enchanting panoramas of red rock spires and massive natural stone arches. When they left the park they headed for Interstate 70 and toward Stephen's home in Colorado. The atmosphere inside the RV was subdued, as everyone tried to grasp all they had seen in the last few days. As they traveled, the landscape shifted from mountains, canyonlands, and deserts to grassy plains and bare rocky areas.

At one point they were traveling through an area that was exceptionally bleak and rocky, devoid of any sign of green life. Kozy, who had been dozing in her window seat, sat up. Seeing the lifeless surroundings she asked drowsily, "Gramma, are we on the moon?"

Maria looked down into the sleepy brown eyes. She felt a tender tightening in her chest as she realized: *I love this child. I will love her forever.*

She lowered her face and placed a soft kiss on the little girl's forehead. "No, honey," she assured her. "We are only in Utah."

***

The next morning they waited in the lobby of the bus station in Fruita, Colorado. Tickets had been purchased, and Maria and Kozy were ready for the final part of their journey home to Cleveland.

"I can't thank you enough, all of you, for what you have done for us," Maria said.

After depositing Maria's suitcase on the floor, Stephen Szabo clasped her hand.

"It was our pleasure," he said, reaching with his other hand to ruffle Kozy's hair.

Maria then wrapped her arms around Bertha and gave her a warm hug. "Bless you, my friend!" she whispered. "You have given a healing touch to my little Kozy. You have taught her to laugh. I will never forget you."

Bertha cupped Kozy's cheek tenderly as she bent to give her a kiss. "I know you will get along fine," she assured Maria as she helped Kozy step onto the bus. "*Isten hozta!*" Bertha took hold of her husband's arm as they waved. "Remember to send us a card at Christmas! With Kozy's school picture!" she called.

Maria nodded. The lump in her throat would not allow her to speak as she waved good-by to her friends. They continued waving until long after the bus had pulled away.

***

Kozy glanced at the clock on her bedstand and was surprised to see that she had been lost in her reverie for over an hour. Those magical four days with the Szabos had indeed been a gift from God. In her mind's eye Kozy had always remembered her first hours with Maria in blacks and whites and grays. But from the moment Maria had agreed to join Bertha, Joe, and Stephen it was as though they had walked through a doorway into a world of vibrant, living color. That trip had been the catalyst for the bonding of her relationship with her grandmother. They never again felt like strangers. They had become family. The Szabo family's obvious love and respect for one another was a role model that became forever etched on Kozy's heart. She began to feel that her newfound cultural heritage was a gift to be cherished. Kozy picked up her prayer journal, chose a deep pink colored pen, and began to write.

My Abba, my friend !

Have I ever thanked you for bringing the Szabo family into our lives that day so long ago? I can still remember how Gram and Bertha found a hundred things to talk about and how funny they sounded to me! They were all three so nice to us! I think I must have decided way back then to become a teacher. I had never even realized it was possible until Stephen suggested it.

Chapter 7

It was early Tuesday morning when Tom Calderon pulled his old blue pickup into the parking lot of April's Diner. Glancing toward the entrance, he spotted the man he was there to meet. The man was already looking over the handwritten menu for the day's specials.

"Hope I haven't kept you waiting long, Vince," he called as he strolled over to his friend. "It's good to see you, old buddy. It's been way too long."

Vince Mateo turned and with a hearty laugh, grasped his friend in a quick bear hug. Vince was a short stocky man, with a swarthy complexion and dark eyes that smiled as brightly as his grin.

"Cal, my old friend! You look great! And as trim and good looking as ever, I see. Lucky you took after your mama's side!" he chuckled as he combed his hands over his nearly bald head. "Course, some of us have been blessed with a more hidden charm."

Fond memories flooded Tom's mind when he heard his friend use the nickname that had been abandoned long ago.

"Thanks, Vince," he answered, "but you'd better be checking into getting some glasses if you haven't noticed the gray in my hair and the extra pounds I've put on since high school!"

In a few moments they had settled into a well-worn booth in a corner of the popular, family-run restaurant.

"What will you be having this fine morning, gentlemen?" asked the middle-aged waitress as she filled the coffee mugs they had uprighted.

"It is a fine morning," Tom agreed. "I'll have the medium special, please. Scrambled, wheat toast." She nodded and turned to Vince.

Vince glanced at the woman's nametag. "Ditto for me, Valerie," he said with a smile. As she turned to the next table, he surveyed the bustling room. "It feels good to be back in Shelby Falls again. Glad to see that April's is still thriving. It always was one of my favorite feeding places." Vince emptied a second packet of cream into his coffee.

"And what place wasn't one of your favorite feeding places?" his friend asked with a grin. "Boy, you could always be counted on to have a good appetite!"

"You're right, Cal. If we had had cell phones in those days, every one of those places would've been on my speed dial, including your mom's kitchen. She was such a good and generous lady, as well as an awesome cook. What I wouldn't do for a taste of her homemade lasagna once more."

"Yeah, it's been four years since she passed on. Driving past the old house, I still sometimes imagine I can smell the aroma of sauce simmering on the stove." Tom thought that it was likely more than just good food that made Vince nostalgic for the Calderon home of their youth. Both of Tom's parents had seen to it that Vince had a refuge in their home during the times when Vince's own father had had too much to drink. Too often Vince's home life was intolerable, if not downright dangerous. Vince's mom, the stabilizing influence in the home, had died about the time Vince was starting high school.

"Both of your parents were true godsends for me. I'll always be grateful."

Valerie soon arrived with their orders. The two men bowed their heads and gave a quick prayer of thanks before starting on their steaming plates of scrambled eggs and home fries. As Vince covered his potatoes with a generous portion of ketchup, Tom added a packet of sweetener to his coffee. "All right, Vince," he began, "So is it true? Are you and Wendy really moving back to Shelby Falls?"

"It's official as of yesterday, friend. We've retired from the mission field. I'll be starting next month as the new chaplain and general manager at Hope Hospice House. Wendy will be nursing part-time at New Dawn Retirement Center."

"Sounds like a perfect fit for you both. I wish you well. As soon as you get settled, Marcy and I intend to have you and Wendy over for dinner. "

"Great! We accept! We're looking forward to meeting the new members of your family. We feel truly blessed to have this opportunity to move back to Shelby Falls. You see, Wendy's folks still live in Shiloh on the Ohio River. They're slowing down now and could use our help with things. Our kids have settled on opposite sides of Akron. It puts us just about equal distance from all three families. We can be there for any of them in less than two hours." He pulled his phone out of his pocket and scrolled through the pictures. "This," he said with exuberance, "is the real prize!" With obvious pride, he showed Tom a round-faced infant with a shock of black hair, sparkling blue eyes, and a toothless smile.

Tom grinned, enjoying Vince's happiness. He noted the pink bow clipped to the child's hair and guessed, "Girl?"

"Yep! Jessica's first. Her name is Adelaide Matilda. What a moniker for such a little girl, but she's 'Addy' to us. Six months old today. I don't want to brag, but honestly, you never saw such a gorgeous kid! And Gabe's wife is expecting their first in February." He gazed at the photo for several more seconds before putting away the phone. "Things were getting a little too intense where we were serving and the mission board decided to pull us out. The timing was perfect to come back to the states for good. Wendy is thrilled to be so close to the kids."

"I'm really happy for you, Vince," Tom said with sincerity, "and glad for myself. I've missed having you around, my friend. But I am curious about your time overseas. Rumor has it that you and Wendy had spent some time in creative access areas. What can you tell me?"

Tom understood that some places were hostile to Christianity and it was impossible for a foreign missionary to get a visa as a missionary. Thus, those wishing to share the gospel had to use "creative" ways to gain access to those countries. Visas could be obtained for skilled workers such as teachers, doctors, nurses, or contractors. Working in these fields, they were often able to develop friendships that would eventually lead to chances to share their faith. Because it was often a dangerous undertaking, it was important that the exact places remain unknown to all but the sending mission board.

"A lot happened in eighteen years, Cal. How much time do you have?"

"If you're going to be living here I don't have to hear everything all at once," Tom smiled. "Just give me a highlight or two so I have something to tell Marcy tonight. She's interested, too."

"Then I'll tell you a story from our one of our first assignments." Vince speared a lump of scrambled eggs as he gathered his thoughts. "We were in a remote village in Africa being mentored by a man who had established a church there. I tell you, my friend, the Bible had never seemed so alive to me as in that little village. If you walked a few hundred yards from the compound where we lived, it was like going back in time. I often came face to face with witch doctors or the demon possessed. The sun shone brighter than I had ever seen, yet I would sometimes get this eerie sense of darkness. It was the witchcraft. I still get chills just thinking about it.

"There was an old woman. I'll call her Tahtee because her full name was practically unpronounceable. Tahtee had come from a long line of witch doctors and she held power over the people in the village because of their fear of her. But a year before, our mentor, Arthur, had brought in a team that showed the *JESUS* film to the village. Tahtee had convinced half of the villagers not to attend, but the rest were curious enough to risk her wrath. A half dozen people had given their souls to Christ after hearing the gospel for the first time. Our mentor had stayed to teach them the Bible and to train one of the men to be a lay leader in the budding church. Soon there were a dozen or more believers. They were the only ones not intimidated by Tahtee; the truth of the gospel had set them free from her power.

"The church had been meeting just outside the village beside a sort of garbage dump of discarded roofing thatch. A tin roofed open-air shelter had been built right beside the rotting vegetation. We were in the middle of a rousing prayer meeting one day when one of the men heard a rustling noise in the garbage dump. Thinking it was some sort of animal, he grabbed a spear and was nearly ready to hurl it into the brush pile when Arthur shouted for him to stop. Walking quickly to the pile of brush, he reached his hand into the slimy mess and pulled an old woman out by the hair! Tahtee. She was scared to death that we would be angry because of her spying. But Arthur told her that she was welcome to stay. It turned out that she was upset when the Christians were no longer in her power. She recognized rightly that they had a greater power than she had, and she wanted it. She offered to pay for the secret information."

"Just like Simon the sorcerer in the book of Acts," Tom put in.

Vince nodded. "Arthur assured her that we would give her the secret free of charge. She could listen without hiding in the stinking garbage." Vince looked earnestly into his friend's face. "It was the first miracle Wendy and I witnessed. Within a couple of weeks of hearing the gospel, Tahtee was transformed into a spirit-filled believer in Jesus Christ. That was seventeen years ago. She has gone on to heaven now, but before she died, she was responsible for rescuing hundreds of souls from the darkness of witchcraft and leading them into the kingdom of God. It was a pretty dramatic way to begin our ministry."

Tom whistled softly. "Wow."

"Our time in Africa was challenging." Vince said matter-of-factly. "Separation from family was hard. It about killed Wendy and me to have to send the kids back to the states for high school and college. And it got dangerous toward the end. There were exciting things happening, but not necessarily things I'm anxious to relive. Yet, I wouldn't want to trade away any of our experiences, either. God had called us, and there were great spiritual rewards in our obedience to his call."

Tom contemplated the fact that he had never had the desire to leave his own hometown, let alone serve in a foreign land. His life by comparison seemed so mundane, and he said as much to Vince.

Vince laughed. "I'm looking forward to 'mundane' in this new job," he said. "I'm sure it will be challenging in its own way, but I don't expect to have too many surprises." He shook his head and looked soberly at his friend. "We go where God sends us, Cal. He can use us as long as we are willing. It doesn't matter where. Even where we were overseas, it became routine at times. We often went for long, dry periods without seeing much progress, especially in the later years. We'd hope and pray that we were making a difference; that we were influencing others for Christ, but we couldn't be sure much of the time. We just had to wait and trust."

Tom looked pensively into his now cold coffee before he took a sip.

Vince continued. "Not all that different from ministry here in Shelby Falls, I would guess. By the way, I've heard good things about your work at Grace Community."

Tom shrugged. "Thanks, but you're right. We do have to wait and trust that God is using us to make a difference. It took me awhile to figure out that I don't have to have all the answers; just try to be obedient to where I think he's leading me."

The waitress came by and began clearing the table. They left their tips and walked over to pay their bills.

"If you have some free time," Tom said, "come take a ride with me. I'll show you some of the changes we've made here since you've been away."

A minute later Vince climbed into the passenger seat of Tom's pick-up, and they took off.

"We were so sorry we weren't able to be here for you after Sharon's passing, Cal. She was such a good woman. I can't imagine what it was like for you to lose her so young."

Tom's eyes focused on the road ahead as he remembered. "The lowest point of my life," he said grimly.

A wave of regret swept over Vince. He and Wendy had made one trip back to Shelby Falls just before leaving for training for their first assignment. Sharon had just been diagnosed with the cancer, and they had spent several hours visiting the Calderons. But soon after, their lives had become a frenzy of activity as they prepared to leave the country. Subsequent furloughs over the years had been jam-packed with visits with Wendy's family and the business of acquiring funding from sponsoring churches.

I should have made more of an effort. The note of sympathy and a few emails over the years seemed pretty inadequate now as he watched the pain flicker over Tom's face.

But his friend's voice held no bitterness. "It was a valley I had to walk alone, Vince, though it did help immensely that I had so many people praying for me."

As they turned onto one of the main streets, Tom pointed out the mall that had opened a couple of years before. Vince gave a thumbs-up. "Lots of baby items available there, I'm sure," he said with a wink.

Tom headed for the edge of town. As they approached the sign for Calvary Cemetery, he asked, "Care to stop?"

"I think I'd like that," Vince answered. A moment later the two men were out of the truck, their shoes making crunching sounds on the gravel path. Leaves were beginning to turn color, the air held the promise of frost, and an occasional chorus of bird calls broke the stillness. They stopped first at the Mateo grave and silently read the names etched in the modest granite headstone: Julia Mateo 1940–1976, Anthony Mateo 1935–1992. Tom stepped aside for a few minutes, giving Vince some privacy.

Next they found the stone for Tom's parents, Ed and Belinda Calderon. "They were like parents to me," Vince said quietly as he put his hand on Tom's shoulder. Tom bent and pulled a few weeds from around the flat brass plaque that sat next to his parents' granite memorial. Under Sharon Calderon's name was engraved: "Safe in the Savior's arms."

"Sharon's wish?" Vince asked. When Tom nodded, he said, "That sounds like her. She was so grateful for Jesus."

Vince lowered himself onto a nearby bench and waited as his friend wrestled with feelings from the past. Tom looked up, his eyes scanning the expanse of sky, brilliant blue with a smattering of wispy white. He perched on the seat, shoulders tense.

"I didn't handle it well, Vince," he said. "I fumbled my way through all the stages: denial, fear, anger … I felt so betrayed by God. How would I raise Nolan by myself? How about my ministry? How could I be strong for my family and my church when I felt so helpless and inadequate?"

A glance at Vince's sympathetic face helped him relax.

"I coped by getting lost in church work. If I was home and had to watch Sharon getting weaker and weaker, I was faced with the sense of my own inadequacy to protect my wife from—life, I guess. I was thirty-six years old. Nolan was barely ten at the time. Sharon and I had planned to grow old together."

"How did she handle what was happening?"

Tom frowned. "Sharon was the one who had to go through the physical pain and the reality that she would not be watching our son grow to adulthood. She coped by grabbing hold of Jesus and not letting go. She accepted her fate with amazing grace. But I was angry with Sharon," Tom confessed. They stood and started strolling on the gravel path. "I wanted her to fight for her life."

Vince nodded, "I've been told that the will to live is a huge factor in survival rates."

Tom stopped abruptly and looked into Vince's eyes. "Early on she had that will to live, for me and for Nolan. But the chemo took such a toll on her. She refused any more treatments. The prognosis was never good. Her chances were slim no matter what, but it might have given her a little more time. It was her choice. She said she wanted to enjoy life in the time she had left, even if it meant having less time. But I wasn't ready. She seemed to sense God's plan in it, but I just wasn't seeing it. While she was looking heavenward, I was scared out of my wits to be left behind. But I should have spent more time with her while I had the chance."

"Did Nolan have any counseling after Sharon died?" Vince was thinking of the feelings he'd had to work through when his own mother had died while he was a teen.

Tom shook his head. "Not really. You see, he was such a compliant kid. He never acted out like most kids do. So I guess I thought he was doing fine. My parents felt differently, but I'm ashamed to say that I was so into my own pain and my own loss that I let a lot of things slip that first year. Frankly, Nolan and I seldom talk about Sharon. It just gets too awkward for both of us. Why is it that I can speak intimately to those in my congregation, when it's my job, but I have a hard time with my own flesh and blood?"

Vince laughed, "My wife would say, 'It's a guy thing!'"

Tom spoke ruefully. "I suppose it is. I'm sure Marcy would agree."

His face grew serious again as he continued. "I started using Sharon's Bible in my daily devotionals soon after she died as a way to feel close to her. She had taken to writing copious notes in the margins and where she ran out of space, she had plastered post-it notes all over the pages. It was beautiful to see her peace and understanding expressed in her own words. I had always believed in the power of the gospel, but I don't think I had ever truly experienced it in such a way until then. I had talked of heaven from the pulpit, but now a part of me was actually there. Sharon's serenity had come from finding God's promises and holding fast to them. I was her husband, her best friend, and her pastor. I should have been comforting her more instead of feeling so sorry for myself. But God had it under control, just as Sharon had tried to tell me.

"My whole approach to ministry changed after her death. I took a good honest look at myself. I wondered how effective I had been as a pastor. I was a hard worker. But was I really feeding my flock the way God wanted me to? I couldn't forget how much the Bible had strengthened Sharon. I thought long and hard, Vince, about just exactly what my calling involved."

He stopped on the path and looked earnestly at his friend. "I came to the conclusion that if Christ is who the Bible says he is—and I believe he is—and if I truly believe in him—which I do—then my focus has to be on him above all. To me that meant that Christ and his Word should always trump church business, finances, programs, building projects, politics— fill in the blank—all the things that had in the past kept me from focusing on my true calling, which is drawing my people, my flock, into a close and saving relationship with Jesus Christ."

Vince's eyes were focused on Tom's face, and he gave a nod to encourage him to continue.

"I made a vow that as long as I am the pastor of Grace Community Church, or any other church for that matter, that the Bible will be preached and taught from my pulpit each and every week. The people can and will reach their own conclusions, but as long as it is in my power, I will not have my flock live in ignorance of God's Word. If the people ever grow weary of that and want rid of me, so be it. I *will* remain true to my vow!"

The moment he finished, Vince stepped up, placed his left hand on Tom's shoulder and pumped his right hand vigorously. "Preach it, brother!" he said with a wide grin. "I can tell you now, as soon as Wendy and I get moved back to Shelby Falls, you're going to have two new people added to your flock!"

Chapter 8

It was lunchtime on a Saturday when Marcy Calderon walked into the Snappy Café, and it was packed. She was accompanied by her new friend Wendy Mateo. Marcy had fair skin and a smattering of freckles across her slightly angular face. Her hair was auburn and cut in the pageboy style. She was barely five foot five, but due to her long legs and lanky frame, she gave the impression of being taller. In contrast, Wendy was a petite five feet and full-figured. She wore her straight, raven-black hair pulled back loosely in a bun. She had dark eyes and a round face that was brightened by a charming dimpled smile.

The women looked in vain for an empty table in the crowded lunchroom. As Marcy scanned the room she saw a hand waving at her from the back. Stepping closer, she recognized Kozy Hanner, the girl who had been helping with the youth project at church. They weaved their way through the restaurant to where Kozy sat with her friend Cathy Dawson. Kozy quickly introduced Marcy to Cathy.

Marcy, in return, introduced Wendy. "Wendy is married to my husband's best friend from childhood. They recently returned to the area, and I was hoping to show her some of the new spots in town. Looks like we came at a busy time though."

"We'll gladly share our table with you," Cathy offered, pointing to the two empty chairs at their table for four.

"Yes," Kozy added. "We haven't even ordered yet. Please, feel free to sit with us!"

"Glad to!" said Wendy as she pulled out a chair. "I'm eager to start meeting people." Upon learning that Kozy and Cathy taught third grade together at Central Elementary, Wendy remarked, "Aw, nice age to work with. I miss those years. I'm an empty-nester myself!"

"Me too," Cathy said. "So you've lived here before, Wendy?"

"Shelby Falls is my husband's home town, so we used to visit quite often, but it's been many years. We just retired from overseas mission work."

"Wendy works as a nurse. Her husband, Vince, is the new chaplain for Hope Hospice House," Marcy added.

"Oh, that's wonderful!" Cathy said. "When my husband died a decade ago, the facility was only in the planning stages. But hospice nurses were available for us during his illness and were greatly appreciated. They were such a blessing to us!"

Wendy and Cathy continued their conversation, and Marcy turned to Kozy with a smile. "So, how is it going with your Wednesday small group?"

Marcy was delighted to have this chance meeting with Kozy Hanner. Kozy had been attending Grace Church on Sundays ever since she had been the kick-off speaker for the special fall teen event. Though Marcy was unaware of the blind date on which the girl and her stepson had first met, she was aware that Nolan had specifically asked to be paired with Kozy as a co-leader for one of the teen groups. It was unusual for Nolan to make such a request since he was normally content to work wherever he was needed. Marcy had noticed that Nolan seemed especially attentive to his new group partner last week during the social time before the Sunday services started. Of course, Nolan was an adult and had been on his own for several years, but Marcy still found it frustrating that he was so reserved when it came to sharing anything about his social life. It would be nice to get to know this young woman better, just in case there might be a budding romance in the near future.

"It's going great, Mrs. Calderon!" Kozy answered with enthusiasm. "The teens seem to be opening up to us. And the Bible study that your husband put together has really seemed to spark their interest."

"I'm glad to hear that, but you needn't be so formal with me. I'd be happy if you just called me Marcy. It's what Nolan calls me."

"Well then, 'Marcy' it is!" Kozy grinned.

By the time the server had taken their orders, all four women were chatting easily with one another. Wendy was not one to let her status as the newcomer in the group get in the way of getting to know people. "So, Marcy, I haven't yet heard about how you and Tom met. There's nothing better than hearing a good love story, right, ladies?" She clasped her hands together and looked eagerly at Marcy.

Marcy's cheeks turned pink, and she rolled her eyes slightly as her three table companions nodded their heads in agreement. "Okay, fine," she agreed finally, biting at the smile on her lips. She paused as she considered how to begin her story. "I had just moved to Shelby Falls, and I hardly knew a soul except for the co-workers in my small office. The ancient desktop computer I had moved to my apartment was about ready for the landfill. I had my heart set on a laptop, but I had myself on a very tight budget. Looking in the paper one day I saw a personal ad for the very computer I was hoping to buy. The ad said it was 'still in the box' brand new from an individual seller, and the price was almost too good to be true. I was sure it had to be a scam, but my frugal mind desperately wanted it to be for real. Finally, I worked up the courage to call the number. A man answered. Nice smooth voice. 'Scam,' I figured, but when I asked questions, his story sounded so reasonable. He had just bought the computer on a super sale and before he had a chance to use it, he had been given a similar computer as a gift. Naturally, to avoid hurt feelings, he had to keep the gift. He didn't need two computers, and he wanted to recoup some of his money on the one he'd bought. So a reasonable story, and a nice voice. Too nice. I was convinced it had to be a scam. But what if it was for real? I might consider checking it out if we met in a very public place. My skepticism must have come through in my conversation. 'If you're interested,' he said abruptly, 'you can meet me at

Grace Community Church, tomorrow morning, any time after nine, but before four. Ask for Tom.' And just like that he hung up."

Marcy looked around the table at the three women whose eyes were focused on her. "Go on. What happened next?" Cathy prompted.

Marcy laughed. "I told myself, 'I can do church.' The next day on my lunch hour I drove over to the address Tom had given me and introduced myself to Helen Troyer, the church secretary. When I asked to see 'Tom', she walked me over to the door that said 'Pastor' and gave it a tap. 'Miss MacCready to see you, Pastor,' she announced as she carefully propped the door open. First thing I noticed, after his handsome face, was the prominently displayed family picture on his desk. It was Tom, his pretty dark-haired wife, and their young son. 'Oh well', I thought. It had been my lot so far in life that the good ones were already taken.

"He was all business. He demonstrated the computer to me, we agreed on the price, and I handed him a check. Then, as I was headed out the door with my new computer, I heard him clear his throat. I turned to face him and with his charming smile, he said, 'Miss MacCready, I'd like to invite you to services on Sunday; that is, if you haven't already found a church home.'"

She chuckled. "I still like to tease Tom that it was a really cheap first date! I liked Grace Church right off the bat; the people were friendly, and I was really touched by Tom's preaching. But it took me several weeks before I figured out that he was a widower."

The server arrived at the table then and the women started on their lunches. The ladies still had questions. Wendy continued. "It must have taken courage though, to date your pastor. Not to mention having the entire congregation watching the process unfold, and deal with a stepchild as well." The other ladies nodded in agreement.

"It was a rather touchy situation," Marcy answered. "But, I'm a preacher's kid myself. I had the advantage of knowing firsthand that pastors are really just people like anybody else. Plus, I couldn't have had a better teacher than my mother, Sarah MacCready, to show me how to gracefully navigate the minefields of life in the pastorate. As for Nolan, he was a delightful kid. My being a 'PK' too made it easier for us to hit it off from the start." She smiled. "I found out months after the fact that there was a group of ladies in the church, my future mother-in-law included, who had made it their mission to meet every week to pray for a spouse for their lonely pastor. How could they not accept the answer to their prayers?"

The rest of the time was filled with easy chatter while the women finished their lunches. When the time came to leave, Kozy stood, donning her light jacket, and turned to Marcy. "Thanks for sharing your story with us, Mrs.—oops, I mean, Marcy. I really, really enjoyed our time together."

"Well, thank you for offering to share your table with us. And it was good to meet you, Cathy. See you soon, Kozy," she said with a wave.

"That was fun," Wendy told her as they walked to Marcy's car. "I enjoyed meeting them both." She looked questioningly at Marcy. "Sweet girl, that Kozy. Pretty, too. So do you think she and your Nolan might be interested in each other?"

Marcy laughed as she put her key in the ignition. "I really don't know, Wendy. But if you happen to find out anything, I'd appreciate it if you'd let Tom and me know!"

Chapter 9

Nolan found himself whistling as he stepped out of the shower and dressed for his dinner date. He stood in front of the mirror to comb his hair and noticed the smile on his face. He turned it into a slight grimace.

Get a grip on yourself, Nolan. She's just another girl, right? He watched the smile creep back on his face and he rolled his eyes.

Forty minutes later, he and Kozy were being seated at Valentini's, a popular new restaurant just outside of town. When they entered the colorful dining room, he was pleased with his choice for, what he considered, the first *real* date with Kozy Hanner. He did not count the less-than-perfect blind date on which they had met three months ago. There were no powder-blue mismatched shoes tonight. Nolan thought the attractive, silky turquoise dress she wore this time was a bit more becoming than the frilly pink and blue outfit she had been wearing the first time they met. She looked stunning, actually. No ruffles and lace in sight. Since their first meeting he and Kozy had spent hours getting to know one another. Looking back, he was amazed that he had failed to notice her wonderful qualities from the beginning.

She looked around the brightly lit room. Servers dressed in white shirts, black slacks and red vests carried large bowls of tossed salad to the tables of cheerful diners. The tantalizing aroma of fresh-baked bread and Italian spices permeated the room. "I've wanted to try this place ever since it opened, Nolan. Thanks for inviting me."

Nolan's eyes followed a dish of steaming lasagna as it was being delivered to the table behind them. "Mmm. I don't think I'm even going to need to look at the menu. That looks too good to pass up. I've heard it's their most popular entrée."

Kozy closed her eyes and breathed deeply. "I think I have to agree, Nolan. It looks and smells wonderful! It gets my vote."

For the next hour and a half they enjoyed the delicious food, cheerful atmosphere, and easy conversation. Though the portions of salad and lasagna were generous, they were still tempted by the server's suggestion to try the cannoli, the restaurant's signature dessert. They opted to take the middle ground.

"We'll try one, but bring us two plates, please," Nolan said to the server.

Kozy cut a small portion for herself from the delicate rolled pastry and pushed the rest to Nolan. She tasted the sweet creamy filling and groaned with pleasure. "A perfect ending," she said, "but if I eat one more smidgen, you'll have to roll me out of here."

Nolan savored the last scrumptious bite and checked the time on his phone. He was surprised at how quickly the time had passed. He looked guiltily at the groups of people still in line waiting to be seated. He was enjoying their time together so much that he wished they were just starting. "I guess we'd better be kind and give up our table," he said reluctantly when the server brought the bill. As they maneuvered their way through the crowd and out to the entrance, they noticed new customers were walking in brushing snow pellets off their coats. Nolan frowned and quickly checked the weather channel on his phone. The temperature had dropped at least fifteen degrees since they had arrived, and a weather front had moved in that suggested periods of heavy snow and wind for the next several hours. As they headed out the door and into the darkness, the wind whipped around their heads and angrily pelted their faces with sleet. Nolan felt his chest begin to tighten. *Oh, no. Not now! Everything was going so well. Please God. Let me get her home all right.*

"I'm sorry, Kozy," he explained. "I'm going to have to cut our time short tonight and take you straight home now. Storms like this make me nervous. I really, *really* enjoyed our time together, but I'd like to get you safely home."

Kozy saw the guarded look on his face, and she sensed that this was not the right time to question him about it. Instead she said, "That's probably a good idea, Nolan. I had a wonderful time with you tonight." She laid her hand on his arm and looked into his eyes with a smile. "But let's get going now. The weather may turn really nasty soon."

Nolan's hands clutched the steering wheel as he drove back through the dark night. Though there was no snow accumulation, he felt unnerved by the flurries that furiously whipped at the windshield. He concentrated on breathing evenly during the six-mile drive back to Kozy's house. He tried to sound casual as they chatted but feared that he was failing miserably to mask his tension. Once he pulled into Kozy's driveway, he quickly walked her to her door. Not wanting to see a questioning look in her eyes, he avoided looking at her face as he said good night and jogged back to his car.

Minutes later he stepped inside his apartment and quickly pulled the blinds on the front picture window. He sat heavily on the couch and shut his eyes with a sigh, relieved to have narrowly avoided a full-fledged panic attack. He was embarrassed about how his perfect evening had ended. His feelings once more under control, he pondered his phobia for what seemed like the thousandth time. It had taken him by surprise tonight. It had been over two years since his last one.

It had started the winter after his mother's death. He had been walking the short distance over the frozen field that separated his friend Ben's house from his own. Though it was early evening, with only a sliver of moon, it was nearly pitch dark. The snow had started suddenly and began swirling wildly around him, exactly as it had been the night his mother died. His chest had tightened, and he had trouble breathing. He didn't know how long he had crouched in the field, eyes squeezed tightly closed, fighting nausea and faintness. When he dared open his eyes, the air was clear. Nolan had sprinted the rest of the way home and let himself into the house. His father arrived home a few minutes later. Nolan, still shaken, had stayed in his room for another half hour, not wanting to worry his dad.

Eventually Nolan learned to focus on other things when the weather conditions were like this. He thought he had conquered his weakness. His dad's marriage to Marcy and the arrival of his two rambunctious siblings had helped ease his anxiety. When he entered high school, his busy schedule with sports and college prep courses kept his mind occupied.

After college, he felt fortunate to have landed a job as an accountant with a large company based in Buffalo, New York. It turned out to be much different from what he expected. He would later confess to his dad that his job title could have been "police dog" rather than accountant. He was to travel to the various branches and sniff out signs of possible fraud or mishandling of funds within the company. He had felt like an outcast whenever he arrived at the next branch on his schedule. He had not been especially popular with his co-workers, which was understandable given his role, and he missed his family terribly. However, he was determined to succeed and stuck with the job for a couple of years. Eventually, the stress of the job combined with the loneliness and isolation he felt took its toll.

It was impossible to avoid snowstorms in Buffalo. Late one winter evening, while returning from one of his assignments, the panic attacks that he had thought were a thing of the past returned with a vengeance. Having lived most of his life in Ohio, Nolan was well used to winter driving. That night the driving conditions were less than ideal, but nothing too serious. However, the combination of the dark and the angry swirl of the snow in his headlights seemed to trigger something inside his psyche. The panic and feeling of helplessness he had felt the night his mother died overtook him once more. Fortunately, the predictions of treacherous road conditions had kept most people home that night. Nolan managed to maneuver himself safely to a vacant parking lot where he gasped for breath and waited for the terrifying symptoms to subside. That scenario repeated itself a few more times that winter and the next.

He was deeply grateful that, while home visiting two summers before, he had the good fortune of having placed his chair next to Mr. Marley's during the Fourth of July parade. Mr. and Mrs. Marley attended Grace Community Church, and they also lived three streets away from the Calderon home. Nolan had mowed Mr. Marley's grass all through middle school and high school, and they had been good friends ever since. Mr. Marley had taken a special interest in Nolan because he was an accountant. When he offered Nolan a job at his small firm that day, Nolan knew it was an answer to prayer. After having worked as a fairly anonymous employee at a huge company, the prospect of being a part of a small but respected company in his own hometown was very appealing. He had always admired Mr. Marley's integrity, and he felt blessed to have the chance to work for him. He was also thrilled for the chance to move back to Shelby Falls and be able to see his family more often. He gave his notice at his job as soon as he returned to Buffalo. Within three weeks he had moved into a duplex on Oak Street and started his job as an accountant at Marley's Financial Services. The panic attacks had not returned, until tonight.

Nolan felt calmer now, but he still sat dejectedly on the couch with head in hands. He thought of how he had rushed Kozy home in his urgent need to escape his fears. *I sure owe her an apology. I just hope I have the courage to explain the next time we're together. I want her to like me. But I need to be honest.*

He picked up his Bible and turned to a passage that he had long ago highlighted. He read the familiar words over again, even though he knew them by heart: Psalm 30: 4-5 *"Sing praise to the Lord, you saints of His, and give thanks at the remembrance of His holy name. For His anger is but for a moment. His favor is for life; Weeping may endure for a night, but joy comes in the morning."*

***

Saturday dawned bright and mild, and Nolan looked in amazement out his kitchen window. The thermometer was inching towards sixty degrees with the sun hinting at even higher temperatures as the day progressed. Gone were the snow squalls and icy winds of the night before.

A typical December in Ohio. Nolan shook his head. *If you don't like the weather, just wait a day.*

His thoughts went immediately to Kozy. The idea of sharing a portion of this beautiful day with her was extremely appealing. And he was hoping to redeem himself after his abrupt end to their time together last evening. He grabbed his phone and punched in her number before he had a chance to change his mind.

An hour later they were walking together down an obscure wooded trail just past the town park. They started out at a brisk pace, relishing the chance to be out in the sunshine and fresh air.

"Good thinking, Nolan, after you filled me up with all those calories last night," Kozy teased.

Nolan grinned. They walked in companionable silence until they reached the top of Oldtown Hill, where they stopped to enjoy the panoramic view of Shelby Falls and its surrounding hills.

"Pretty!" said Kozy as she removed her hat, loosening her golden curls in the sunlight. "I can't wait to see it in the spring when the leaves are back on the trees." She looked at him with a happy smile.

He stepped behind her and pointed over her shoulder toward a spot right below a stand of evergreens. "Now is the best time to show you where Shelby Falls got its name. If you look over to our left," Nolan pointed, "you'll see it."

Kozy squinted at the spot. "Okay, I can see what looks like a big grayish rock, but I can't make out any water."

Nolan laughed. "About two hundred years ago there was a small stream cascading over that gray rock. A Mr. Josiah Shelby from Pennsylvania traveled here, bought a few hundred acres of land surrounding the waterfall, and built a gristmill, intending to spend the rest of his days grinding grain for the local farmers."

Kozy turned to face him, her eyes twinkling in anticipation. "What happened?" she asked, clearly intrigued with the mini history lesson.

"Within a short time, a flood changed the course of the stream. Overnight, the poor man's intended livelihood had literally dried up. He still owned the surrounding land and realized that the location was well suited for a town. So he hired his brother-in-law, who was a surveyor, to lay out plans for the streets. Then he went back to his old home and talked a couple dozen brave souls to move west with him to where the game was still plentiful and the land fertile. He sold plots to each of those original pioneers, and the town was born. Funny thing was, Josiah soon decided to move on west to the wilds of Indiana. As far as anybody knows, he never set foot in the area again. But the name 'Shelby Falls' stuck even though we no longer have a waterfall nearby, or a Shelby descendant for that matter."

Kozy smiled, chewing on her lip. "I never dreamed you were such a history buff, Nolan! What would I have to do to convince you to give a little talk to my class?"

"Hmm," he teased, looking at her with narrowed eyes. "I guess I'll have to think about that proposition."

He could not help but notice the glimmer of her hair, and the pink glow in her cheeks from that last push up the steep hill. He felt his pulse quicken. Reluctantly he looked away.

"Oldtown Hill was part of my old stomping grounds as a kid," he explained. "Ben and I put in lots of time roaming this part of town, mainly because his family owned some of the surrounding land. This hill really is a killer; I'm afraid I may feel the results in my calf muscles tomorrow. It's hard to believe that I used to sprint it back in my cross country days."

"Well, I am impressed, believe me." Kozy chuckled.

Nolan pointed to a large fallen log that sat in an open space. "Let's rest for a while." They sat side by side, enjoying the warmth of the sun in the cool air. When she remained silent, he began. "I wanted to explain about last night; about why I was acting so weird." *There. I've started. Now I have to finish.* He struggled to find the words. "I have a problem. I thought it was over with, but it seems to be coming back." The words came easier as he continued. Kozy's eyes stayed steady on his face as he told her about his panic attacks, from the time they had started years ago until the one he nearly had after their dinner the night before.

When he finished, she placed her hand on top of his. "I'm glad you shared this with me, Nolan," she said. "Now I'll know how to pray for you. Let's both ask God to reveal to you the reason behind all of this." Her brow wrinkled as she thought about Nolan's revelation. "Hmm. I can understand how stressful your job in Buffalo must have been, but you say you really enjoy working at Marley's. I wonder what could be affecting you now. Is something at work bothering you?" Her eyes grew wide as she thought of a new possibility. "Oh, I hope being with me wasn't too stressful!"

"Now you're being silly," he chuckled as he shook his head. With his index finger he tapped her lightly on the nose. "Meeting you has been one of the nicest things to happen to me in a long while." He was rewarded with a wide smile. "Let's get going now. Your nose feels a little cold."

Kozy giggled then and they headed down the hill at a leisurely pace. Nolan was glad he'd opened up to her about his fears. He felt lighthearted there in the sunshine and ready to put aside his problems at work. He was determined to ignore his annoying co-worker and enjoy this day.

"So, 'Kozy' isn't a name you hear every day. Is there a story behind that?" he asked.

"My name comes from my mother's maiden name, Kozma. I barely remember my parents, but somehow I've retained the memory that I was named after my grandparents. No matter where I ended up in foster care, there were always kids who taunted me. 'Where's your dad? Where's your mom? I'll bet you don't have a *real* family, do you?' I hated those questions, and hated even more that I didn't have an answer. But I had my name, 'Kozy'. I clung to my name as proof that I really did have family out there somewhere. Still, it hurt." Her mouth twisted as she muttered, "I slugged plenty of kids for teasing me in those days."

Nolan's eyebrows lifted in surprise. "It's hard to picture you as a brawler, Kozy," he said with a grin.

"Well, I lived in some pretty rough neighborhoods. One of my many foster brothers, Raúl, taught me how to have an advantage over the bigger kids." She answered the question in Nolan's eyes.

"And yes, once Gram got hold of me, the fighting did stop. She kept a pretty tight rein. She did everything she could to make our home stable. That's not to say that I got everything I wanted—not by a long shot. I didn't mind, really, because I always felt loved. Not just by Gram, but by the whole group of 'paprika ladies' from the church."

"Paprika ladies?"

She grinned. "My pet name for her Hungarian friends. I was in college before I realized that not *everyone* has paprika shakers on their kitchen stoves alongside the salt and pepper." She laughed at the confusion on Nolan's face.

"Paprika is the premier spice in Hungarian cooking. Indispensable! Virtually any dish that calls for salt or pepper, also calls for paprika, at least according to Gram and her 'Old Country' friends." She placed her fingers on either side of her face. "See these rosy cheeks?"

"Uh-huh."

She gave him a mock sober look. "Directly proportional to the amount of paprika eaten," she whispered conspiratorially.

"Ahh, so *that's* the secret!"

Once they reached Kozy's house, she invited Nolan to sit on her porch while she went in to fetch them bottles of water. When she returned, Nolan was perched on the porch rail with a wry smile on his face.

Wrinkling her brow Kozy asked, "What?"

He shook his head and chuckled. "It's just that I'm still having a time picturing you in a scuffle. I'm trying to see it in my mind, for instance, you as an eight-year-old punching me for teasing you."

"I don't think *you* would have done something like that would you?

"True enough. I always tried to do what was right, on the outside at least. But that doesn't mean I wouldn't have *wanted* to tease you."

She studied his face. "I forgive you, Nolan," she said at last.

"I believe you would." Then he laughed. "I wish I could have seen you though, taking on the big kids. You, with your frilly pink clothes and lacy socks; it must have been a sight!"

Kozy was silent for a while as she looked soberly at Nolan. "Well," she finally said. "Here's the thing, Nolan. When I was little, I had to wear hand-me-downs from my foster brothers. Plain boy jeans and oversized black t-shirts with ugly monsters, cars, or robots on the front. How I envied all those little girls who got to wear pretty pink or purple jeans and with all the lace and glitter! I wanted sparkly shirts with Disney characters on them. I wanted clothes that would make me feel like a princess. I pretended it didn't matter, but it hurt. It was just one more thing that made me think the mean kids might be right; that I had no family and no one to truly love me."

Nolan's heart sank and he wished he could take back his last words. "Oh, Kozy, I'm sorry. It never occurred to me that you'd not get to dress like the other kids. Once your grandma got custody of you, were you finally able to wear the clothes you wished for?"

"No, not really," she answered. "Gram's idea of appropriate clothes and mine differed quite a bit. She was on a pretty limited income, and she needed to get me practical things that wouldn't go out of style. That hunger for glitz and fluff stayed with me even after my friends had outgrown them. When I began my student teaching, I got the wild idea that, as a third grade teacher, I might be able to indulge in the things I had missed out on as a little girl. So I had the idea that, once in a while, I would dress like the little girls in my class. I ran my idea past my instructing teacher. She happened to be a free-spirited soul herself and gave me permission to give it a try. Turned out the kids kind of liked it. The little girls in my class love my clothes! So I stuck with it. Someday I expect I'll get my fill of lace, glitter, and frills, but until then, I'm going to enjoy what I missed out on."

Nolan stepped forward and looked into her eyes. "I feel like an insensitive oaf. I just didn't think … I'm sorry."

"You are not an insensitive oaf, Nolan. You have nothing to be sorry for."

He reached over and pulled gently on one of her curls. The silky strand slipped from his fingers and as it did he allowed his fingers to lightly trace the curve of her cheek. The touch nearly took his breath away. "I should leave now," he said abruptly, and turned to jog back to his car. "See you at church tomorrow."

Thank you for giving me the courage to tell her, Lord. She's so easy to talk with. I'm feeling pretty bedazzled. I guess you know that, don't you, Lord? Help me keep my head on straight!

Chapter 10

"Yes! This is the one!" Kozy announced. She passed her hand back and forth horizontally from her chin to the top of the Frasier fir. "It's perfect, don't you think, Nolan?"

Nolan pursed his lips and stared at the four and a half foot tree. "Um, ah, it's ah, tiny."

"I'll take it!" Kozy said excitedly as she handed the money to the Christmas tree lot attendant.

Nolan grimaced slightly as he carried the tree in one hand and carefully placed it in the trunk of Kozy's Hyundai Elantra. Lying flat with its branches folded in, it looked even more miniscule. *More like a broken twig than a tree. What is she thinking?* He wisely kept his thoughts to himself. After all, she seemed so happy. No sense spoiling her fun by pointing out a real Christmas tree should be huge. The Calderons never had a tree less than eight feet tall. The bigger the better.

"Thank you for offering to come with me, Nolan." Kozy said shyly. "This will be the first time I've put up a tree on my own. I didn't have the heart for it after Gram died, but this year I feel it's time."

Nolan smiled. *Just as I suspected. The poor girl just doesn't know anything about choosing the right kind of Christmas tree!*

They made it back to Kozy's house and carried the tree inside. Nolan used a handsaw to make a fresh cut off the end of the tree's trunk, a job that took him less than five seconds. Carrying the tree into the living room, he saw that Kozy had already placed a plastic cover over the small oak table that sat in front of the picture window. Nolan centered the tree in the small metal stand and tightened the screws, then rotated the tree until Kozy was convinced that its best side was facing inward.

"It smells so wonderful!" she said, sniffing the fragrant branches and lightly stroking the soft needles. "The lights are the most tedious part. Would you like to put on some music, Nolan, while I wrestle with these? I'm afraid I'm a bit of a perfectionist when it comes to the lights."

Nolan picked an instrumental Christmas CD and sat on the couch to watch Kozy as she painstakingly wove the string of miniature white lights evenly through the branches. Humming softly along with the music, she stepped back every so often, checking and readjusting until she felt the lights were nicely balanced.

Nolan took this time to take a better look at the living room of Kozy's modest ranch home. He had only glimpsed this room from the kitchen in his prior visits. The small space was uncluttered and welcoming. The walls were painted in a pale yellow that seemed to mimic natural sunlight. Her cream colored couch and armchairs were enlivened by bright cushions in solid primary colors. Displayed inside a small oak china cabinet was an array of cheerful patterned platters and dishes. Nolan stood and examined the eclectic collection of artwork on the walls. There were a couple of tasteful floral prints and a peaceful pastoral scene with cows grazing by a stream. By the door was a framed print of a poem by the popular early twentieth-century poet, Edgar A. Guest called "Home." The atmosphere in the room made him think of his late grandparents' home.

"Gram's little house had to be torn down for a strip mall," she explained, "but I was able to keep all the pieces that were dearest to me. One of Gram's friends let me store everything in her garage until I got my teaching job and moved to Shelby Falls. I was able to get enough for Gram's house to pay off my school debt and have a down payment on this little place. It's small, but it's really all I need for now."

The uniqueness of the room seemed to fit so well with her personality. "It's charming," he said, though he was thinking of the girl as well as the house.

"What do you think of the lights now, Nolan?"

He gave a thumbs-up and nodded. "Are we ready to decorate?"

"Yes," she said. "We are ready to make a traditional Hungarian Christmas tree." Kozy pointed toward a cardboard box that was sitting on the armchair. "You can open that box while I run into the kitchen."

Nolan was intrigued as he lifted the lid from the box and peeked inside. On top were dozens of small, heart-shaped ornaments made of red and white felt. The white side of each heart was embroidered with colorful flowers and vines. He lifted the ornaments from the box and discovered several small costumed dolls with pretty, delicate faces nestled in the bottom of the box. He looked up as Kozy came back into the room.

"Chocolate fudge with walnuts," she announced as she set down a large tray. "The first batch turned out too runny; I saved that to use on ice cream. These turned out just right."

Nolan admired the little squares of creamy fudge. "Why so many?"

She pointed to the pile of red and green metallic paper squares sitting next to the candy. "For the tree," she said. "We wrap the pieces and tie them on with red ribbons."

"Every single piece?" Nolan teased.

"Well, I guess we could spare one or two!" she grinned, popping one into her mouth and then offering the tray to Nolan. "They're supposed to be eaten by my guests during the holiday season and you are my first guest. I just hope I have the willpower to leave the rest alone until Christmas!"

Twenty minutes later, they were putting the finishing touches on the tree with some gilded walnuts and dried slices of oranges and lemons. Kozy wrapped a long piece of green felt around the tree stand and pronounced the job finished. Nolan sat back on the couch to admire their efforts. After turning off the lamp, Kozy sat down beside him. Christmas carols were playing softly, and the little tree glowed with the soft white lights. The effect was subdued and peaceful. Nolan admitted to himself that he had been wrong about Kozy's choice. Sitting on the table top, and framed by the picture window, the tree was perfect for the small room.

"Decorating the tree this way makes me feel connected with Gram. She was proud to be an American, and she cherished the freedom this country gave her, but she couldn't ignore her Hungarian heritage. It was what made her the unique person she was."

"Tell me more about her."

Kozy sat studying the tree for a moment before responding. "She was courageous, wise, creative, and fun. It couldn't have been easy for her to take on raising an eight-year-old at her age, but she made me think I was the best thing that ever happened to her. Of course, she didn't take any nonsense from me, either. When I wasn't acting my best, she would try to teach me by weaving a little homespun wisdom into her stories. Or she would do absolutely silly things to make me laugh when I got myself into a bad mood. Most of all, she made sure that I was surrounded with love.

"Gram arrived here, after the Hungarian Revolution, all alone. The Hungarian church that sponsored her became her family. The Buckeye Road neighborhood eventually became too dangerous, and by the early nineties the church had moved out to the suburbs. Gram and many of her dearest friends settled close to one another in the Heights. I was surrounded by those little Hungarian ladies while I was growing up. Gram and her friends seemed so old-fashioned compared to my classmates' parents." She let out a wistful sigh, "I realize now how much I was loved."

"I wish I could have known her," Nolan said softly. "And I wish you could have known my grandparents. They sound a lot alike. They were great encouragers." He looked at his phone and whistled. "Wow, I didn't notice how late it was getting. I should be heading home. Thanks for sharing this time with me, Kozy." He hesitated a moment. "Umm, I was thinking, that maybe you would like to come to my folk's house tomorrow evening for the Calderon tree decorating? We have a little different style. Actually, with my brother and sister involved it's always pretty rowdy, but still lots of fun. I think you'd enjoy it, and my family would love having you."

"I'd like that, Nolan," she said with a bright smile.

***

Tom and Marcy Calderon peeked out their front window the next evening as Nolan walked Kozy down their driveway and helped her into his car. The decorating was finished, the twins had just left to go caroling with a family down the street, and Kozy and Nolan were headed to another Christmas party.

"Did I have that same look on my face when we started seeing each other?" Tom wondered.

Marcy grinned. "Smitten, you mean?" she asked.

"It does appear that way, doesn't it?"

Marcy chuckled as she studied her husband's smiling face. "Yes," she said finally. "I do seem to remember that same look on your face a long, long time ago."

"I'm still smitten with you, and you know it," he countered with a sound kiss on her lips.

She wrapped her arms around him and drew him close. "And you are still my handsome hunk of a man," she whispered in his ear. His smile widened in anticipation.

Later, they settled next to each other on the soft sectional in the family room and enjoyed the quiet. The dust had settled following the joyous, though noisy, tree-trimming event that had taken place an hour earlier. The majestic nine foot white pine, fat, full, and slightly askew, now dominated the far end of the room. Hundreds of brightly colored lights blinked through the tinsel-covered branches. Here and there glittery construction-paper stars shown through with crudely printed greetings from years past: "Merry Christmas from your little angel Kelsey!" and "All Zane wants for Christmas is two front teeth!" The volume on the Christmas CD had been turned down and Patsy and Elmo were singing "Grandma Got Run Over by a Reindeer" as Marcy cuddled up to her husband.

"I think it went well, don't you?" Marcy mused. "I mean, the kids really like Kozy, and she seemed to be enjoying herself. As for Nolan, every time I peeked at him he was gazing at Kozy with a goofy smile on his face."

"Mmm-hmm," Tom agreed. "I'm surprised that Zane and Kelsey didn't tease them unmercifully. Maybe they really are growing up."

"Or maybe Nolan bribed them to be good!" Marcy considered with a giggle. "At any rate, I am glad to see Nolan so happy. And I really, really like Kozy. She's been good for Nolan."

"Amen," said Tom.

Chapter 11

The air was clear and cold on Christmas Eve. A smattering of fresh snow sparkled on the lawn beneath the street lights. Kurt Walker peered from behind the shade in his darkened living room. Nolan Calderon had just stepped off the front porch of the duplex and was making his way down the shared driveway to his car. He balanced several brightly wrapped presents on one arm and held a shopping bag in the other. With some quick acrobatics he managed to punch the key to unlock his doors and open the driver's side to deposit the gifts onto the backseat. Kurt's expression was blank as he stared at the man who was both his next-door neighbor and his co-worker. Only after Nolan had started backing the car out of the drive did Kurt turn from the window and snap on a lamp. He sat heavily on his couch and reached for his phone. He scrolled through his contacts and found the one he had been looking for. He stared at the number a long while with finger poised, trying to decide. Finally with a low growl he tossed the phone aside.

"What's the use?" he muttered. Then he walked to his small kitchen and opened a cabinet door. He grabbed a bottle and a glass, poured a drink, and tried to forget the fact that it was Christmas Eve and he was alone.

***

Nolan fidgeted on the sofa as Kozy took her time admiring the brightly wrapped package in her lap. She looked up at him smiling and then continued admiring the package.

"I didn't wrap it myself," he confessed. "I don't exactly excel at wrapping, so I asked Marcy to help me."

"She did a beautiful job, but I would have been just as happy if you had done it, no matter how it looked," she assured him.

"Go ahead and open it," he urged.

She carefully removed the paper and lifted the lid from the box. Gently, she unfolded the tissue paper and removed the object inside. To her surprise, tears formed in her eyes when she realized how much thought had gone into the choosing of the gift.

"Oh, Nolan," she cried softly as she held up the heirloom quality Christmas tree skirt.

"It's so beautiful!" The rich black satin was hand embroidered with traditional Hungarian stylized flowers and hearts in bright colors. The hem was finished with a thick gold braid. Her fingers caressed the silky threads. She guessed from the quality of the workmanship that the piece was handmade. She leapt to her feet and rushed over to the tree. She tossed aside the circle of cheap green flannel that she had used to cover the tree stand and carefully arranged the new skirt around the base. She stepped back to admire the effect. The size of the skirt was perfect for the small tree, and its ornate beauty gave the tree a finished look that was charming.

She looked back at Nolan. "Thank you," she whispered, the warmth in her eyes proving her sincerity. Breaking her gaze, she looked back at the tree. "I've never seen anything like it before, Nolan," she said with wonder. "How did you ever find it?"

Nolan had fretted over finding the right gift which would be personal, yet not overly forward. He was overjoyed when the idea finally came to him. Relieved now, seeing that she was touched by the gift, he shrugged and said, "I happened to see a site for an internet Hungarian store. I was a little worried that it might not get here in time, but it arrived yesterday."

"It's so beautiful," she repeated. "I have something for you, too, but I'm afraid it isn't nearly as special as your gift," she apologized as she shyly handed him a maroon package tied with a large silver bow.

"It doesn't matter. I don't need a thing," he said with a shake of his head. "I wanted you to have something special. Seeing your enjoyment is all I really cared about." He tore at the paper to reveal the latest book of one of his favorite writers.

He was touched that she remembered. "Perfect!" he said with genuine pleasure. "I'll have something to relax with on the days we close the office for Christmas." He took that as an opportunity to step over and thank her with a kiss on the cheek.

"I guess we should be going soon if we don't want to be stuck in the back row for the candlelight service," he said reluctantly. She nodded before pulling on a fuzzy, powder-blue knit hat. "So, you'll still be spending the day with Cathy and her family tomorrow?" he asked.

"Yes," she assured him. "Cathy's son and daughter actually requested me as a guest. They both think they have a chance of beating me in Scrabble this year."

"And?"

"Not a chance!" she scoffed with a flick of her hand.

"Well, well, I've not seen much of your competitive side before. If you manage to retain your championship title, I just might have to challenge you to a game." He chuckled as she lifted her brow.

He had hoped he could spend some time with her on Christmas Day, but the Calderons would all be traveling to Marcy's parents' house this year. Marcy's dad was still recovering from a hip replacement and couldn't yet manage the trip to Shelby Falls. Nolan was thankful that the Dawsons had invited Kozy to spend the entire day with them. He hated the idea of her not having anyone to spend Christmas with. Nobody should have to spend Christmas alone. Suddenly, an image of Kurt Walker trudging out of the office the day before flashed in his mind. Nolan realized that Kurt would likely spend Christmas day alone, but he quickly brushed the thought aside.

Not my problem. He walked Kozy to his car and held the door as she climbed inside. He paused, frowning in the darkness. *Not my problem.*

***

Happy birthday, Jesus! What must it have been like for you that night? Were you aware of the angels praising you? Was it frightening for you to leave heaven to come down to live with us? I hope you were comforted by Mary's tender love for you. I hope she was able to keep you warm.

The candlelight service was so beautiful tonight! Thank you that Nolan wanted to share that time with me. He went to such a lot of trouble to find me a gift that was so very special. It's what I would call a "forever gift."

Kozy paused in her writing. Aside from that first awkward meeting with Nolan, she had enjoyed every moment they had spent getting to know one another. Lately it had become evident that he was becoming interested in more than mere friendship. She was elated at the thought, but it also worried her. Would she ever be able to rid herself of the insecurities that had haunted her since childhood?

It scares me a little. Maybe our relationship is progressing too quickly. Help me to figure things out. And please, I ask you again to help Nolan resolve the problems he's having at work and figure out what's behind these panic attacks. Help him to know that he doesn't need to be perfect for you to love him.

Always and forever your child, your Kozy

***

"Now who could that be?" Kozy asked herself when she heard the knock at her kitchen door one Sunday in early January. She relaxed as she recognized a familiar profile behind the sheer lace curtain.

"Hope I'm not interrupting anything important," Cathy Dawson apologized as Kozy offered her a seat at the small table.

"Not at all!" she said. "You caught me at a good time. Nolan and I stayed after church awhile to discuss the new ideas we'd like to implement with the teens this year. I just got home minutes ago."

Cathy noted the confident smile and bright-eyed look that was evident at any mention of Nolan Calderon lately. *She's so happy.* Cathy looked around at the sunny room as she considered how to break the news that would certainly ruin her friend's day.

Kozy had already sensed her hesitancy. "What's wrong?" she asked weakly as she sank into a chair opposite her friend.

"I didn't want you to hear about it first thing in the morning and then have to immediately face the kids in class. It hasn't hit the paper yet, but—" She took a deep breath and plunged ahead. "Shaina's mom and her live-in were arrested late last night. They were cooking meth in their apartment." She watched as the color drained from Kozy's face.

"Shaina's safe," she answered the unspoken question in Kozy's eyes. "I ran into our principal at the store just now. Children's services notified her that she's been put in foster care in another county. She'll be officially withdrawn from our school system in the morning. Janet was glad she saw me. Word will get around like wildfire, and the kids are sure to have questions. She wants to meet with us early to discuss how we can be discrete as we help them deal with all the rumors."

Kozy squeezed her eyes shut in an attempt to stem the tears. Cathy patted her tightly clenched fists and said softly, "I know this hits close to home for you, but Shaina will be all right."

"I know exactly what she's feeling right now, and it's not all right!" Kozy snapped. She covered her face with both hands and moaned. "I'm sorry, Cathy. It's not your fault. But how did we miss this? I should have sensed what was coming."

"There's no way we could have done anything to prevent this, Kozy. People make terrible choices that, unfortunately, often involve innocent kids." Cathy sighed, wishing she had the power to take away all the hurt she had witnessed in her two decades of teaching.

Kozy lowered her hands from her face, and choked back her tears. "Do you think I'll be able to see her?"

Cathy shook her head. "You of all people know how unlikely that would be," she said calmly. "She was taken to another county for her own safety. Those two ran with some pretty unsavory characters. It'll take a while for the courts to work things out. For now, Shaina is where she needs to be. Meanwhile, you're going to have to trust that God has everything under control." She stood up to leave. At the door she turned and smiled sadly at her friend.

"You have such a passion for kids, Kozy. It'll do my heart good to see you with a few of your own someday."

Kozy's eyes remained focused on the table as Cathy let herself out. She sat immobile, trying to ignore the bitterness that enveloped her. *Kids of my own? With one parent dead from a drug overdose and the other killed in a prison riot, should I even take that chance? What if I were to fail my kids the way my parents did me?*

Chapter 12

Nolan stepped into his dad's office waving a paper bag. "Do you have some time? Marcy said you didn't have plans to go home for lunch today, so I thought maybe we could eat together."

"Of course I have time for you. Come on in," Tom said. It had been years since he and Nolan had eaten lunch together in the church office. When Nolan was in high school, it was a ritual they had whenever Nolan had a problem he wanted to discuss privately with his dad. Tom brushed aside some clutter from his desk and motioned for Nolan to pull up a chair. Seeing Nolan extract two burgers and two boxes of fries from the bag, Tom immediately began wrestling with his conscience about whether or not to inform Marcy about the fast food. Except for a few times during the holidays, he hadn't overindulged much lately.

"It's all right, Dad," Nolan chuckled. "Marcy asked, and I wouldn't lie to her."

"So I guess it'll be a big green salad for me tonight," Tom said ruefully.

"Probably," Nolan replied as he popped a French fry into his mouth. "So enjoy."

Ever since Tom had experienced some health issues a few years ago, Marcy had been diligently monitoring her husband's diet and exercise. She allowed for an occasional indulgence. Nolan was grateful that she cared. After all, he wanted to keep his dad around as long as possible.

Tom stepped over to the tiny refrigerator in the corner of the room and pulled out two bottles of water. Nolan waited as his dad asked a blessing for the food and their time together.

"So, is there anything special you wanted to talk about, Nolan?" Tom asked before taking a bite of his sandwich.

Nolan drummed his fingers a moment on the desk before answering. Tom waited, wondering what might be on his son's mind. He thought at once of Kozy Hanner. *Perhaps he wants to talk about his feelings for the girl.*

But when Nolan spoke, it was about something entirely unexpected. "Sometimes I feel I've been drifting away from God, Dad. I've tried so hard to be a good person, to love others the way a Christian is supposed to, but I have a hard time with it."

Tom tried to mask the unease he felt. He cleared his throat before responding. "Well Nolan, God doesn't expect that we'll be perfect all the time. He knows our weaknesses and loves us still. He loves you, Nolan, just as you are. If it were possible for us to be good enough on our own, Jesus wouldn't have had to die. Of course, you already know that. You've known that since you were a child."

Nolan looked solemnly at his father. "I know that in my mind, Dad, but lately it's been hard for me to feel it in here," he said, pointing to his chest. "I think that God may be expecting more from me that I've been willing to do, and I'm struggling."

Tom pondered how best to respond to this. Something told him to just let it go for now. Instead, he asked, "Is there a particular person you're having a problem with?"

"It's my office mate, Kurt Walker, Dad. I try to be civil with him, but the guy just rubs me the wrong way."

"I don't think you've mentioned this fellow before. What's he like?"

"Kurt started at Marley's this summer. He's smart and knows what he's doing as far as the job. But we have totally opposing lifestyles, which he's very vocal about. Early on he invited me to go gambling with him at one of the casinos. I told him that, as a Christian, I had no interest in gambling, drinking, or carousing after the kind of women he likes. Since then, when we're alone in the office, he's been nearly unbearable."

Tom cringed slightly at Nolan's words, but he let him continue. "He knows I don't want to hear of his exploits with the women he hooks up with, but he tells me anyway. Now, every so often, he invites me to go with him somewhere, just to hear me refuse. Then, he calls me a 'goody-two-shoes' or 'holier than thou' and mocks me for my convictions. Of course he does all of this in the privacy of our office. I'd just as soon stay away from him, but it's hard when you share an office with somebody. And to make matters worse, I can't even get away from him after work because he rents the other half of my duplex! How's that for an unfortunate coincidence? Sometimes I'm forced to know what's going on at his place, whether I want to or not, because of the thin walls."

Once Nolan was finished with his rant about Kurt, Tom tried to advise Nolan as he would any of his parishioners. "Well, Nolan," he said, "perhaps you're not looking at the situation from every angle. Maybe when you refused Kurt's invitation the first time, he may have interpreted it as a slam on his own worth. Maybe he was just trying to be friendly, and you may have hurt his feelings by the way you reacted. If he's not a Christian, he probably doesn't see the harm in his lifestyle. He just thinks you don't like him. Everyone wants to be liked."

"I know, Dad," Nolan admitted with a wry grin. "Kozy told me pretty much the same thing. She says that I should try to see Kurt the way Jesus sees him and that I should lift him up in prayer whenever I feel angry with him. She's praying for God to make a way for me to show Kurt that I do care about him. That's one of the things that I really admire about Kozy, Dad. She seems to have a genuine capacity to love all kinds of people."

"Well, I'm glad you two have become friends." Tom couldn't think of another thing to say that wouldn't seem like prying, so he remained silent. He dug into his fries as he watched his son devour his sandwich. Nolan's eyes wandered around the room as they finished eating. After he folded the wrappings from his lunch and tossed them in the trash can, he stood to leave.

"Kozy told me it might help if I talked with you about it, and I think she was right," Nolan said with a smile. "I've got to get back to work now. Thanks, Dad."

He was out the door before Tom had a chance to respond. Tom shut his office door and pulled down the shade on the window, his signal to Helen not to disturb him unless it was an emergency. Then he spent several minutes in prayer for his son.

Chapter 13

Helen Troyer had tried to get back to sleep after being awakened by yet another hot flash. The temperature outside was hovering near ten degrees and she knew the bedroom was still a comfortably cool sixty-eight, yet she had suddenly felt like she was wearing a fur coat in a sauna. She carefully lifted the sheet from her side of the bed as she waited for her body to cool down. Her hand reached out to grab the tiny battery-powered fan that her son had given her as a joke on Christmas. Using the tiny fan to dry her sweat-soaked face she thought with a wry smile, *Some joke. It's just what I needed! Oh, the joys of middle age.* Just as she had begun to feel drowsy again, her right hand started to throb. She was going to have to do something about that soon. Maybe it was time to finally schedule the carpel tunnel surgery her doctor had suggested. She opened one eye and squinted at her digital bedside clock. *Four-thirty.* She sighed. Maybe if she got up and read a little, she might be able to nod off in her chair for an hour or two before having to get ready for church.

She eased out of bed, taking care not to awaken her husband Jerry, who snored softly beside her. Jerry was newly retired from the Shelby Falls police department. In all his years on the job he had tried his best to be considerate of her while he worked the crazy swing shifts required in the small department; she tried her best to reciprocate his thoughtfulness. She grabbed her Bible from the stand and tiptoed out of the room, carefully shutting the door behind her.

She shuffled out to the living room in bare feet. She rested her forehead on the cold glass of her large front window as she surveyed the peaceful scene outside. Three houses down on the left she saw an upstairs light pop on. *That nice young couple, the Henrys. The new baby must still be getting them up for night feedings.* She smiled tenderly, remembering those nights that she had spent getting up with her own babies nearly thirty years ago.

Her eyes settled on the duplex directly across the street. All quiet on Nolan Calderon's side of the building. She thought she could see a light through a gap in the living room drapes on the other side where the fellow named Kurt lived. She knew he worked at Marley's with Nolan. She frequently noticed that Kurt had a light burning late into the night, particularly on weekends. She turned from the window and sat in her recliner, Bible in hand. The quiet of the street was soon disturbed by the faint sound of a siren in the distance. *Hopefully, just a false alarm.* A few moments later, she frowned as the sound moved closer. She rose from her chair and peered once more through the window just in time to see Nolan Calderon, still clad in his pajamas, stumble out of his front door. She could see him clearly in the streetlight. He appeared to be all right. *Thank you, Lord!*

In an alarmed voice she called, "Jerry! Jerry! I think there's something wrong at Nolan's house!" She could hear the siren getting closer and the sound of her husband's footsteps moving swiftly across the bedroom floor. She ran to the hall closet to get his boots and set them beside the front door. She could now hear frantic shouting from across the street and a muffled pounding. The sound of glass shattering sent her rushing back to the window. Smoke was now pouring out of the open front door of Kurt's apartment. She watched in horror as Nolan disappeared inside.

Jerry had stepped into his boots and was now sprinting across the street. Helen grabbed her phone and punched the Calderon's number. She hated to awaken the pastor so early on Sunday morning, but this was Nolan. Tom needed to know, and he needed to know now. As soon as she had hung up from her frantic call, she thought of Kozy Hanner, the young woman that Nolan had been seeing. She still had her number in her phone from the time she had arranged for Kozy to speak at the fall youth event. *She'll want to know, too.*

***

Nolan had awakened from a sound sleep to the high-pitched shrill of a smoke alarm. His heart thumping, he turned on the bedside lamp, shaking his head in confusion. It wasn't the alarm outside of his bedroom door, he could tell that much. Perhaps it was the one in the basement. Phone in hand, he ran barefoot downstairs searching his entire apartment. Nothing, yet he could detect a faint odor of smoke. He quickly surmised that the alarm must be coming from Kurt's side of the house. He dialed 911 and reported the situation. In seconds he was back upstairs and pounding on the thin wall that separated Kurt's bedroom from his own. His shouts and pounding brought no immediate response, so Nolan raced back down the stairs and tumbled out the front door. In the street light he could see the smoke that was snaking its way from under Kurt's doorway. He pounded on the door and shouted for Kurt but with no effect. He searched frantically around the small porch for anything he could use to smash the window. He spotted a brick underneath the downspout for the gutter. He snatched up the brick, and with one hard swing he shattered the glass of the front door. In a second he unlatched the door and was inside.

Kurt's apartment was a mirror image of his own so Nolan knew exactly where to find the master bedroom. He made his way up the stairs, crawling on hands and knees. He made it to Kurt's bed and was hit with the pungent odor of alcohol, vomit, and smoke. The smoke was rapidly filling the room. As he suspected, Kurt had been drinking heavily and was now completely unconscious. Kurt outweighed Nolan by at least forty pounds.

No way am I going to be able to carry him out of here. Nolan grabbed hold of Kurt's shirt and dragged him off of the bed and onto the floor. Kurt hit the floor with a heavy thud, a slurred curse word slipping from his lips.

"Sorry, Kurt," Nolan coughed. "This may hurt a little, but at least the stairs are carpeted." Nolan kept his face close to the floor, taking shallow breaths where the air was clearer. Then he dragged Kurt by his feet down the stairs. He cringed with each clunk of Kurt's head on the steps. Nolan was surprised to see how far the fire had spread in the mere seconds it had taken him to get to Kurt. Through the smoky blackness he could see flames lapping close to the stair rails and consuming the draperies. He didn't tarry. He gave Kurt one final great pull and deposited his leaden form onto the front porch. Jerry Troyer appeared and helped him hoist Kurt off the porch and onto the brown grass.

At that moment, the fire engine whipped into the driveway. Four men spilled out of the truck; three ran straight toward the blaze; the other ran to Kurt and Nolan and began assessing the two men for injuries. Jerry stayed beside Kurt while the firefighter escorted Nolan to the curb at the far corner of the lot, commanding him to sit where he would be safely away from the action.

Two ambulances and a police car arrived with sirens blasting and red and blue lights flashing, adding to the already chaotic scene.

"Anybody else in the house?" the firefighter shouted to Nolan.

Nolan glanced at Kurt's driveway. The vehicle that had been there when he had turned in for the night was now gone. Only Kurt's car remained. He hadn't seen anyone else in Kurt's bed, but he hadn't looked elsewhere. He shook his head. "I don't think so. I know my side, the one on the right, is empty. You'd better ask the other guy about his side to be sure."

The man ran off to talk to Kurt. It was only then that Nolan realized that his chest felt tight, and he was shivering in the freezing air. Two EMTs approached him and administered oxygen. Helen soon arrived with a furry red blanket in her arms.

"Hey, Helen!" The older technician greeted her cheerfully. "Did you and Jerry order all this excitement on Oak Street?"

"Certainly not, Ed," Helen answered with a huff. "I was scared out of my wits to watch Nolan going into a burning house to rescue his neighbor. You just see that you take good care of him. And wrap this blanket around him! Can't you see he's freezing?"

The first ambulance took off in a rush, carrying Kurt to the hospital. Just then, Tom and Marcy arrived, breathing heavily with faces tense. The police had made them park a block away. Tom let out a sigh of relief when he saw Nolan sitting on the curb. Helen was bent over him, helping him pull on a pair of heavy wool socks.

"Nolan! Thank God you're safe! Thank you, God!"

Marcy blinked back tears and knelt to give her stepson a quick hug. Aside from his uncustomary rumpled look and a layer of black grime on his face, he looked fine. As soon as she was convinced that Nolan hadn't been hurt, she turned to her husband. "Honey, I'd better get back home. I don't want the kids to be frightened if they awaken and find us gone. Now I'll be able to tell them that their brother is safe. She looked at Helen. "Once Nolan has the okay from the EMTs, would you and Jerry mind giving Tom and Nolan a ride home?"

"Of course, Marcy," Helen assured her. "You get on home to the twins. We'll take care of these two."

Marcy looked back at Nolan. "I'm making up the bed in the guest room. We want you to stay with us until you can get back into your place."

It was only then that it dawned on Nolan that his apartment might be uninhabitable for the time being. As Marcy took off, he and Tom watched the frenzy of activity in and out of both apartments. Eventually, a young firefighter in full gear lumbered over to them, taking off his protective helmet before he spoke. It was Gary Lawson from the church.

Gary nodded to Tom. "Hi, Pastor. I sure didn't expect to see you this early on a Sunday morning!" He patted Nolan on the shoulder. "You got your neighbor out of there just in time. He's got some smoke in his lungs and a couple of burns from falling debris, but he'll recover. Looks like he's going to have a whale of a hangover, though," he chuckled as he walked back to the engine.

Tom sat down beside Nolan, who was looking pretty dejected by now. Placing his arm around Nolan's shoulder he shut his eyes and prayed silently. *Thank you again, Lord, for protecting my son. Please guide him through the challenges that might come from this. Lift his spirits now and surround him with your love.*

"Nolan!"

Tom's eyes popped open. Kozy Hanner appeared before them, her bare head a jumble of blond curls, her coat unzipped, and with furry blue slippers on her feet. Nolan, who had been slumped over with head in hands, jumped up so quickly that Tom nearly tumbled over onto his back. The two were in each other's arms in an instant.

"Oh, Nolan, I was scared to death when I saw the ambulance pass me! I'm so glad you're okay! You are okay, aren't you?" Kozy looked at him intently as she stepped back.

"I'm fine, really," he assured her, already missing the comforting feel of her arms around him. "They took Kurt to the hospital. He's going to be all right, just a few minor injuries."

"Helen said you went in to rescue him. I don't know whether to commend you for being so brave or kick you in the shin for taking such a risk!" Her eyes filled with tears then, and she stepped forward to bury her head in his shoulder.

Nolan looked over the top of Kozy's head and locked eyes with his dad. Tom could see that it was more than just the flashing lights from the fire truck that lit up his son's face.

"Well now, if that wasn't a quick answer to prayer!" Tom murmured wryly to himself as he walked over to chat with Jerry Troyer.

***

Pastor Tom, along with the twins, managed to make it to church on time, but Marcy stayed home to keep an eye on Nolan. The EMTs hadn't felt that a trip to the hospital was necessary, but they advised him to take it easy for a couple of days. Marcy made a run to the store and picked up a couple of frozen pizzas to have for lunch. When church was over, Tom called to say he had invited Kozy over. Everyone was eager to learn the details of last night's happenings. A half hour later they were all seated around the Calderon dining table eating pizza and the tossed salad Marcy had added to the meal.

Zane and Kelsey had picked up a few details about the fire from Gary Lawson's younger brother. Kelsey couldn't wait to tell what she knew. "Brady said that whoever Kurt had over earlier in the evening had dropped a lit cigarette onto his couch. Kurt told the firefighters that they thought they had put it out, but Brady says they put chemicals in cigarettes to keep them from going out when you smoke them."

"People pick up the cigarette and think they've taken care of the problem," Zane quickly added when his sister stopped to take a breath, "but sometimes an ember will get deep into a crack of the sofa, and it can smolder for hours before it catches fire."

"And," Kelsey resumed with a dramatic flair, "that's exactly what happened!"

"If Nolan hadn't gone in when he did, Kurt might have not awakened in time." Tom looked proudly at his son. "And it was quick action from Nolan that got the fire department there to knock out the fire before it did any structural damage to the house."

"Anyone would have done the same, Dad," Nolan said modestly. "It all happened so fast. I don't remember thinking much except that I had to get Kurt awake and out of there somehow. It was instinct more than anything."

"Well, we all think you were super brave," Kelsey said as Zane reached for the last piece of pizza. "Hey," she frowned. "Don't you think you should save that for Nolan?"

Nolan waved away the offer with a grin. Looking at Kozy he asked, "Would you want to go over to the hospital with me to check on Kurt? I'd like to know how he's doing."

"Of course I'll go," she answered.

"I'd be happy to go along, too, Son," Tom said impulsively, just as Marcy's warning kick reached him under the table.

"Thanks, Dad, but that won't be necessary," Nolan responded without taking his eyes from Kozy's face. After a moment he looked up brightly at his dad. "But if and when the time comes that Kurt is ready to see a pastor, you'll be the first one I recommend."

***

Kurt was sitting up in the hospital bed gloomily watching a sports program when Nolan and Kozy tapped on his door and walked into the room. His face registered surprise at his unexpected company, and his countenance brightened immediately. "Hi, Calderon," he said in a hoarse voice. "Who's this pretty gal you brought with you?"

As Nolan introduced Kozy, he took note of the bandage on Kurt's right wrist and one on the side of his shaved head. He grimaced slightly.

"I'm sorry you got burned, Kurt. By the time I got you downstairs, the drapes had caught fire and fallen to the floor. I didn't have time to do anything but pull you through."

Kurt dismissed Nolan's apology with a wave of his left hand. "You risked your neck to get me out of there. These little burns will heal in no time." He looked straight at Nolan and said with uncustomary humility. "If you hadn't broken in and got me out when you did, I might not have made it. If you'd waited for the fire department to find me, I probably wouldn't be here right now. I was out cold, dead to the world. I owe you." He looked down and muttered. "It's going to be a long, long time before I let myself get that drunk again."

Nolan wondered why anybody would seek drunkenness in the first place, but decided to let the comment pass. "Anyway, I'm glad you're okay."

"Thanks," Kurt replied. After a few moments he added, "Sorry about your apartment. I know mine's a total mess and they said yours had some smoke damage, too."

Nolan shrugged, "My family's putting me up until things get fixed, so it'll work out."

Kurt decided to change the subject then. "So, how about those Cavaliers?" he said as he pointed to the television screen. "They're always surprising us, aren't they?"

The three spent several minutes in an animated discussion of basketball with some easy banter and laughter. When a nurse came in to check on Kurt's wounds Nolan and Kozy stood to leave. Before they walked out, Kurt motioned them to the bedside.

"Uh, Nolan," Kurt coughed and spoke in a low voice. "I know I've been giving you kind of a hard time at work. Pretty unprofessional of me, I guess. I'll try to do better from now on. And hey, thanks for coming to check on me. I really enjoyed meeting you, too, Kozy."

***

Kozy tried her best to put Shaina's troubles out of her mind. It was a busy time at school and she had eighteen other students from her morning classes and twenty from the afternoon who needed her attention. It was not easy, especially when one of the Shaina's friends would mention her name or ask her when their friend would get to come home. Somehow, Kozy managed to hold back her emotions while she tried to reassure the students. However, when she was alone, her pessimism threatened to take over. She managed to rally her enthusiasm for the teen meeting the following Wednesday night, but as she and Nolan left the church afterwards, her fatigue and hunger had put her in a funk. Being in a rush, neither of them had eaten before church.

"I'm starving. Think we could pick up some carry-out and maybe go back and eat at your place?" Nolan asked hopefully.

She considered for a moment, vacillating between her desire to be with Nolan and her need to be alone to sulk. "Sure," she agreed finally, "but you're positive you don't need to go home and rest? It's only been a few days since the fire."

"Do I look sickly?" he asked incredulously.

"No," she admitted with a smirk. "You look pretty nice, actually."

"Well, then," he grinned. "It's settled."

A few minutes later they were headed back to Kozy's house with carry-out bags of food. They sat at her kitchen table eating bowls of chili and drinking milk while they discussed the earlier study meeting with the teens.

"That was just the ticket," Nolan said as he scraped the last spoonful from his bowl. "Thanks for eating with me." He gave her a smile. "With all the commotion, I forgot to ask. Have you heard any more news about Shaina?"

Her shoulders slumped. "Nothing new," she answered. "But thanks for asking." She smiled sadly. "The whole situation seems so hopeless."

He inched his fingers over on the tabletop until he had hold of her hand. "Hey, don't feel so bad. It's not hopeless. I know it seems personal for you, but you know Shaina is better off where she is now."

She stared glumly at the tabletop. "I guess so," she admitted. "But it is personal for me." She blinked back tears. "Oh, never mind," she sniffed, pulling her hand back. "You wouldn't understand." She stood abruptly to clear the table.

Nolan followed her to the sink and stepped close as she rinsed the two glasses. "Try me," he said in a low voice. "I want to understand. Talk to me, please."

She turned. Nolan placed his hands on her shoulders and drew her close. "You know how much I care about you, don't you?" He lifted her chin and touched his lips to hers. She enjoyed the kiss so much that it took all of her willpower to step away a moment later. She leaned against the counter, arms folded tightly across her chest.

"Ever since this happened to Shaina," she explained haltingly, "I've felt furious at her mother for not being more responsible. I haven't been able to let it go. I wake up in a panic, feeling guilty; like I should have done something to stop it." She frowned. "I thought I was so well adjusted. I thought I had conquered my anger toward my own parents. But what's happened has made me feel so powerless."

Nolan started to speak, but she stopped him with a wave of her hand. "I know. I know I shouldn't feel this way but I can't seem to get it under control. Maybe I don't even want to," she ended in a whisper. Turning her head, she frowned into the darkness outside her kitchen window.

He reached a tentative hand toward her but she shook her head. "I care about you, too, Nolan. I really do. Our relationship is special to me. But I feel so confused. I think I need to be alone now, okay?"

She stood leaning against the counter with her hands covering her face. He wanted to take away her pain, but didn't know how. Reluctantly, he donned his coat. "Promise you'll call me if you want to talk?"

She let down her hands and gave him a weak smile. "I will," she said.

Chapter 14

"I'll be out to help you in a minute, Marcy," Nolan called as he sat on the couch, eyes fixed on his laptop. His dad and siblings had left for the Tuesday youth meeting as soon as supper was over.

Marcy Calderon stored the leftovers in the refrigerator and finished wiping the countertop. She walked into the Calderon family room and sat down in the chair across from her stepson. "No need, everything's done," she said with a smile as Nolan looked up in surprise.

"Boy, I must have been deep in thought," he admitted. "I'm sorry. I honestly intended to help out. I really, really appreciate you and Dad inviting me to stay in your guest room while my apartment is being fixed. I don't mean to take advantage."

Marcy looked into his eyes. "Nolan, we're your family. We wanted to help you. That's what families do. It's wonderful having us all under the same roof again. Your dad loves it. I love it." She grinned. "Your brother and sister are thrilled to be able to annoy you at will. Don't think you have to pay your way the moment you walk in the door. I can handle the kitchen just fine. I appreciate the offer, though."

"Thanks, Marcy."

"So, what had you so involved? Are things working out with your insurance agent?"

"Actually, everything seems to be going fine. In fact, since you guys are taking me in, I think I'm going to have a little bit of extra cash, even after paying for a new mattress and couch. About everything else can be cleaned, even most of my clothing. I'm thinking I'd like to invest in a new desk. That's what I was looking at online. The old one I've had since high school was pretty shabby to start with, and after the fire I think it's a complete ruin.

"Oh, wow, Nolan. What perfect timing! Before you make up your mind about the desk, you may be interested in what I have to show you." Marcy stood and motioned for Nolan to follow as she led the way to the storage area above the attached garage. "Since the twins will be turning thirteen this spring, your dad and I have decided to utilize this space as a game room, maybe buy a used pool table, so they can have their friends over."

"Very cool," said Nolan. "They'll love it for sure."

She opened the door to the large rectangular room, explaining their plan to repaint and carpet the storage space, and add more lighting. "We've been working on clearing things out. Your dad took the cribs, playpen, and double stroller to Goodwill last week. Loads of toys, too. I just couldn't give up all the books though. We'll build some shelves. After all, I'm hoping to read to grandchildren someday," she finished lightly. Though Nolan's thoughts flew immediately to Kozy, he strove to keep his expression blank. Realizing she wasn't going to get any pertinent information, Marcy pointed to a sheet-covered object in the corner under the eaves. "It's your mom's desk, Nolan," she said. "Your dad said your grandparents had given it to her before you were born. Frankly, we'd forgotten about it. It's been sitting here covered up since we moved in, right after your dad and I married. I hadn't had a chance to mention it until now, what with all the excitement of the fire and you moving in."

Nolan looked intrigued. "I forgot about it, too, I guess. What's it like?"

"I only got a peek the other day, but I think it has promise," she said. "Help me move it out into the light and we'll take a look."

Once she and Nolan had dragged the desk from its corner, they carefully lifted and folded the dusty sheet that had protected it for fourteen years. Marcy waited as Nolan took in the clean, classic lines and rich tones of the sturdy mahogany desk. "I like it," he said after a few moments. "I like the size and the style. It seems to be in good shape. Do you think it will need to be stripped and refinished?"

Marcy ran her fingers over the wood. "The finish is a little dull, but it actually looks pretty well preserved. It might just need a little polish. My Aunt Mae had a formula that she used to revive varnish on older furniture. I believe it was a tablespoon each of turpentine, olive oil, and vinegar to one quart of water. She'd just rub the mixture in with a soft cloth, and you'd be surprised at the difference it made. It would be worth trying, don't you think?"

"Yes, I'd like to try it. This is great. I would much rather use a family piece like this than buy something new." He began pulling out the drawers to see how well they worked. They all glided smoothly until he tried the top middle drawer, which stuck after opening a few inches. "This one may need a little sanding or some wax on the tracks or—no, it seems like there's something stopping it inside."

"Here, let me check." Marcy inched her slender arm into the partially open drawer. Stretching her fingers as far as possible, she caught hold of some paper and tugged. "Tada!" she sang as she pulled a long thick envelope from the opening. "No wonder it was stuck. Oh my …." Her voice trailed off and she looked up, wide-eyed, from the yellowed, tattered envelope and then to Nolan's face. "I think it's a letter from your mother. It must have been caught in here all these years."

Nolan stared at the sealed envelope that Marcy had just placed in his hand. On the front was the familiar handwriting of his mother: *To my son, Nolan.*

Nolan stood immobile and silent. Marcy rested her hand gently on his shoulder. "I'm thinking you'll want to be left alone to read that," she said as she quietly left the room.

The guest room door was still shut a half hour later when Tom brought the twins home from church. Though the two were hoping to spend a little time with their brother, Marcy convinced them that Nolan still needed time to rest after the fire and it would be best if they would attend to their homework tonight and give Nolan some time to himself. There would be plenty of time to spend with him in the weeks to come.

Zane nodded philosophically. He was the more introspective of the two and seemed to understand the occasional need for solitude. Kelsey, on the other hand, was extremely social, and she loved the attention she usually received from her older brother. She exhaled a deep sigh before reluctantly agreeing to give him some space. After noisily raiding the refrigerator for leftovers, the two headed to their rooms to tackle their homework.

As soon as the twins' doors were shut, Marcy explained to Tom about the letter she and Nolan had discovered in the desk drawer. His expression told her that the existence of the letter came as a surprise to him as well. "It could have been something written when he was born, I suppose, like the letter I wrote the twins at their birth," she said, "but it seems more likely it was written close to when she died. Either way, it may have quite an emotional impact on Nolan. I wanted you to be forewarned. Nolan needs to know you're available for him if he wants to talk. He needs you." *And you need him as well.*

Tom's face was pensive as he took his wife in his arms and gave her a hug. "I'll check on him right now," he said quietly as he walked to Nolan's door and lifted his hand to knock.

***

"It's me, Nolan," Tom said. "Can I come in?"

Nolan responded after a few moments, and Tom walked into the room. Nolan sat on the bed, his back pushed against the headboard and his arms hugging his knees. He pointed to an upholstered chair across from the bed and Tom sat down. Tom's eyes traveled to the letter lying open on the bed by Nolan's feet. "Marcy told you what we found," Nolan said flatly.

When Tom nodded, Nolan reached over and offered the letter to him. When Tom hesitated, Nolan said softly, "It's okay, Dad. I'm fine."

Tom ran a gentle hand over his late wife's familiar handwriting. He sighed, surprised at the sudden rush of emotion he felt at the sight of it. He looked at the date on the letter: January 8, 2000. "Interesting," he mused, "that you very nearly found this on your birthday." They had celebrated Nolan's birthday last week just a day before the fire. Shaking his head he began reading:

Dear Nolan,

I'm writing this on your tenth birthday, but by the time your father passes this on to you, you will be a grown man. I smile to think about how you might look by now and what kind of man you have become: a very good one, I trust, if you grow up to be anything like your father and your grandparents.

I'm praying that your grandparents live for many years to come so they can continue to be an influence on your life. Without Ed and Belinda Calderon, I wouldn't have had the privilege of being your mother. They not only rescued me; they took me into their home and introduced me to their Savior, Jesus. And I made him mine.

Then your dad came home from college. I never meant for it to happen, but we fell in love. Your grandparents had taught me that God promises that we become new creations once he redeems us. When your grandparents saw what was happening and that we were determined to marry, they accepted me unconditionally as a daughter-in-law. I knew then that their God was real, and I had truly become a child of God.

Your dad and I felt it best that we wait until you are grown to explain to you about my past. A child of ten shouldn't have to deal with those sordid details. I hope you understand and can accept what happened to me with the same understanding and love that your dad and grandparents did.

Doctors had told me there was very little chance that I would be able to conceive. But God gave us a miracle! Oh, you have been a delight, Nolan, from infancy until now. I'm enclosing in the envelope the little cap you wore in the hospital after you were born. You will think me silly that I could never part with it. And I'm giving you a list of the books you loved as a young child. Maybe you'll want to read some of those same books to your own children someday. I'm also including the songs and lullabies we used to sing together. I want you to remember the good times we had, not just my illness. My prayer for you is that you will stay close to God as you grow. I pray that your life will be blessed with love and laughter. I hope and pray that you will have a heart for God and people, even "the least of these," just like your grandparents did.

My illness has been so hard for your dad and for you. I fought it as long as I could, but I'm just so tired and I want to go home now. Your dad has had a hard time accepting this, I know. But God has promised me that everything will be all right. Whenever God chooses to take me, I'm ready. Years from now, hopefully after you are an old man and have lived a good and happy life, I will be waiting for you when you get to heaven. I love you, Nolan.

Mom

Tom brushed away a tear. Nolan looked away, waiting, blinking at his own tears. After a few moments Tom was able to speak in a husky voice, "I'm sorry. Seeing this out of the blue like this, it's just hitting me kind of hard."

"Me too," Nolan said sadly. "It seems like the kind of letter she would write. Sweet and loving, just like I remember her. But, Dad, I don't understand. What was she talking about? What did Grandma and Grandpa rescue her from? And why haven't you ever told me about it?"

Tom sat in the chair, his head down, hands over his face. It took a full minute before he looked up and faced his son. He took a deep breath, wondering where to begin.

"Please forgive me, Nolan. I see now that I should have said something years ago. I had no idea that your mom had written this letter to you. She must have meant to give it to me to save for the proper time, but she died so suddenly. We had discussed telling you, but as she said, we agreed that you were too young. Then later, after she was gone, I guess I felt it wasn't necessary for you to know."

Nolan's eyes were still fixed on his dad's. "But now, Dad, I want to know. Maybe I even need to know. What exactly happened to my mother that she needed to be rescued?"

Tom shut his eyes, trying to decide what and how much to reveal. "By the time I was into my junior year in college," he began, "your grandparents were in their fifties and were both newly retired from teaching. Grandpa had taught what was then called 'shop' and Grandma had taught math.

"That's why Grandpa was always so handy at fixing things," Nolan remembered. "And you always said I inherited Grandma's mind for math."

Tom nodded and continued. "With me away at college, they felt called to get involved in mission work. They got connected with an evangelical ministry that worked in homeless shelters and crisis centers in some of the larger cities. For a couple of years they made numerous trips to New York City with that organization. Dad used his skills in plumbing, electric, and carpentry to do general repair work at various shelters. Mom used her math skills to help people study for their GEDs. They used their hands and minds to demonstrate the love of Christ to those less fortunate. Mom loved the people she helped, but there was one girl in particular she was especially drawn to. She had been orphaned in her mid-teens and was taken in by her uncle. When he turned abusive, she ran away. She was extremely bright. She managed to survive on her own for a while. Once she got into the shelter, she started working on her GED. Grandma was thrilled to be able to help her."

Nolan still sat motionless on the bed, his eyes fixed on his father's face.

Tom answered the unspoken question with a nod. "The girl was your mother. Your grandparents looked for her during their next mission trip to New York and subsequent trips, but she had disappeared. Then on their final one, they were sent to help at a home for battered women and children, and there she was." Tom's voice broke and he paused before continuing. "The physical bruises were mostly healed by then, but when they looked into her eyes, they knew she had suffered from more than physical wounds. The man had found her and snatched her from that first shelter. He used her for months to make money for his drug habit. He kept close tabs on her and beat her every time she tried to run away. Eventually, she was able to escape from him and find refuge at the women's center. Your grandparents were heartbroken when they found out what had happened. They decided then and there to offer their own home to her and to help her heal here in Shelby Falls, so that the man who had controlled her would never find her again."

"I'm so sorry," he whispered. "Do you understand why we couldn't tell you when you were a child?" He didn't wait for an answer but continued on. "I came home that summer after I graduated from college, and there was your mother. As she said in her letter, your grandparents had taken her in, and with the love they showed her, they had wooed her to Jesus. Her newfound faith radiated from her.

"In a short time we had fallen in love. Her past didn't matter to me or to your grandparents. She was a new creation in Christ, and he took away all of our doubts. Not to say that our lives were perfect from then on; your mom had a lot of fears to deal with. But we were very happy."

Nolan ran his hands over his head and shut his eyes. Finally he shook his head, trying to make sense of all he'd learned. "But Dad," he began, his voice full of pain. "I can't, I just can't think of my mom that way. She just couldn't have been a …." His voice broke and he couldn't finish.

"She was a victim, Nolan." Tom's voice was low, but firm as he went on. "She didn't deserve the life that man put her through. Besides forcing her to do unspeakable things, he messed with her mind and tried to make her think it was her fault. It weighed her down with a load of guilt and shame. Once my parents explained the gospel to her, she realized that no one is good enough on his own to stand before God; that we all have fallen short. She soon recognized that she needed the grace of Christ to rid herself of the anger and bitterness in her own heart. Most of her life she had longed for love and had never felt worthy. When she came face to face with the cross and realized the price that had been paid for her, she surrendered completely. She was overflowing with gratitude. Her life from then on reflected that gratitude, even when God chose to take her away from us at the age of thirty-four."

Nolan sat quietly for several minutes, taking in Tom's words. "Mom wrote that it was a miracle that she had me," Nolan said. "What did she mean?"

"The injuries she suffered while she was being abused had caused scarring. Doctors had told us that the chances were slight for her being able to get pregnant or carry a child to term."

"But here I am." Nolan gazed at his dad, a ghost of a smile on his face.

"God had other plans, obviously." Tom returned the smile. "She was healthy during the entire pregnancy and didn't have a bit of trouble delivering. And it's true, Nolan. You were a delight to her and to all of us." He looked back at the rest of the contents from the envelope. "Mind if I read the lists of books and songs your mom gave you?"

Nolan handed them to his dad. Tom scanned the papers, smiling occasionally as he remembered while Nolan stared at the wall. After a minute or two, Nolan reached over and picked up the letter once more. He sighed, shaking his head grimly. "I don't know, Dad. I think God may be trying to get through to me with all that's been going on." He hesitated before looking once again in his father's eyes. "I didn't know how to put it into words at the time, but Mom always seemed kind of like a fragile flower. Now I can understand why she never liked to leave the house much. To find that she had this stuff in her past, stuff that I'd be quick to judge in others; yet I still love her just as much as ever. She's my mom. But would I have been able to do what Grandma and Grandpa did? I doubt I would have taken that risk and brought her home."

"I don't think I was mature enough in my faith then either, but I'm sure glad Grandma and Grandpa were. Otherwise, you wouldn't be here."

Tom sat staring at the floor, quietly thinking before venturing another look at his son. "Nolan," he said at last, "I should have told you long ago about your mom's past, but I'm glad that it's all out in the open now."

"It feels weird to be talking about Mom at all." Nolan's voice was almost a whisper. "It's just something we never did after she was gone."

Tom felt a sudden crush of regret. It was clear to him now that keeping his pain to himself all those years ago had been a huge mistake. In those first months, putting words to the loss seemed too risky. He thought he might break if he had to see Nolan's pain when his own was still so raw. Better to just talk of other, safer things. Then it became a habit to avoid speaking about Sharon at all, much less her death. Now, he saw that in not sharing his feelings with Nolan about the illness and loss of his mother, he had cheated him out of the reminiscing about the good times they had shared. He was heartsick to think of how cowardly he had been. Early in his relationship with Marcy, she had tried to warn him that he needed to keep Sharon's memory alive for Nolan, but it was so easy to put off. Nolan had seemed fine. The twins arrived within a year of his marriage to Marcy. All of a sudden, they were a new family, the five of them, and life got hectic. All of those thoughts struck him with lightning speed, and as clear as if they had been written in outline form in his sermon notes. *What have I done, Lord? Please, forgive me!*

"I guess that wasn't the healthiest way to handle it." Tom shook his head. "I thought I was trying to protect you, and I was just tired of feeling so bad. Maybe we would have healed better if we had allowed ourselves to feel the pain. It was my fault, Nolan. I was the adult. I should have been more helpful."

"It's okay, Dad. I don't blame you for anything." Nolan said. "Marcy's been great for us. I've always been grateful that she's made you so happy. I love that she never tried to push herself on me, or try to take Mom's place. And I always wanted to have siblings. For that alone, I love her as much as I love Mom."

Tom nodded and smiled.

"If you don't mind, we'd better call it a night," Nolan said. "I need to try to get a little sleep before I have to get up for work tomorrow." Tom stood and walked to the door.

"Dad?" Nolan spoke, causing his dad to pause. "Thanks for coming to talk with me."

***

Nolan wondered if he should say anything to Kozy about the letter from his mother. However, that Wednesday evening at church, she sensed right away that something had happened. She waited until the last of the teens had gone home to ask him about it. Any apprehension he had about sharing with her dissolved as soon as he began to confide in her. She listened in silence, occasionally touching his hand as he struggled to sort out his feelings about finding the letter and the revelation of what his mother's life had been like before she moved to Shelby Falls.

When Nolan paused she spoke. "Oh, Nolan. Your poor mother."

"My mom had a mild form of agoraphobia," he said, rubbing his chin with his hand. "I mean, she did what she had to do. She went to church and to the grocery and took me places I needed to go, but we were all aware that the only place she was truly comfortable was at home, or at my grandparents' house. I always accepted that as just the way she was. I never thought about what might have been the cause behind her fears."

Kozy nodded. "She must have been so scared that that awful man would find her again. Fears have a habit of wanting to stick around, even after the danger has passed." *I should know.*

"I guess you never know what kind of things a person has had to deal with that makes them do the things they do," he said with a frown. "I'm really feeling convicted now that I shouldn't have been so quick to judge Kurt without really trying to find out what makes him tick."

"Well, you just risked your own life to get him out of his burning apartment," she said in his defense. "I'd say that's a pretty good start to make it up to him."

He shrugged as he stood to leave. They locked up the church and walked to their vehicles. "Thanks for caring enough to let me talk it out," he said. "But I shouldn't be whining to you. You had it so much tougher as a kid than I did, losing both of your parents, and having to live with strangers for years."

Nolan's phone chirped. "It's Ben." He grinned as he scanned the text. "He and Nikki invited us to see what they've done with the nursery. Friday at six. Will that work for you?"

She nodded. Nolan made a quick response and pocketed his phone. As he opened her door he cocked his head to the side.

"You okay?" he asked. "I didn't mean to bum you out with my problems."

"I'm fine," was her automatic response. "I guess I'm just a little tired. I'll see you in a couple days." Her mood was somber as she drove home. Her heart ached for what Nolan's mother had suffered. And the story was all the more tragic because the abuse had come from someone who should have been protecting her. *Like Shaina's mother should have protected her.* Her thoughts shifted from Shaina to her own situation so many years ago. She allowed herself only a few moments of reflection before she chased away the images. She tried instead to focus on the upcoming plans to meet with Ben and Nikki, but even that didn't lighten her mood.

Nolan always seems so elated when he sees how excited they're getting about the baby.

Chapter 15

Kurt had been on his best behavior at work in the weeks following the fire. He was released from the hospital after only two days, the burns on his arm and scalp healing nicely. Nolan had relished the peaceful atmosphere at work the few days that Kurt was off. Now that Kurt had returned to work, Nolan appreciated that he was actually keeping his promise to drop the personal digs and sarcasm and keep things at a professional level. Nolan felt more energetic and productive and he was getting caught up on some of the projects for which he and Kurt shared responsibility.

He had come in early today to do some of that work and to also have a time of quiet meditation away from the hustle and bustle of his parents' house. It always seemed too hectic with the twins getting ready for school and his dad preparing to go to the church. He loved the time he was spending with his family while he waited for his apartment to be restored, but he also missed his quiet time.

He sat peacefully now, behind the half wall in the office he and Kurt shared. The street light outside illuminated his desk as he prayed. He thanked God for the good that he had brought from the disaster of the fire. *I still can't say that I like Kurt, but at least things have improved in our relationship. Thank you for using me to keep him from harm. Now help me to be the kind of friend that he needs so he might see Christ in me in the future.*

He had almost reached his hand to the light switch when he heard a stumbling noise and a muttered curse from the hallway. With a sinking heart he accepted that his reprieve from Kurt's obnoxious side might be ending. Now he hesitated to make his presence known, wishing that he could just spend a few hours working without even having to acknowledge him while he was in a foul mood. Kurt would certainly have some snide remark if he guessed that Nolan had been sitting in the dark praying. Kurt had turned on the overhead lights now, unaware that Nolan had arrived at the office before him. The low cursing continued. Huddled in his hidden corner, Nolan decided to don ear buds, begin his work, and ignore his officemate. It would be awkward for him to reveal his presence at this point. He would wait until Kurt left the office for a cup of coffee, and when the rest of their coworkers arrived, he hoped that Kurt would assume that he had just arrived as well.

Nolan silently looked over his schedule for the day. Although they each had their own responsibilities, he and Kurt were supposed to work in tandem on their jobs, each having access to the other's work as an accountability measure. Giving a cursory glance at the next file on his agenda, he was surprised to notice a glaring typographical error in the report on the Miller account that Kurt had finished the day before. It wasn't a huge deal, Nolan reasoned, but it made the report look unprofessional. It would be a bad reflection on the company, and on Kurt, if not corrected before it was turned in. Though Nolan couldn't change it himself, he felt obligated to inform Kurt so he could correct it. Ignoring it wouldn't be the right thing to do, but pointing out the error would take some diplomacy on Nolan's part.

It serves me right for hiding myself to avoid his unpleasantness. I may as well speak to Kurt before the others arrive.

He rounded the partial wall and approached Kurt's desk. "Kurt, I noticed a problem with ...." His voice trailed off as he took in Kurt's reaction to his sudden appearance. It took Nolan a second to take in the scene. *Something is up.* This was much more than mere surprise at finding that he wasn't alone in the room; he knew from the cry of dismay, the guilty expression, and the shaking hands that tried to shield something on the desk. As Nolan watched, Kurt's eyes moved furtively, judging the distance to the paper shredder on the other side of the room.

Before Kurt could stand up, Nolan blocked him with a hand on the shoulder, and then slammed his fist on the paper that Kurt was frantically trying to hide. With piercing eyes he stared at the alarm on Kurt's face. They heard the sound of the back door opening and the click of heels on the hardwood floor as the secretary walked down the hallway to the front office.

In a terse whisper Nolan threatened, "Make one move, and I promise you I will tackle you, and yell loud enough to be heard across the street."

Kurt's face finally crumbled in defeat, and he lowered his head to his hands. Nolan quickly snatched the paper and his eyes scanned it. He walked to the office door and shut it firmly. In the tense silence he turned to face Kurt. "Do you mind explaining this?" he asked coldly.

Kurt ran his hands over his face and answered in a near whisper, "You don't understand, Calderon. You can't understand the pinch I'm in. It was just temporary. I planned to pay it back soon."

Nolan eyes moved from Kurt's face to the paper in his hand and back again. "And just what kind of a pinch are you in that you would risk professional suicide and maybe even jail time? Not to mention doing irreparable harm to the reputation of the firm you work for and betraying your clients' trust. To write a check to yourself on a client's account for ten thousand dollars! This is unbelievable! What were you thinking?" Nolan shook his head at the thought. "Spill it, Kurt. Everything."

Kurt looked down at his trembling hands. In a low voice he began. "The weekend of the fire, I had a loss at the casino, a big loss. Plus, I owe a bundle to some guys that aren't very patient. Then the fire." He started to ramble. "I should never have gotten involved with that woman. I should be all right with the hospital bills. My health insurance ought to pay for that, but now I'm living in a motel until the apartment is fixed. And I lost about everything I owned in the fire. My pay can't cover all I need."

"But your renter's insurance," Nolan interrupted. "Surely they'll pay for the motel and help you with at least a portion of your loss. They would have to, even if it was a result of your carelessness. What have they told you?"

Something in Kurt's expression made Nolan ask, "You did have insurance didn't you?"

Kurt looked down again in shame. "I never got around to getting insurance."

Nolan shook his head, his practical mind trying to grasp how anyone with even a basic intelligence could get himself into such a fix.

Seeing a hint of sympathy on Nolan's face gave Kurt a ray of hope. "You see, Calderon, I'm in a real bind. But I figure that ten grand will cover me. Just enough to pay off the loss, pay on the credit cards, and leave me enough stakes to pay everything back before anybody is the wiser. I wasn't going to keep the money. I just need to borrow it for a few days."

Nolan was flabbergasted. "Let me get this straight. You were planning to gamble some of the money you stole in order to pay back the money you stole?"

"I've got a sure system, Calderon. I just need a little more time and cash!"

"Is this the same system you used two weeks ago, Kurt when you had the big loss?" Nolan asked.

Kurt had no answer. His shoulders sagged in defeat. "I never should have got involved with that woman. She's brought me nothing but bad luck. Then she sets my place on fire besides. I should have dumped her weeks ago. She's bad karma!"

Nolan had to stop himself from rolling his eyes. "You may think it was bad karma, Kurt. That's your choice. But I believe that it was the God who created you, and who loves you. I believe he had me walk in on you at the precise moment I did, so that he could stop you from doing something absolutely insane that could end your career, your freedom, and your self-respect." He stood watching Kurt and trying to take it all in. "Now I need to know something, and you need to be absolutely straight with me. Have you ever done anything like this before?"

Kurt shook his head vigorously. "Never! Never! I swear this was the first time."

Nolan looked at him hard and long. Finally he said, "Funny, but I actually believe you. And, I believe God has placed me here to save you from your own foolishness and to give you a second chance."

Kurt looked up with surprise and hope. "You'll give me back the check so I can shred it?" he asked.

"Absolutely not!" Nolan answered as he carefully folded the evidence of Kurt's deceit and placed it in his wallet. "You need to get to work, Kurt." He glanced at the clock on the wall. "In about three hours, we are going out to lunch, my treat, and then we will talk." He spelled it out in terms that Kurt was sure to understand. "The high cards are in my hand, Kurt," he told him. "I don't believe you have any more aces up your sleeve. If you will listen to me, I believe I have a plan to save your sorry hide and stop you from destroying yourself. If you refuse to abide by my rules, I will turn you in!"

Nolan turned on his heel and walked the few steps past the partition into his own office space. He looked down at his hands and saw that they were shaking. He sank to his chair, slowly letting out his breath as he put his head on the desk. *What now, Lord? What now?*

***

Three hours later Nolan and a subdued Kurt walked into April's Diner and sat down in a corner booth. Nolan noticed that Kurt was looking around at the unfamiliar room.

"No booze served here," Nolan commented sharply. When he saw the wounded look on Kurt's face he repented. "I'm sorry, Kurt. That was uncalled for and mean-spirited. I apologize."

Kurt nodded grimly. "No offense taken. I've come back buzzed from lunch enough times to deserve the dig."

Nolan decided to let it go without further comment. They remained silent as they waited for their orders to arrive. The tantalizing odor of that day's lunch special, chicken pot pie, did little to whet Nolan's appetite. His stomach felt as though it was tied in knots. He could only imagine how bad Kurt was feeling.

Kurt stared intently at his plate, picking at his food. "So, what's the verdict, Calderon? What do you want from me?"

Nolan drummed his fingers on the table a few moments before he spoke. He had spent most of the morning carefully scrutinizing every account that Kurt had been involved in. He had found no evidence of prior misconduct.

"There are some conditions you must agree to if you want me to help you. Hear me out before you put up any arguments." He paused as Kurt shrugged lightly and then nodded. "Number one: You must immediately start attending a gambler's support group. I know of one here in town that you can try. This is nonnegotiable. You have got a big problem, and you need to face it. The casinos have seen the last of you, Kurt. You will need to get another hobby!"

Kurt opened his mouth as if to speak, but closed it with a resigned look.

Nolan continued. "Second condition: I want you to write me an itemized list of what you actually owe, with no gambling stakes included. We're going to get this debt taken care of ASAP."

"But I've tried to get a loan." Kurt interrupted, "No bank will touch me. I've tried the payday loan places, but it's like throwing money down a well. The other guys I owe are already threatening me. That's why I'm desperate!"

"I'm going to take care of that."

"You'll loan me the cash?"

"No, I won't," said Nolan. "I have a better plan. We're going right to the top man."

Kurt glared at Nolan and then blurted out sarcastically, "You're going to pray for your God to hand me the money?"

Nolan had to smile in spite of the seriousness of the situation. "Well, that wasn't who I meant, Kurt, although I have prayed for God's help. But I like how you're beginning to think. No, by 'the top man' I meant Mr. Marley, the owner of the company."

Kurt was dumbfounded. "No! Please! I thought you said you were going to help me, not destroy me!"

"I am going to help you, Kurt. We are going to Mr. Marley and ask him for a loan for the exact amount that you need."

Kurt looked warily at Nolan. "How do you know that he's not going to laugh in my face and then fire me to top it off? Or have me arrested?" he finally sputtered.

Nolan responded with calmness he had yet to feel. "Well, I can't guarantee anything. However, I have known Mr. Marley for most of my life. I trust him to be a fair and compassionate man. With me advocating for you, you just might have a chance." Nolan forced himself to ignore the trembling of Kurt's lips and the pallor on his face. "I can understand your fears and your doubts. You are just going to have to trust me. I know it's not going to come naturally for you, but you really have no choice, do you?" He took a bite of chicken. "This is really quite good. I suggest you try to eat. We have a whole afternoon of work ahead of us. I'll need you to stay over and write me that itemized list of what you owe on your own time." He took another bite. "I had a hard time focusing on work this morning, and I imagine you did, too. We're going to owe Mr. Marley some extra time once this is all settled."

Chapter 16

Kurt decided to arrive early the next Tuesday night for his first gambler's support meeting, not because he was anxious to attend, but because he wanted to avoid being noticed. Kurt slithered into a seat at the back of the still empty room and pretended to focus on his phone.

He still couldn't believe that Nolan had pulled it off. He had never met the founder of Marley's Financial Services until last night. Kurt's interviews and hiring had been conducted by the present CEO who was a nephew of the man. Nolan and Kurt had met at the old man's home and, to Kurt's amazement, Mr. Marley had agreed to loan him the money he needed—at a very fair interest rate. Kurt was to pay back the loan within six months, which was a guarantee because Nolan had insisted that the payment come directly from Kurt's paycheck. Initially, Kurt was tempted to argue with the terms Nolan had come up with. How could he live on such a steep pay cut? But Nolan had quickly pointed out that Kurt wouldn't be needing money for the casino while he was paying off the debt. Plus, Nolan was able to find him a furnished efficiency apartment that would cost him a third as much as what he had been paying at the motel. Kurt knew he was lucky to have gotten off this easy. He could get by for six months. He was sure he could stay away from the casino for that long. Pretty sure, at least.

Nolan had spoken with Mr. Marley ahead of time. Kurt still didn't know if Nolan had spilled anything about the check. He thought not, but he was frankly too scared to ask. Marley seemed to be a pretty nice guy, but Kurt had his doubts about whether Marley would have agreed to the loan if he had known of his intentions to "borrow" the money from a client.

Who am I trying to kid? It would have been embezzling. Might as well call it what it was. He sighed. *I'm going to owe Calderon big time once this is all over.*

He was startled when a hand suddenly settled on his shoulder. He looked up into the face of Mr. Marley. His heart sank. "Mr. Marley!" He nearly stumbled getting to his feet. He felt his face heating up. "I, uh, I didn't know you'd be here."

The elderly man shook Kurt's hand and looked deep into his eyes. "Perhaps Nolan failed to mention that I was the one who formed this group twenty-five years ago. I'm glad you made it tonight, Kurt. Now, if you'll excuse me I see some others who have arrived that I'd like to greet." He started to walk away but turned back. "And Kurt, just to let you know; we don't use last names here."

Kurt took some deep breaths, trying to get his heart to slow down. He studied the people who were starting to trickle into the room. It was a varied group of young, old, male and female. Some looked down and out, others looked prosperous. Fifteen minutes later, he watched with interest as Mr. Marley walked to the front of the room and addressed the crowd.

"Good evening," he said. "My name is Fred, and I am a compulsive gambler."

***

The morning after his first gambler's support meeting, Kurt's mind was still reeling from the things he'd heard. The biggest revelation to Kurt was Mr. Marley's own story. Marley had lost his father during World War II, and his widowed mother could barely support herself and her four children. He had worked his way through high school and college with little help from family. It took him several extra years to finish his degree, working multiple jobs to support his wife and two young children at the same time. Once the children started school, his wife had worked to help him start his own accounting firm. Mr. and Mrs. Marley made sacrifice after sacrifice to build up the company and their struggles paid off as Marley's Financial Services grew to be prosperous and respected in the community. But success had left him feeling restless and unfulfilled, and he sought a distraction in the gambling casinos that were starting to pop up all over the country.

Listening to Marley's story, Kurt remembered the first time he had walked into a casino years before. There was energy in that dark cavernous room that pulsed with light and sound. It had pulled at Kurt and drawn him in. Fred Marley had described the feelings that gambling had given him. The feelings were uncannily familiar to Kurt: the euphoria, the thrill of winning, and the overwhelming urge to go on. Marley understood.

Marley candidly spoke of the toll his gambling compulsion had taken on his family, friends, and his business. It was only when his wife threatened to leave him that he was forced to face his addiction. Marley went on to talk of his struggle and his miserable failure to gain control of his actions. He had come close to losing his family, career, and self-respect before finally facing the fact that it was something he couldn't conquer on his own. Marley had credited God with intervening in his life and giving him the power to overcome his weaknesses.

Kurt wasn't ready to accept this part of the story, but he did have much to mull over as he considered the similarities between Fred's experiences and his own. Kurt never knew his real father, who had chosen to distance himself from parental responsibilities before Kurt was born. The succession of stepfathers in his boyhood had spent his mother's hard-earned paychecks as fast as she could bring them home, usually at the neighborhood tavern. Kurt's dreams of college would have gone unfulfilled had he not been born with an exceptional aptitude for math. The combination of his good high school record, high test scores, and extra low family income landed him a decent scholarship at a state school in Nevada. Kurt earned the rest of the money he needed to finish school by working on a construction crew during summer breaks and as a waiter during the school terms. He worked hard to accomplish his career dream. Being able to work at something that he enjoyed, was good at, and paid him a decent wage gave him great satisfaction. He had headed east after graduation to put some distance between himself and his mother's actions. He secured a job with a large firm in Cleveland. His college struggles were over, and he now made good money, yet Kurt, like Marley, felt restless and unfulfilled.

His social life in Cleveland had consisted of partying on weekends at various casinos with his single co-workers. He met a few women there, but none who seemed genuinely interested in him. He had lots of buddies who shared his love for a good time, but the times when Kurt looked with honesty at his life, he realized that he wanted more. He wanted true friends who would be willing to stick with him in good times and bad. He doubted that any of the people he now spent his time with would ever be that kind of friend. Discouraged and lonely, he decided to change jobs. When he had seen the online ad for a position in Shelby Falls, he thought this might be the place where things could change. It was a small company where he could be more than just a number. Maybe, just maybe, this could be the place where he could begin to feel a sense of belonging. He had hoped it would be a place where he could find a true friend or two and maybe even begin a lasting relationship with a woman.

Kurt enjoyed the work at Marley's and the slower pace of life in Shelby Falls. Since it was within easy driving distance to several casinos, he could still enjoy his gambling hobby and meet with his old co-workers on weekends. He was disappointed that his overtures of friendship to Nolan Calderon, the only other young single male at the office, had been rebuffed from the start. Kurt had reacted to Nolan's priggishness with cutting remarks that he knew made Nolan uncomfortable. Kurt realized that his behavior with Nolan was unprofessional, and he was careful to make sure no one else heard his remarks. But with the fire, things had changed. In less than two weeks' time, Nolan had saved Kurt's life, caught him in the act of embezzling, and threatened to expose him if he didn't explicitly follow his rules. Then he had gone to great lengths to help him out of his financial bind. He arranged for the loan and helped him work out a stringent budget so he could pay off his debt in a reasonable time. He was totally confused trying to figure out Nolan's motives.

Whatever they are, I'm stuck for at least as long as it takes me to pay back that loan to Marley and get that check back from Nolan.

"Good morning, Kurt," Nolan greeted him cheerfully as he walked into the office. "How was your meeting last night?"

Kurt studied Nolan's face. He could detect nothing but a friendly curiosity in his manner. "It was pretty interesting," he admitted after a moment. "You could have warned me though, Calderon. I about jumped out of my skin when Marley showed up there."

"Sorry, Kurt," Nolan frowned slightly as he poured himself a cup of coffee. "I thought it best to do it the way Mr. Marley asked me to."

Kurt chewed on his lip. He mulled over whether to ask if Nolan had come clean with Marley about the entire situation. Surely he hadn't told the whole story or Marley would never have agreed to help him. Thinking about it made him nervous. He stirred some creamer into his cup of coffee and turned to his desk without another word.

Chapter 17

The mid-thirties temperature was not ideal running weather, but the sun was shining, the air was still, and the snow had melted off of the track. Nolan's years of cross country and track had conditioned him to run in all seasons. When it came down to it, he preferred the cold to sweltering heat. Typically, he favored the more interesting trails or back roads, but today he welcomed the mindless circling of the track. He needed rest from the turmoil he was feeling. If only he could roll back time and undo what had happened last night. He deposited his coat on a stadium seat and did some stretches before slipping a second long-sleeved shirt over his head and pulling on gloves. He took off at a medium pace and concentrated on his rhythm. As his body adjusted to the effort, his breathing came easier, and he felt the tension releasing. After every two laps around the track, he'd break into a short sprint. It only took a few laps before he had to shed the extra shirt and gloves, tossing them on the seat by his coat. He finished lap twelve with a fifty-yard sprint at his peak speed. Huffing, he slowed to a walk for his cool down.

With his body energized, and his mind rested, he allowed himself to ruminate over the developments of the past month. He had expected things to slow down after the holidays. Instead, beginning with the fire at his duplex, his normally well-ordered life seemed to be taking him on a series of detours. Finding out the secrets of his mother's past had forced him to look more closely at his own Christian walk. On the heels of that revelation was his discovery of Kurt Walker's attempted theft. He was surprised at himself when he decided to go to Mr. Marley as an act of mercy towards a man he previously thought of as nothing more than an annoying pain in the neck. And now his romantic relationship with Kozy Hanner, which he had assumed was progressing nicely, had taken an unexpected turn.

Nolan cringed as he relived the conversation from last evening. They had spent a couple of hours with Ben and Nikki, sharing a pizza and checking out Ben's handiwork. The nursery was freshly painted and decorated down to the last detail for the soon-to-arrive baby girl. The room was awash with the glittery and lacy stuff that Kozy loved. Nikki kept a steady narrative on the uses of all the special gadgets and equipment that they had acquired. Nolan and Ben enjoyed watching a basketball game together while the girls chatted. It had been early enough when they left Ben and Nikki's that they decided to have some hot chocolate at Kozy's house.

Thinking back, Nolan recalled noticing that Kozy had seemed a little quieter than usual, but he figured she was just tired from teaching all week. And she had been a little down ever since she had confided to him that she still harbored anger from her childhood. He hadn't broached the subject since then. The reluctance to open up about their deepest fears was one characteristic that they seemed to share.

He remembered how she looked as they sat together on the couch. The cold had brought color to her cheeks, and her soft sweater and jeans flattered her figure in a way that made his heart flutter. It didn't matter what she wore; she always looked good to him. But the attraction was more than merely physical. For months they had been working together with the teens from church, and their spiritual connection had deepened considerably. Her honest assessments had encouraged him to examine his own heart. Her intelligence, maturity, and love for people impressed him more every day. Her sense of humor had brought back his ability to laugh. He was completely comfortable with her, yet at the same time realized that she was a person who would always keep him intrigued. Their personalities complemented one another well. He could no longer imagine his life without her at his side.

That was the problem; he had thought too far ahead. Seeing Ben and Nikki with stars in their eyes as they anticipated becoming parents for the first time had put thoughts in his head. He should have been more attuned to Kozy's feelings.

"Nolan, you're staring at me," she had said with a giggle. "Stop it," she said. Her cheeks flushed even more as she fumbled with the empty mugs on the coffee table.

"I'm sorry," he told her, though he didn't mean it. He scooted closer and reached his hands to draw her face close to his. "It's just that you look so gorgeous." He kissed her mouth and drew back to smile at her. "It was fun tonight, wasn't it? Catching the excitement of waiting for their baby to be born?"

He should have quit there, but he hadn't been able stop himself. "Kozy," he blurted, "I can see us being at that point, maybe in a year or two, can't you? I love you, and I hope …."

His voice trailed off as she stiffened. "Please, Nolan. Don't say any more." Her voice shook as she put a hand in the air to stop him. "I'm not sure if I even want to have children. My parents failed so terribly. I couldn't live with myself if I turned out like them. I know how important having kids is to you. I'm sorry. I should have said something before we started caring too much. I don't want to disappoint you."

Nolan's face was unreadable as he took in the words. When his eyes wouldn't leave her face, she leaned forward in her seat and, elbows on knees, covered her face with her hands. When he finally found his voice, it was calm. "That is the most irrational thing I've ever heard." He stood and raked his fingers through his hair. When the moments ticked by and she didn't look up, he sighed and spoke softly. "You love kids, Kozy. That's why you're such a great teacher. And you are not your parents. You're a wonderful, loving, responsible woman of God. The choice whether or not to have children is yours, of course, but you can't use your parents as an excuse."

He frowned and waited for a response. When she didn't speak, he went on. "Kozy, are you seeing someone else?"

She peered at him over her fingertips. "Of course not," she said in a wounded voice. "Is that what you think this is about?"

"Well, I didn't really think so," he answered. "But I need to know exactly what I'm up against—whether it's another guy I'm competing with."

"Of course not," she repeated. "It's not about you, Nolan. It's me. Maybe I sound crazy to you, but I know how I feel. Ever since Shaina was taken away, I've had trouble sleeping, I wake up in a panic, and I feel so angry when I let myself think about it. I guess I shouldn't expect you to understand. I don't even understand it myself. But it isn't fair to you. I think … I think we should stop dating."

He stared at the floor for a long moment before standing and reaching for his coat. He threw it over one shoulder as he stalked across the room to the front door. He could hear her sniffling behind him as he gripped the handle.

She needs you. You can't leave her like they did. He didn't hear an audible voice, but the message was unmistakable.

Releasing his hold on the doorknob, he turned and walked back to the couch. "There," he said. "We just made it through our first fight."

She looked up, swiping at her eyes. "We did? What do you mean?"

"I mean I'm not giving up on you, Kozy Hanner, not as long as you can stand having me around. I love you. But I promise not to pressure you into any commitment. Once you've had time to work through your feelings, that'll be time enough to decide where we go from there. No strings attached."

She was dumbfounded. "I don't know what to say, Nolan."

He put on his coat. "You don't need to say anything. Nothing you've said has changed how I feel about you. Look, how about we just forget the presumptuous stuff I said earlier? We are friends. We go to church together and lead a group of teens. We hang out on our days off. There's no reason we can't just continue on as we've been, as the good friends we've become." His eyes studied her face, noticing the dark circles under her eyes and the trembling of her mouth. "Get some rest. You talk about fairness. It's not fair for you to dump me now while you're confused and tired. I would like you to think on what I've said. I won't bother you tomorrow, but you can let me know what you decide."

He had driven around for over an hour after he left her house.

You have a plan for me Lord, and I was so sure that plan included Kozy. Can you let me in on the plan? 'Cause I don't understand what just happened.

He was grateful that, by the time he had arrived home, his family had already turned in for the night. He was so weary that he dropped off to sleep as soon as he fell into bed.

It was a new day, and his workout had cleared his head. The situation didn't look quite as bleak to him as it had the night before. She had admitted that she cared about him. She hadn't absolutely refused to continue seeing him. If only there was some way to help her work through the feelings that were causing her to doubt herself. He determined to give her all the understanding and love that she needed and see what happened.

Lord, please give me patience.

***

Tom had spent the early morning hours putting the final touches on his sermon while Marcy took the twins shopping for new sneakers to replace the ones they had outgrown. After finishing his sermon, he gathered his income tax folders and set them on the kitchen table. Marcy usually did their taxes, but since Nolan was more attuned to the latest changes in tax laws, he had offered to help them complete their returns in appreciation for their providing him a place to live after the fire.

"I think that's everything you'll need, Nolan," Tom announced. He noted that his son had showered and shaved as soon as he had returned from his run. "Are you sure you don't have better things to do with your time today?" he hinted with a smile.

"I won't be seeing Kozy today, Dad," he said, "if that's what you're wondering."

Tom's smile faded at the painful look on his son's face. "I don't want to seem like I'm prying into your life, Nolan. It just seemed like you two were getting along so well, and Marcy and I kind of thought, well, we really like Kozy, and so do the kids."

"I care about Kozy a lot, Dad," he admitted, "more than anyone else I've ever dated. But our relationship is kind of on hold right now." He sighed. "She wants to keep things on a friendship level until she figures some things out. Kozy still has some issues from her childhood that she hasn't quite resolved."

"You're disappointed."

Nolan nodded. "Disappointed and confused, but maybe this is for the best. Maybe we both still need time to work some things out before we're ready to commit. I won't push her into anything she's not ready for, but I'm convinced we have a future together, and I think she's worth the wait."

Nolan's determined look as he reached for the tax folders made Tom realize he wasn't going to get any more details. "Sounds like pretty wise thinking," he said as he pulled his chair to the table. "Well, how have things been going at work lately? Are you making any progress in your quest to be more of a friend to Kurt?"

Grateful to change the subject, Nolan chewed on his lip, wondering how much he could say without revealing too much of Kurt's predicament. "Some things have happened in the last few days, Dad." He went on to explain that Kurt had confessed to him that his gambling had landed him in quite a financial mess. "I'm not at liberty to elaborate, but Kurt agreed to let me help him. I took him to meet Mr. Marley, and Mr. Marley was willing to loan Kurt the money he needs, with the agreement that Kurt will attend Gamblers Anonymous meetings until he's paid off his debt."

"Wow. That's very generous of Fred. But of course, he's always had a special interest in people caught in addiction. I'm surprised that you were able to talk Kurt into getting help so quickly. Usually it takes a real crisis to get people to accept that they have a problem."

"Well, it was kind of a crisis, and I did have to do a lot of praying about the situation," Nolan conceded as he started sorting through the tax documents. But he stared at the same page for five minutes and couldn't recall a word he had read. *Kozy's not the only one with unresolved issues. Maybe it's time I faced my own. Is that what you're telling me, Lord?* He brushed the folders aside in frustration.

Tom's brow wrinkled as he glanced up from reading the newspaper. "There's plenty of time to work on our taxes another day, you know. Got something else on your mind?" he asked as he folded the paper and set it down. Something in Nolan's expression made him ask, "Is it something about your mother?"

Nolan looked up, surprised that his father had guessed. He tried to summon the courage to speak.

"I'm sorry, Dad," he uttered at last. "I'm sorry I let you down the night Mom died."

It was Tom's turn to register surprise. He sat staring at his son whose eyes were carefully focused on the tabletop. "I don't understand Nolan," he said in confusion. "How could you think you let me down?"

Nolan's face was grim as he began. "I didn't do what I was supposed to that night, Dad. If I had, maybe things would have been different."

Tom began a protest, but Nolan quickly cut him off. "No, Dad, you've got to let me finish. You have to let me explain." Nolan took a shaky breath and continued. "You had to go to the board meeting that night. My job was to stay with Mom. I checked on her two or three times while I was doing my homework. Each time she said she was fine, just really sleepy. I asked her if I could run over to Ben's just for a minute to get an assignment I'd left at school. She said I could but that I should come right back because of the weather forecast."

Nolan looked up for a moment and met his dad's eyes. "He'd just got a new video game. We only wanted to try it out. We got so involved in it, and before I knew it, the storm had started. I raced as fast as I could across the field. The wind had kicked up and that wet snow pelted me in the face. I checked on Mom the minute I got in. She was having trouble breathing. She asked me to call you at the church. As you know, that's when the power and phone lines went out."

Except for the detail of the few minutes Nolan had spent on the video game, none of this was news to Tom. He was well aware of how Nolan had found a few candles and lit them for his mother so she wouldn't be in the dark. Then the boy had rushed over to the closest neighbors to use the phone, remembering too late that they were gone on a vacation. He had frantically tried the elderly woman on the other side of the road. Her power was out, too, and she didn't own a vehicle. After checking on his mother again, he had run back across the frozen field to his friend's house where the lights were still on. Ben's dad first called for an ambulance and then called the church. Before either of them had gotten back home, it was over. Sharon was gone. Now Tom desperately wanted Nolan to stop reliving the painful scenario, but he sensed that Nolan needed to talk it out.

He didn't even notice the tears running down his own face until he looked down and saw the newspaper was wet. He stood, stumbled over to Nolan and embraced him.

"I should have been there with her, Dad," Nolan said brokenly. "She shouldn't have had to die alone. If I hadn't stayed so long, I could have called for help before the power went out. Maybe they could have saved her."

With a jolt of pain, Tom realized the guilt that Nolan must have carried with him all these years. He struggled now to convince his overly conscientious son that he had done nothing wrong. He had been a mere child overtaken by the simple desire to enjoy a moment of fun, and no one had ever blamed Nolan for the tragedy.

Tom himself had lamented a thousand times the fact that he had left home at all that evening. The church board hadn't expected him to attend every meeting, as they were well aware of Sharon's fragile condition. To this day he still couldn't pinpoint the reason he had chosen to leave his ten-year-old son alone to carry the burden of staying with his terminally ill mother that night. Was it pride in his position as pastor? The fear of his own weakness in dealing with the impending loss? Was it anger that Sharon had given up on fighting the cancer? He had beaten himself up enough times over each possibility.

There had been no prior indication that Sharon would draw her last breath that night. Her condition had remained stable for weeks. No one could have predicted that an ice-covered branch would fall at such an inopportune time and knock out the power and phone lines. No one could have guessed that the circumstances would play out so tragically that night. Tom had been left with a tremendous sense of loss and shame.

But Pastor Tom Calderon had long ago given his shame to God. Not that shame didn't still resurrect itself occasionally, as it was doing now. But Tom knew for certain where it belonged: buried at the foot of the cross.

Forgive me again, Lord, for doubting your worthiness to cover my guilt. Please begin a healing in Nolan today, that he might once again experience the fullness of your grace. Bring him peace. Please bring him peace!

***

Tom and Nolan continued talking for some time, and during that time Nolan's burden slowly dissipated. Father and son were still reminiscing over sweeter and happier memories when Kelsey breezed through the kitchen door carrying bags from the mall shoe store. Zane followed close behind. Kelsey's bubbling chatter ended abruptly when she noticed Nolan's red-rimmed eyes, and then her dad's.

She was suddenly frightened. "Is something wrong, Daddy?" she asked timidly.

Kelsey was used to seeing her dad get emotional. She had often witnessed him shedding tears along with his church family as they suffered through various crises and trials. But it had been years since she had seen Nolan cry, not since the deaths of their Calderon grandparents. She waited breathlessly as Tom reached over and squeezed Nolan's shoulder.

"Everything's fine, sweetheart," he told her as he smiled at Nolan. "We've just been remembering Nolan's mom and talking things over. It was a good talk."

Blinking hard, Kelsey stood watching her older brother. She rushed over to where he sat at the table and threw herself into his arms. "I've been such a selfish sister! I hardly ever even think about how sad it must have been for you to lose your mom when you were so young. You were just a child!"

"Hey, kiddo," Nolan patted Kelsey's back and gave her a quick kiss on the forehead. "Don't feel bad. I'm fine, I really am." They were all used to Kelsey's frequent emotional outbursts, but Nolan was touched with her show of sympathy.

"We don't mind sharing our mom with you, right Zane?" she sniffed.

Zane silently stepped up and gave Nolan an awkward one-armed hug.

Still embracing his siblings, Nolan looked over their heads at Marcy, who stood silently witnessing the scene from the doorway. He winked at her. "Don't worry, kids," he said with a smile. "Just because I call her 'Marcy', doesn't mean I don't love her just as much as I do my own mom. She was being a mom to me long before you two were even born." He grabbed a tissue from the table and dabbed at Kelsey's tears while acknowledging Zane with a gentle punch on the arm.

He spoke with mock severity. "Now that doesn't mean that you're allowed to call your mom 'Marcy', though. That's just for me and Dad. She's still to be 'Mom' to you two! Got it?" He waved them away then with a smile. "Okay, now. I had better get busy if I'm going to get these taxes finished this afternoon."

***

Kozy awakened late on Saturday morning, feeling out of sorts. Though she had turned in shortly after Nolan left the night before, her sleep had been sporadic. After dragging herself out of bed at nearly noon, she wandered aimlessly inside her house. The rest of her day loomed long and empty. Ever since she and Nolan had begun dating in earnest in December, they had rarely spent a Saturday afternoon or evening apart. Telling him that they should stop seeing each other had seemed like a good idea last night; the only fair thing, really.

If only he hadn't hinted at marriage and children.

They could have just continued enjoying one another's company until she figured things out. Her conscience just wouldn't let her continue on, letting him think that she had the same dreams and aspirations as he did. Maybe she used to, but now she had begun to feel so unsure and broken.

She stared gloomily into her closet as she remembered what Nolan had said last night just before he left. "Think about it and let me know." *But thinking about it just makes me more confused.* She wished she had the courage to face her fears. She turned from the closet and instead pulled a tattered gray sweatshirt from the laundry basket, one that she wore when doing her dirtiest chores. An equally shabby pair of jeans completed her outfit. She glanced in the mirror with a frown. *There. Now I look just like I feel.*

The idea came like a flash. She padded to the kitchen and took stock of her refrigerator. By one o'clock she was in her car and headed for the supermarket where she did her weekly shopping. After collecting everything she had on her list, she stored her bags of groceries in her trunk and then stopped at the small meat market at the end of her street.

"Do you have any nice soup bones today?" she called to the white-haired man working at the butcher block in the back room.

"For my favorite teacher, I'll find the best!" he answered.

"How's Jaxson doing in middle school?" Kozy asked.

"He's doing great. He even made the honor role last semester! My daughter is still singing your praises for the extra time you spent with him. He loves to read now."

"Well, your grandson was a pleasure to work with," she said modestly. "Please make sure to tell him I asked about him, okay?" She gave a nod of approval for the meaty beef bone before the man wrapped it in white paper.

"Thanks so much, Mr. Beaber," she said as she handed him the cash. "This is exactly what I need."

Back home Kozy dug her largest stockpot out of the cupboard and set the soup bone in a gallon of water to boil. She washed and peeled several carrots, a couple of potatoes, and an onion, adding them to the pot. She hummed as she worked. Next, she rummaged in the refrigerator until she found the remains of a stalk of celery and a small head of cabbage. She rinsed the bitter celery leaves and dropped them into the pot. She lowered the heat on the boiling pot to a medium simmer, then chopped off a chunk of the cabbage and plopped it into the soup. She chewed on her lip. *What's missing?* Her eyes landed on two Roma tomatoes that sat ripening on her window sill. She grabbed a paring knife and scraped it all over the surface of each tomato until the skins loosened. Once she had slipped them from the skin, she chopped them on a cutting board and slid them into the pot. Smiling now, she placed a small iron skillet on the stovetop and started melting a blob of butter. Just as she had watched her grandma do a hundred times, she carefully browned the butter and reached into the ever-present red tin for a tablespoon of paprika. She stirred in the resulting roux and smiled as the broth took on a beautiful rosy hue. *You taught me well, Gramma.* She grabbed another pot, filled it halfway with salted water, and set it to boil. Then she expertly stirred a mixture of flour and egg into the proper consistency for making hard dumplings called *nokedli.* By the time the teaspoon-sized drop noodles had been rinsed and placed in a bowl in the refrigerator, her soup had filled the air with a rich aroma. She turned the burner to the lowest setting and let it simmer while she indulged in a long hot bath. It was only then that she allowed herself to think.

Kozy had spent a good part of her life trying to ignore any lingering memories of her parents. When she had given her talk for the teens, she had used the court records to reenact the events that led to her stint in foster care. She knew the history was an essential part of the story and needed to be told for the testimony to be compelling. So she had memorized the bare facts and somehow managed to sidestep any real feelings from that time period. She had an obscure sympathy for the little girl that she had been. The girl she had been seemed a shadow now, but her little third grade student was real. When Shaina's life was suddenly shattered by her mother's actions, a tiny crack began to form in the protective wall Kozy had spent years building around her own heart. A few memories from her childhood were trying to seep through, and Kozy didn't like it one bit. Yet she knew the anger she was feeling wasn't good either. She thought she had released it all when she had become a Christian. But the rage had been lurking there all along as though to ambush her. Was it possible God wanted her to remember so she could purge her fears once and for all? Part of her wanted to obey. But another part of her was scared to death of what she might find. All this had left her with the convictions she had revealed to Nolan last night.

She was nonplussed that Nolan would consider her confessions "irrational." *Apparently he doesn't think my feelings are valid.* But she knew that wasn't so as soon as the thought surfaced. One of the things that had drawn her to Nolan in the first place was his sensitivity to her feelings. That's why it was so easy to open up to him. She felt safe with him and cherished.

The water in the bathtub had cooled and she shivered as she dried off and dressed in her most comfortable jeans and a pink flannel shirt. Back in the kitchen she chose a tangerine colored bowl from her cabinet. She placed a few dumplings in it and ladled some of the clear crimson broth on top. Fishing a couple of carrots, a potato, and a leaf of cabbage out of the pot, she placed them on a lime green plate and smiled at the picture they made.

Her Gram used to say, "When you face something that takes extra courage, you should always pray. God will help you. But it never hurts to sit down to a good bowl of hot soup, either."

Kozy bowed her head and prayed. Then she took a sip of the rich broth and began to eat. Later, feeling fortified, she picked up her phone and took a deep breath.

The Calderons were all gathered in the family room after dinner, and Nolan was just finishing the tax return when his phone vibrated. As soon as he saw Kozy's name, he jumped up and headed for the guest room. "Hey," he said softly.

"Hi. Uh, I've been considering what you said last night, Nolan. Could you, um, explain to me again why you think it's okay for us to keep dating?"

"Well," he started.

Her heart raced as seconds ticked by. *Maybe he's changed his mind. Maybe he doesn't want to see me anymore. What have I done?*

Not sure of her frame of mind, he was afraid of saying too much. He didn't want to make things worse by once again prematurely declaring his love for her. His mind clicked over the arguments he had given her the night before. In the end he chose to be honest.

"Because," he said at last, "if I can't see you anymore, it'll break my heart." He waited breathlessly; when she was slow to respond, he went on. "I meant what I said before. I promise not to pressure you. I'll give you all the time you need to work through your feelings." He tried to keep the desperation from his voice. "Please, don't throw away what we have because of fear."

"Oh Nolan," she said, voice breaking. "I don't deserve you, but I accept the terms. I would hate to no longer have you as a friend." She sniffed, her emotions threatening to overwhelm her. "I missed being with you today."

He squelched the disappointment and let out a slow breath. *"Friends" was not exactly my first choice but it's better than nothing. Thank you, Lord!*

In an attempt to lighten the mood and make things seem normal he asked, "So, did you do anything special without me?"

"I made a pot of Hungarian beef soup," she said, "with dumplings. Remember? The kind I made you on your birthday?"

Nolan took a deep breath. "Mmmm. Why, Kozy, I believe I can smell it from here."

She giggled. "That must be some smart phone you have."

It was a relief to hear her laugh. "Yeah," he quipped. "You know how they have an app for everything now."

Chapter 18

That evening in the privacy of their bedroom, Marcy held her husband tightly in her arms as he recounted his conversation with Nolan that afternoon.

"I never dreamed that Nolan had been suffering all this time with false guilt over not being there when his mother died. And when he told me about the panic attacks he's had in the winter storms …." He groaned. "If only I had talked more with him at the time, tried to draw him out or seen to it that he'd had counseling."

"There now, hush," she whispered as though he were a child to be comforted. "You can 'if only' 'til the cows come home, and it won't change a thing. The fact is, Thomas Calderon, you are a wonderful father, and you did the best you knew at the time. Nolan loves and respects you, and he knows you love him. Otherwise, he wouldn't have confided in you at all."

"But he held in his feelings for so long, Marcy. I hate that—"

"That he's so like his father?" Marcy interjected. When he didn't respond, she elaborated. "Tom, you were married to Sharon for fourteen years. That was a huge portion of your life. I would never ask you to share the intimate and private things from your first marriage. I realize that her illness and death were traumatic for both you and Nolan, but …." She paused to rub her thumb tenderly on the sandpaper texture of his cheek. "You were happy in your first marriage, weren't you?"

"Very much so," he admitted with a sigh.

"Then it's okay for you to talk about the happy times, Tom. We owe it to the woman who had a part in making you the man you are today. I don't want Sharon Calderon to be the elephant in the room any longer. I don't want to ignore the fact that she lived just because she's gone for now. You and Nolan will see her again. And the day that I meet her in heaven, I intend to thank her for making you happy enough to want to marry again and for giving me the most wonderful stepson a woman could ask for!"

He turned his head to kiss her hand. "Nolan has loved you from the beginning, you know. You always knew the best way to reach out to him."

"I love your oldest son just as though he came from my own womb, Tom." She smiled in the darkness. "I've always sensed that he loved me back, but it sure was nice to hear him say it today."

***

"Hey, how about lunch?" Nolan asked Kurt one morning the next week. "I was thinking of Dagwood's on Front Street. They make a great Rueben sandwich. I'll buy."

"Sure," Kurt answered after a moment's hesitation. "Sure. That would be great. Thanks, Nolan."

"Good," Nolan said as he rounded the wall to his own workspace. "I'll drive."

***

"You're right. This is a good Reuben," Kurt admitted after tasting his sandwich. They had decided to work a little longer to avoid the lunch rush. At one-thirty they had the place nearly to themselves and didn't have to vie for a seat with a bunch of noisy high school students.

His mouth full, Nolan nodded as he looked through the large window. A man with a plow on the front of his pickup worked in an adjacent parking lot clearing the snow that had fallen the night before. Nolan tried to recall whether it had been snowing yet late yesterday afternoon when he left work. If it was, it must have been a gentle snow, he decided, because Nolan hadn't given much thought to the weather, and he couldn't recall any uncomfortable feelings of impending panic. He turned his attention back to Kurt.

"I think I understand now why you thought Marley might be willing to help me," Kurt was saying. "I was really floored that first night when he told his story in front of that room full of people. I would never have guessed that he would be able to understand, but he's been there. I have to admire him for his willingness to give a guy a chance."

"As I told you before, Kurt, I've known Mr. Marley since I started mowing for him in grade school. I know the kind of generous-hearted person he is. He was the only one I could think of to go to for help with the situation that we found ourselves in."

Now Kurt was the one gazing out at the parking lot. "I can't believe how stupid I was to try something like that." He looked glumly at Nolan. "I didn't think so at first, but I am glad that you caught me before it was too late." He gripped the edge of the table and leaned forward. "I'd like to know, did you tell Marley everything?"

Nolan studied Kurt's face a moment before answering. "I had to tell him, Kurt. It wouldn't have been right not to."

Kurt looked down and contemplated the revelation. So he was doubly indebted to the old man. He exhaled slowly as the realization sank in.

"I had to tell him." Nolan repeated. "But I promise you this: as long as you keep up your end of the bargain, no one else—and I mean no one— needs to know about your error in judgment. Just the three of us. We truly want to help you, Kurt."

They continued eating in silence. Before they stood to leave, Kurt spoke again. "Marley invited me to church. He caught me off guard, and I couldn't think of a single excuse. He told me it's the same church you go to. I feel weird asking, but would you be willing to meet me there? I think I'd feel really awkward sitting with Mr. and Mrs. Marley."

"No problem, Kurt. I'll be going with Kozy. How about if we just pick you up? That way you won't have to walk in alone." They got into Nolan's car, and Nolan inserted the key. Before he put the car in gear, he turned to Kurt. "I'd like to apologize for never inviting you to our church myself. I've worked with you for all these months and had plenty of opportunities but never did it."

"To be perfectly honest, Nolan, if you had invited me I most likely wouldn't have accepted."

"I know, and I wouldn't blame you. But it still doesn't excuse me. I had something happen in my own life lately that has shown me that I have been guilty of acting like a self-righteous jerk around people whose lifestyles differed too much from my own. I'm sorry for that." He started the engine and headed back to the office. After a moment he continued. "If you're willing, Kurt, I'd like to wipe the slate clean and be friends with you."

Kurt was at a loss for words. As he sat with his mouth open, figuring out how to respond, Nolan glanced over and chuckled.

"I'm glad you're coming to church with us. You're going to love my dad. He's a good preacher. He really knows how to bring the Bible to life."

"You mean to say your dad is the preacher?" he asked incredulously. He shook his head and grinned. "Calderon, you are really something else. I'm glad you at least told me that before I had a chance to stick my foot in my mouth." He laughed for the first time in weeks.

***

Nolan had told Kurt that anything from a suit to jeans and flannel shirt would be appropriate for church, but he didn't want Mr. Marley to think he was being disrespectful by dressing too casual. Kurt decided on his light blue shirt, black slacks, and a gray-and-red-striped tie topped with his new gray sports coat. Not that he had all that many casual clothes since the fire had destroyed all of his belongings. A top priority with the budget Nolan had helped him with had been clothes for his job. He examined his reflection in the mirror as he waited for Nolan's text. He barely had time to worry when he heard the chirp. They were in the driveway.

"Looking good, Kurt!" Kozy smiled and gave him a thumbs-up as he climbed into the back seat.

"Thanks, Kozy," he said gratefully. "I had a hard time deciding what to wear, even though I have few choices right now.

"Well, I'm sure you'd look terrific no matter what you would've chosen. You'll have all the single girls in church wanting to sit in our row today," she teased.

Kurt let out a laugh, and Nolan could see him smiling when he glanced in the rearview mirror. *Trust Kozy to know just what to say to make a person feel at ease.* He looked at her, hoping he was keeping his longing for her out of his own expression. *Just friends*, he thought miserably. *Lord, give me patience! I just hope she isn't thinking that she's in the single-girl category.* He grinned as Kozy gave him a quick wink and a smile. Peace settled over him.

At least a dozen people greeted the trio as they made their way into the sanctuary. After introducing Kurt to several of their friends, they headed for a space midway up the left aisle and scooted in toward the center of the row. Nolan nudged Kurt and pointed to Mr. Marley, who was seated across the aisle a few rows back. Kurt gave a slight wave as he saw Marley nod and smile at him. As he was turning back to speak to Nolan, he heard a female voice on his right.

"Well, I don't believe I've seen this man here before. Is this a friend of yours, Nolan?" Kurt turned his head to see a small elderly woman with snow-white hair plop herself down beside him. "I hope you're not saving this seat for someone else," she said with a mischievous grin. "I often end up sitting next to bald men," she continued, indicating Kurt's shaved head, "but those men aren't bald by choice like you, and they aren't anywhere near as good-looking. Margaret will be envious that I got here first." She pointed toward her friend, who was slowly shuffling up the aisle with her walker. "Welcome to Grace Church, young man. My name is Ruby. What's yours?"

Ruby and Margaret kept Kurt in lively conversation until the service began with announcements and a few worship songs and hymns. Though the songs weren't familiar to Kurt, he followed along reading the words on the overhead screen. Once the service started, the time seemed to go faster than Kurt had anticipated. He had to admit Nolan had been right. His dad did know how to bring the Bible to life. He had a thoughtful and yet authoritative manner of speaking. Kurt was intrigued at how Tom Calderon managed to make a several-thousand-year-old story seem relevant for the twenty-first century.

There was something about the whole atmosphere there as well. For the most part, the people seemed totally engaged in what was happening; they seemed to want to be there. He contrasted this with the people he'd seen in the casinos whose faces were so often bored and empty and lacking something. He tried to put his finger on what it was the people at Grace Community Church had that the people in the casinos did not. The word that came to his mind was joy. *Was that it?*

Afterwards, on the way home, Kurt took Kozy's teasing with good humor. "You see, Kurt? I was right about the single girls wanting to sit with you. Ruby and Margaret are both widows, so technically they are single!"

"Very funny, guys," he said with a laugh. "Both of them have to be pushing eighty!"

"Believe it or not, Ruby just celebrated her ninety-second birthday," Nolan said. "And Margaret's not too far behind."

"Well, they were very nice, and I enjoyed meeting them," Kurt admitted. "Actually, Ruby reminded me of someone I used to be quite fond of," he said thoughtfully. "Bobbie was the grandmother of 'Stepdad Number Two' who, luckily, only lasted a few years as a member of my family. Bobbie was just the opposite of her cruel grandson. She was kind and spunky too, like Ruby. She didn't take any bull from him. Before he and my mom split, Bobbie would take me to her place on weekends every so often. Even took me to Sunday school. I'd kind of forgotten about that until today. When 'Number Two' and my mom split, Bobbie was the only one I missed."

Kozy looked back at Kurt with sympathy, but his gaze remained focused out the side window. He didn't say anything more, and a few minutes later Nolan pulled into Kurt's driveway.

"Will we be picking you up next week?" Kozy asked, as Kurt eased his large frame out of the backseat.

Kurt hesitated. "I'm not sure," he hedged. "I'll think about it. Thanks for the lift, Nolan," he said as he waved them off.

"Happy to do it, Kurt," he answered. "See you at work."

Chapter 19

Something in Vince Mateo's straightforward personality and friendliness made people feel comfortable opening up to him. At times he need only ask a simple question such as "What's your story?" to those under his care at Hope Hospice House. In the end stage of life most people just wanted someone to care enough to ask. They needed to explain the essence of their lives before it was too late. Every resident had a unique story. Some were happier than others. It was always heartening to see those who had family and friends to surround them in their final days.

Joni Farnsworth was not one of those. When Vince first scanned the brief Hospice House file for the woman, he had been dismayed to learn that she had listed no next of kin, and until recently, had lived in another part of the country. She would likely have no loved ones to help her through her last journey on this earth. Vince was determined to become a friend. She had, thus far, remained reluctant to share much about herself.

"You don't want to hear my pitiful story," she declared any time he tried to focus the conversation on her.

Yet her eyes had lit up with interest when he told her he had served in missions before moving to Shelby Falls. After that, each morning the frail woman was wheeling herself past his office on her way to the chapel, he made it a point to share with her a brief story of his overseas experiences.

The first time he did this, Joni was very pleased. "Now I have something good to think about the rest of the day."

As the weeks passed, Joni had remained reticent about her past. It wasn't his job to probe but rather to be there for her when she needed reassurance. Still, they had become friends. He felt in his heart she had things she needed to say, but he was having a hard time getting her to that point.

But one day she surprised him with a question, "Do you listen to confessions, Vince?"

"I'm a nondenominational chaplain, Joni, not Catholic, but if you need a priest, I'd be happy to arrange that for you."

"No, I'm not Catholic either. I meant confessions in a general sense, I guess. I was just wondering, in case I would want to sometime."

"Of course. I'm here to listen, Joni. And as a friend in Christ, I want you to feel you can trust me. I'm not here to judge you. I'm here to try to be a comfort to you. You don't need to be alone." He waited in anticipation for her to say more, but she merely nodded and headed her wheelchair down the hallway toward her room.

Later, he was still deep in thought about Joni when he looked up to see Tom Calderon stroll into his office.

"Welcome, Cal! What brings you our way this blustery winter morning?"

Tom reached to clasp his friend's hand. "I'm just on my way to check on Bill Johnson. How're you doing, Vince?"

"Good, very good," he answered. He stood, hesitating a moment before asking, "Tom, my pastor and friend, do you ever get an overwhelming feeling of curiosity, wondering what surprise God is working on bringing into your life next?"

Tom laughed. "All the time, Vince," he said. "All the time."

Chapter 20

"We're going to miss having you at home, Nolan," Tom said as he set the last of the bags of groceries onto Nolan's new kitchen table. He and Marcy were helping Nolan move back into his apartment. In the weeks since the fire, the landlord had washed and painted all the walls, and the carpeting had been replaced. The place looked nicer than it ever had before the fire.

"I enjoyed being home, and I really appreciate that you guys were so nice about putting me up." He opened the refrigerator and began filling it with his groceries. He grinned. "But it'll be good to be able to spread out a little."

"I guess Kurt's side will take longer to renovate," Tom commented. "Of course, your landlord may not be too keen on inviting him back, anyway."

Nolan shrugged. "I wouldn't even want to speculate on that," he said. "But Kurt is really better off where he is right now, renting that furnished efficiency. It's half the cost of the duplex, and he doesn't have any furniture of his own anyway."

"It was great seeing him in church Sunday," Tom said.

"Yeah, it was." Nolan agreed. "The only reason he went at all was because he thought he owed it to Mr. Marley. He was expecting the whole experience to be really uncomfortable. The fact that everybody was so friendly and warm surprised him. And I think he was surprised by your preaching, too, Dad. He told me at work that he was impressed that you really seemed to believe what you were saying."

Tom digested that thought in silence.

"Anyway," Nolan continued. "I've been praying like crazy that God will give Kurt the strength to conquer his gambling problem and change his life for the better. Since I've I gotten to know him better I'm seeing a lot of good qualities. He's really smart, and he's actually pretty fun to be with. He just never had the right guidance to help him use his intelligence for things that are good for him. I'd really like to see him live up to his potential." Nolan put the last of the groceries in his cabinet and shut the door. "I've come to the conclusion that he's really pretty lonely. I don't think he's on the best of terms with his family, and they all live way out in Nevada, anyway."

"You and Kozy are due to come over to eat with us this week after church," Marcy interjected. "If you pick up Kurt for church again, why don't you bring him along, too? He'd probably enjoy a home-cooked meal."

"That's a great idea, Marcy. I'm sure he'd love that. I'll tell him at work that you invited him." Nolan tapped his foot as he looked around his bright new apartment. "If Kurt is having any qualms about coming back to church," he smiled, "that could be the clincher to convince him."

***

Kurt readily accepted the invitation to dinner. A delicious aroma greeted them as they stepped into the Calderon kitchen after church the following Sunday. Chicken breasts, potatoes, and carrots, lightly seasoned with the rosemary that Marcy had grown and dried herself the summer before, had simmered all morning in a huge crockpot. Marcy enlisted the help of Nolan and Kozy in setting the table and with putting the finishing touches on a salad while she placed brown and serve rolls in the oven. She assigned Kelsey the job of entertaining Kurt, a job the young teen took very seriously. Marcy chuckled to herself as she overheard the polite conversation Kelsey was making with Kurt. Her little girl was growing up.

When Tom and Zane arrived home a few minutes later, Marcy herded everyone to the dining room table, and after Tom asked a short blessing, they began eating. Kurt noted that Tom listened thoughtfully to each person, whether child or adult, as they commented on any and all aspects of the morning service, including the pastor's message. Kelsey thought it was hilarious that her dad had accidentally used the word "prostate" in place of "prostrate." Zane quickly pointed out that they had only last week learned the difference between the two words in a vocabulary lesson, or Kelsey would never have noticed. Kurt imagined it must be an especially sensitive subject, especially for a man in his fifties, but Tom merely narrowed his eyes and made a silly face at his daughter.

The conversation didn't center solely on church. There was a liberal sprinkling of jokes, laughter, and gentle teasing among the siblings. Kurt was surprised at how the Calderon family was able to make him feel included, as though he had as much right to be there as they did. He recalled the typical Sunday afternoons at his childhood home, when Kurt would normally be eating his microwave dinner alone in front of the television while the adults slept off the effects of the previous night's drinking binge. He would never have been comfortable inviting his school friends over to his house to hang out, let alone share a meal.

It was an unseasonably warm afternoon for February. As soon as the meal was over, Marcy shooed everyone outside to the basketball hoop in the driveway while she cleaned up the kitchen.

"Are you sure you don't want some help?" Kurt asked Marcy after he had changed into jeans and sweatshirt. "You've done so much already."

"I appreciate the offer, Kurt," she answered. "I really don't mind the work, but I do relish the peace and quiet. You go on and enjoy the sunshine with the others. It won't take me but a few more minutes."

He hesitated, taking in the cheerful lived-in look of the kitchen and Marcy's sincere smile. "Thanks again for inviting me, Mrs. Calderon. It's been a really good day."

The twins were the first to beg off, asking to go spend some time with friends after a half hour or so. Nolan and Kozy were next to wander inside to watch a movie with Marcy. Tom, still craving the freshness of the outdoors, challenged Kurt to a game of HORSE. An hour and a half later, when the movie ended, Nolan looked out the window to see his dad and Kurt leaning against the garage, deep in conversation. "Hmm," he said.

Kozy stepped up beside him and peeked out.

"Uh huh. I totally agree."

***

It had been a month since Joni Farnsworth entered into Hope Hospice House and Vince was not any closer to learning anything much about her past. Not that it should concern him. They had talked enough that he was convinced that her faith was strong. Still, he had a nagging sense that she had unresolved issues that were keeping her from experiencing the peace he wanted for her. He had others to minister to, home calls to make, and office duties that were a part of his job. He couldn't give her as much time as he felt she needed. He could see that her physical condition was deteriorating. He wished again that she had some loved one from her past who could be here to help her through her journey.

Chapter 21

Every visit to the gambler's support group left Kurt with plenty to think about. The testimonies he had heard thus far helped him to recognize a hard truth—that he had been traveling a dangerous road. Not to mention the definitive proof of Kurt's recklessness that Nolan Calderon carried in his wallet. If only he hadn't started drinking that morning after plotting that utterly stupid plan. The alcohol must have dulled whatever common sense he thought he had left. He chastised himself every time he thought about it. If Nolan had not discovered what he was doing and stopped him, the consequences would have been unbearable. He washed down the last bite of doughnut with the remainder of his coffee and tossed the cup in the trash. He waved to the small group that still lingered after the social time and headed for the door.

"See you next week, Kurt?" one of them asked as he zipped his jacket.

"Sure thing," he answered. *Not that I have a choice.* He held out his hand to push open the door when his eye caught a handwritten sign on the wall.

AA meetings 7:00 Mondays, Wednesdays, Fridays—this room—all welcome."

No thanks! He laughed as he walked out.

At home later that evening, Kurt's mind was still spinning with the stories he had heard at the meeting. *Time to relax.* He opened the cupboard where he kept a bottle of bourbon and took off the cap. Frowning, he noted that there was barely a teaspoon left. He thought back to when he had purchased the bottle and scowled. *This is NOT happening. I am NOT an alcoholic!* He angrily threw the bottle into the trash and stomped into his small bathroom. He looked in the mirror to see if he needed to shave his head before going to bed. He turned away in disgust at the expression on the face that confronted him. Without bothering to brush his teeth, he stormed into the bedroom and threw himself onto the bed.

He had expected that he would toss and turn half the night, but he fell into a deep sleep almost the moment his head hit the pillow. He awakened with a start. He turned off the bedside lamp that had been left on and lay back down in the dark, his eyes wide open. Unbidden, the answer came to him why he had been so disturbed by his own face in the mirror. The meanness in his eyes had reminded him of someone he would rather forget. Someone he had long ago vowed to never imitate. Stepdad Number Two. The man who had used his mom as a punching bag every time he had too much to drink.

Kurt covered his face with his hands and groaned. *Oh God.* And then the tears came.

***

From the moment he spotted the sign on the wall, Kurt had known, somewhere deep inside of himself, that he would be walking into that AA meeting the next night. He shuffled into the room and saw that a circle of chairs had been set up in the center. He looked around at the other attendees. Good, none of the faces were familiar. Perhaps he was the only one in town with both a gambling addiction and an alcohol problem. After his initial scan he lowered himself into one of the chairs in the circle and dropped his eyes to the floor. Maybe if he didn't make eye contact with anyone, he would go unnoticed. He truly didn't believe he had an alcohol addiction—at least, not a chemical addiction like his mom and her string of boyfriends seemed to have had. He was smart enough to know the potential was there.

The meeting began much the same as his gambling group. The discussion leader, Phil, called the meeting to order. Several people stood and talked about their struggles with sobriety and some about their recent successes. One man shared a brief story of his life and he, like Mr. Marley, attributed his success in overcoming his addiction to the God of the Bible. Kurt focused intently on all that was said. When the man sat down, there was a lull.

"Anyone else?" Phil finally asked.

Silence. Sweat trickled down Kurt's temple as the moments ticked by. He didn't understand what finally compelled him to stand. Aside from the social time, he had not yet said a word at his gambler's support group. But now, here he was standing in front of everyone.

Kurt swallowed hard. "I—ah, my name is Kurt," he finally choked out. "Uh, you've probably heard this before, but I really don't believe I'm an alcoholic. I mean, I don't think I'm physically addicted, at least not yet." He looked down and saw that his hands were clenched tight into fists. Forcing himself to relax, he continued. "I do have a gambling addiction. I attend the meetings here on Tuesday and Thursday nights. Alcohol had a part in some messes I've gotten myself into lately. Last night I realized that I'm in danger of becoming just like a person from my childhood who made my life, and my mother's life, a living hell. That scared me to death. I need your help. Please."

Kurt waited a few seconds in the silence that followed. Feeling foolish, he lowered himself back down on his chair.

"Hey, we've got your back, buddy," said a heavily bearded man sitting across the room.

"That's what we're here for," said another. "We'll help."

Others were soon piping up with words of encouragement.

The group leader finally called for quiet. "All right, Kurt. I know that took courage to admit you need help. Now, if you're really serious about making a change in your life, we'll see about finding you a mentor, a sponsor to whom you'll be accountable." He looked around the room. "Is there anyone who's currently free? Anybody who's willing to mentor Kurt?"

Once again there were moments of silence. Kurt held his breath, willing himself to not fidget. He could hear feet shuffling and a few people cleared their throats. Then, out of the corner of his eye, he saw a hand rise tentatively to his left. The tall, bulky form of a middle-aged woman in yellow sweats partially blocked his view. Kurt strained to see who had raised a hand. Finally, a slim form stood up. A young woman with straight, jet-black hair and dressed in plain jeans and a flannel shirt stared down at the floor. Then with a slight frown on her face she focused her dark eyes on Kurt and said grimly, "I can do it. I'll mentor him."

"Thanks, Lila," Phil smiled. "I was hoping you'd be ready to get back in the game." Looking to Kurt he said, "I'll let Lila give you her number and explain the rules during our social time." He looked at the wall clock. "And it looks like it's time to close the meeting now. Let's all join in the serenity prayer."

"God grant me the serenity to accept the things I cannot change; courage to change the things I can; and wisdom to know the difference …."

Once the group had finished reciting the prayer, Kurt waited for Lila to approach him. When she made no move toward him, he slowly walked over to where she sat. She looked at him warily, unsmiling, and finally stood. She was tall, just a few inches shorter than his six feet. She looked evenly into his eyes.

"These are my rules," she began. "We check in with each other daily. You'll need to try to learn your trigger points and avoid them, if at all possible. If you have to talk anything through, you can try calling anytime, day or night. If I'm not available right away, I'll call you back as soon as I'm free." She paused to see if he had questions. When he said nothing she continued, asking, "Do you have regular work hours? I need to know when it's okay for me to call you."

"I work a regular nine to five job with weekends off," he answered. "How about you?"

"My hours are less predictable," she said, with a ghost of a smile. "But I can usually answer, even if I'm working, if you need to talk." After a moment she said pointedly, "Socially, we will see each other at the meeting and that's all. Is there anything else you need to know for now?"

He wanted to ask why she had volunteered to mentor him when she seemed so guarded. In fact, she was almost unfriendly. But he kept his thoughts to himself and shook his head. Maybe after they knew each other a little longer she would warm up a bit. He turned to leave and then remembered. "Oh, Lila. Your phone number. I'll need that."

She stuck her hand into the pocket of her jeans, fished out a slightly tattered card, and handed it to him.

"Check in with me after you get home from your job tomorrow," she told him before slipping into her jacket and walking quickly away.

He watched her disappear out the door before turning to the card in his hand. His eyes widened as he read the bold letters:

LILA THE PLUMBER

RELIABLE *HONEST ESTIMATES *REASONABLE RATES

He let the information sink in a moment before adding the number to his contacts.

***

"Ever heard of her?" Kurt handed Nolan the business card he had received from Lila the night before. They were just about to get to work, but Kurt was curious and did not want to wait.

Nolan glanced at the card. "Lila the Plumber," he read aloud. "I think I've seen the advertisement before, but I figured the name was just a gimmick to get business. Do we really have a female plumber in Shelby Falls?" When Kurt hesitated Nolan said with a grin. "Hey, wait a minute. Since when do you need a plumber in your rented efficiency apartment? Have you found yourself a new romantic interest?"

"Hardly," Kurt answered. "She's my new mentor." He took a deep breath and let it out slowly. "I joined an AA group last night."

"Ah!" Nolan gave one nod of his head. He waited as Kurt grabbed the chair from his desk and sat in front of Nolan's.

Kurt elaborated, confessing what had led him to admit to his alcohol problem. "I hated that man, Nolan. He's the last person in the world I'd ever want to imitate. Seeing his meanness in my own face, I knew then

I couldn't continue drinking. It was like someone tapped me on the shoulder and said, 'It's time.'"

Again, Nolan nodded knowingly and said, "Ah."

Kurt clenched his teeth. "I know what you're thinking. You think it was God tapping me on the shoulder." He shrugged. "Who knows? It was kind of creepy."

"Well, whatever it was, I'm proud of you, Kurt. Admitting you need help and asking for it takes courage." *Another answer to prayer!* Kurt smiled sheepishly and looked away. "So, this plumber lady, what's she like?"

"Pretty. More than pretty even," Kurt responded thoughtfully. "Very feminine though she tries to hide it with the clothes she wears. But she might as well have a wall built around her. She's not only all business, she's one step away from downright hostile. I don't know what kind of trouble brought her to Alcoholics Anonymous, but I'll be interested if she ever lets down her guard enough to tell me about it."

"I'd truly like to see you free of all the destructive influences in your life, Kurt. I think this is one more step in the right direction. I'll be praying for things to work out."

Kurt rolled his chair back to his own side of the wall and stuck his head back around the corner a moment later. "Nolan? Thanks."

***

Kurt grimaced and flexed his fingers nervously before punching the number for "Lila the Plumber." He forced a grin as he waited for her to pick up. When she did, he fumbled for what to say. "Um, it's Kurt from the meeting last night. You said I should check in with you when I got home from work." When she didn't speak, he continued lamely. "So I'm home now and I thought I'd check in, if that's okay." He heard a small sigh before she finally responded.

"It's all right," she said. He was afraid that was all she was going to say, but after a few moments she asked, "Have you disposed of all the alcohol in your house?"

He thought of the nearly empty bourbon bottle still in the overflowing trash can in his kitchen. Wanting to be completely honest, he laughed

166

nervously. "Does a drop or two in the bottom of the bottle count? Garbage pickup isn't until tomorrow."

"Yes it does matter," she said severely. "Kurt, if you're not going to be serious about this, then we're both wasting our time." She waited to give him time to think before continuing. "Now I'd like you to get the bottle, pour out what's left and rinse it out."

He rolled his eyes as he fished out the bottle, but he did as she said. "Okay, I did it."

"Is there anything else?"

"No," he started. But then he walked over to his refrigerator. "Wait," he confessed. "I think I have a couple of beers in the fridge." He really didn't like the taste of beer all that much and wouldn't have thought it a problem. But he opened the cans, making sure that the phone was close enough that she could hear the fizzing sound as he poured the contents down the sink and rinsed out the cans.

"Thank you," she said. "You might not see the importance, but it makes a difference to me, and it helps me to trust you." The tone of her voice changed, softened. "Now, if you want to talk, I'm willing to listen."

"I don't really know what to say. I'm new at this."

"Why don't you tell me what it was like for you growing up?" she suggested.

Kurt wasn't used to reminiscing about his youth, let alone talking about it. But something had been working in him the last few days. The little bit of information he had revealed both at the AA meeting and to Nolan, seemed to have opened a floodgate. After a few faltering starts, he found himself opening up to Lila. He told her about the succession of men in his mother's life and his feelings of frustration and helplessness when she inevitably got hurt.

"They hit you, too?" she asked, already knowing the answer.

"'Number Two' was the worst. He had an uncanny control over her. He made her think she deserved to be treated that way. I was still a scrawny kid, but I tried to defend her, and I paid for it. That is, until I learned to be faster and wiser." The pain was evident in his voice. "Mom seemed to be drawn to all the losers. I could never understand it."

She waited a moment. "Yeah," she said finally. "That stepfather of yours, 'Number Two'?" She sighed. "Five years ago I was in a relationship with a virtual clone of that man. I'm still trying to figure out how I could have been that stupid."

Before he could ask a question, she stopped him. "Hey, are you going to be all right? I have a clogged sewer waiting for me. I need to get on it as soon as possible."

"Sure, I'm fine," he assured her. "It was good to talk, Lila. Thanks. I feel bad for you though. Sewer work doesn't sound like much fun."

"Pays the bills," she quipped as she ended the call.

***

"Hi. Mind sharing your table?"

Lila looked up to see Kurt standing beside her, a tray laden with burger and fries in hand. For a moment she looked as though she was considering, but the restaurant was filling up fast with the Sunday church crowd. Finally, she shrugged and motioned for him to sit. She peered across the small table at him and lifted a brow. "Is this just a chance meeting, Kurt?"

He chewed on his lip before admitting, "I just happened to see your van pull in. You can't blame me for getting a sudden hankering for a bacon cheeseburger, can you?"

When she didn't answer, he went on. "Look, Lila, I'm not trying to stalk you if that's what you're thinking. I just don't see the harm in us seeing each other face to face once in a while out in public. Besides, I hate eating alone all the time."

"Fine," she relented as she focused on opening her packet of light Italian dressing.

"Rabbit food? When you could be having the best burger in town?" he asked with a smile.

"Hey, this is a great salad. If you tried it you just might like it."

He gave a noncommittal grunt as he took a big bite of his sandwich.

"I don't have anything against a burger and fries, Kurt. If I eat wisely most of the time, I allow myself an occasional indulgence. But I owe it to myself to stay fit and healthy. The better I feel physically, the easier it is for me to stay sober."

"It's still a struggle for you then?"

She gave him a steady look. "I've learned it may always be a struggle." She frowned. "I'm not willing to take any chances. I'm a new creation. I'm determined to never drag the new me down that old road."

"'New creation.' That sounds like something my friends would say." He saw the question in her eyes. "I've started attending church with one of my coworkers. Kind of a result of a recent mess my gambling got me into."

"And are you paying attention to what you're hearing there?"

He stared out the window for a moment before turning back to face her. "I've been giving it some thought. The pastor's even got me started reading some of the Bible." He shrugged. "I may not know much, but I know I really am ready to try to change my life. Maybe it can help."

She watched him without comment. He took another bite and leaned back in his seat, realizing he was going to have to tread carefully if he wanted her to open up to him. He picked what he hoped was a neutral subject.

"So, I'm curious. Why plumbing, Lila?" he asked lightly. She looked away. As the seconds ticked by she seemed to be struggling with a decision. Finally she lifted sober eyes to meet his.

"I quit school my senior year to go live with my boyfriend," she began. "It was convenient. He was old enough to supply me with booze. I spent my twentieth birthday in the emergency room." She gave a bitter laugh. "Two black eyes and a broken jaw, a birthday present from the guy who claimed to love me. That was my great awakening. The next day I moved into a shelter for battered women. That night I attended my first AA meeting. Couldn't say anything, but I didn't need to. My face told my story."

Kurt's fists clenched, imagining how the beautiful young woman in front of him must have looked that day. Then he tried to ward off the memory of his own mother as she had appeared after some of "Number

Two's" drunken rages. He wanted to say something to take away the pain and regret he saw in her, but no words came to him.

"At that first meeting they paired me with George," she went on. "He was a grisly, rough looking geezer in his mid-seventies, but that rough exterior masked a heart of gold. He'd been sober for two decades. He became my mentor, my friend, and so much more. While I worked on staying sober, I needed a means of support. George was a semi-retired plumber, still doing small jobs for some of his older customers. He offered to take me on as an apprentice."

She picked nervously at her salad for a minute before continuing. "Turns out I had an aptitude for the work. It's fun for me, like figuring out a puzzle. And I didn't have to settle for a job waitressing somewhere where alcohol was served. I made enough to get by. Whatever George couldn't teach me about the newer products, I learned from the vocational school."

"And now you're on your own?" Kurt asked.

She nodded. "George died about a year ago of heart disease. He left me the business, tools, references, and even the van. It was his idea to change the name from 'George the Plumber' to 'Lila the Plumber.'" She smiled. "But that's not the best gift he gave me," she said. "George introduced me to his Savior, and that's made all the difference."

Once again Kurt found himself at a loss for words. He settled for a nod to encourage her to continue.

"Like I said before, I'm a new creation. The new Lila intends to stay sober. The new Lila intends to stay independent. The new Lila wants desperately to live within God's will. I'm mentoring you, Kurt, because I want to help you and because I think I felt God nudging me to volunteer that night. But I just need to be straight with you. We're going to stick to my rules about socializing."

Kurt rubbed a hand on his chin as he considered her declaration. He wanted to smile at her candor, but he managed a neutral look. "But we can be friends at least, can't we?" he asked with a tilt of his head.

She tried to hold onto her fierce expression, but after a moment she shut her eyes and a tiny smile played at the corner of her mouth. "Yes, Kurt," she conceded. "We can be friends."

Chapter 22

"If you don't mind my asking, Vince, what do you feel was the turning point in your life?"

Joni Farnsworth was sitting in the lounge that overlooked the courtyard at Hospice House when Vince stopped by to chat. She wrapped her hands around her mug of tea, savoring the warmth on her slender fingers. Vince took a sip of his morning cup of coffee and stared at the small islands of bright snow in the otherwise bleak winter landscape. He had grown used to Joni steering conversation toward his life rather than hers.

"I was a junior in high school," he began the story that he had shared many times before. "We had lost Mom a couple of years before, and it was just me and my dad. Dad wasn't handling life well. He had always been a drinker. A mean one. Things escalated after Mom died. It didn't take much to get him enraged. I tried to stay out of his way and spent a lot of time at my best friend's home. One evening Dad came after me with a kitchen chair instead of just his hands. I could have been seriously injured, but he was so drunk that his aim was poor. He was strong, but I was fast." He looked up to see Joni's eyes fixed steadily on him.

"I took refuge at the Calderon home, as usual. I was frustrated and ashamed that I hadn't had the guts to fight back. Mr. Calderon took me aside to calm me while I ranted on and on about my hatred for my dad.

'Don't succumb to the temptation to hate,' he told me that night. 'You think your dad doesn't deserve your love and maybe he doesn't. But the enemy wins if he gets us to hate those we're born to love. Don't you see? Your father is in a trap with his alcoholism. You can hate what's happened to him but don't give in to the temptation to hate the man. Love is the only thing that has a chance to change him.'"

Vince paused, caught up in bittersweet memories. With a shake of his head he continued. "The advice from that godly man was the beginning. I couldn't get his words out of my mind. The next day I was back in our kitchen warily keeping an eye on my dad, trying to determine his mood. Suddenly it appeared just as clearly as I see you sitting here in front of me. God sent me a vision. My dad's form disappeared, and instead I saw a scrawny, mangy, filthy-looking dog. Its leg, all bloody and torn, was caught in a steel trap. It whimpered pitifully, struggling to pull free. I could smell the blood, feel the raw fear, dread, panic, and the sense of helplessness. It had the saddest, loneliest face I ever saw. It made my heart ache. Then as quick as it had appeared, the vision faded, and there was my dad with his bloodshot eyes and foul breath."

He raised his eyes to find Joni still focused intensely on his every word. "I knew that God was telling me I had to forgive my dad. Part of me wanted to rebel, to ignore what he had shown me. But I couldn't shake that vision. I struggled for weeks. In the end, I told God that if he wanted me to forgive, he had to help me. I wasn't capable on my own. Long story short, I started finding ways to show my dad I cared. It didn't happen overnight, but he eventually got help with his drinking problem. By the time he died he was a much different man. And I loved him."

She smiled at the thought. "So the vision was the defining moment."

"The first of several, I would say. God caught my attention for sure. Eventually, Wendy and I felt the call to go into overseas ministry. The vision reappeared many times for me on the mission field, whenever I was tempted to judge harshly the people I was sent to serve. It was a gift I learned to use, and it helped me see people with compassion, to see beyond the sins that sometimes repulsed me. It helped me to see the people as Christ sees them, and I realized that, but for the grace of God, it could have been me in that trap."

Her eyes were shut and he thought for a moment she may have fallen asleep. But then she whispered, "Thanks for sharing that, Vince." Then she set down her mug and slowly wheeled herself down the hall.

***

A few days later, Joni asked for a private meeting in Vince's office. Vince readily agreed. Joni arrived for their meeting with a determined expression. Vince was curious but said nothing. He took a moment to pray for guidance while he was getting her situated. He offered her tea and cookies, trying to put her at ease, but she declined. He grabbed a cup of coffee and a couple of cookies for himself and sat down across the desk from Joni.

"Okay, Joni, what can I do for you today?"

She closed her eyes for a moment, breathing deeply. Voice shaking, she began. "First off, my name is not Joni Farnsworth. I stole the identity of my friend, and I have been living a lie for close to two decades." She looked at Vince, the shock evident on his face. After several failed attempts to speak, he nodded for her to continue. "We were heavy into drugs and had been sharing an apartment. One morning I woke from a binge to find that Joni had overdosed.

"She looked odd, so still, and I was spooked, I was afraid to touch her. I got a small mirror from the bathroom and thought I'd put it up to her nostrils to see if she was breathing. I remember how my hands shook. I stared at the glass for a long time, willing the mirror to fog up from her breath. When it didn't happen I had to accept the fact that she was really dead. I forced myself to look at her face. All I could think was that it could have been me lying there."

"It was at that moment that the bizarre idea began to form in my mind. She looked so peaceful. She never again had to face the humiliation of needing a fix so bad that she would do anything to get it. I was so tired of living in the shame of what I had done with my life. In my warped reasoning, I thought it would be better if I could just disappear. Maybe disappearing would be preferable to continuing being me."

She sat wringing her hands, remembering. "I knew that Joni had no family, and that no one other than her pimp would come looking for her. I called the police from a pay phone. While I waited I found Joni's driver's license and compared it with mine. Our features were remarkably similar, and people had often mistaken us for sisters. But neither of us looked much like our photo IDs anymore. The drugs had aged both of us considerably. As it happened, I had colored my hair black a few days before the overdose, and I looked more like the woman in her driver's license picture than she did. I made the decision. I thought if I could get away from the guy who controlled me, I might be able to get clean. By the time the cops arrived, I had taken Joni's IDs to use for my own and gathered the stuff I wanted them to see. They believed me when I identified her and handed them my ID. The guy in charge barely looked at me. It was an obvious overdose in a place where it happened often. It was amazingly easy. If they ever came back to follow up, I didn't know. Within a few hours I was on a bus, and my new life began."

Vince sat speechless at his desk, the coffee and cookies untouched and forgotten. Covering his face with his hands he gave himself some time to absorb the ramifications of what the woman was revealing. This was a situation he was pretty sure was not covered in the Hospice Handbook. He looked into her eyes and saw her uncertainty. "What can I do, Joni?" he asked at last. "What, if anything, are you asking me to do with this information?"

She sighed. "My file says I have no living relatives. That's a lie, too." She lowered her eyes and Vince felt a stab of sympathy for the shame he saw. "I have a child who lives here in Shelby Falls. I'm asking you to help me to meet with her before I die, so I can tell her how sorry I am."

His voice was almost a whisper. "Who are you?"

"My real name is Elizabeth Hanner." A single tear escaped from her eye and ran down her face. "I'd like you to be my advocate and help me see my daughter, my Kozy."

Vince sat back in his chair, letting out a soft whistle as he processed the information. The last piece of the puzzle clicked into place. *Kozy Hanner is the girl Nolan Calderon is dating.* He remembered Tom telling him a little about the girl's testimony and her work with the teens at the church. Joni's move from a large city in California to little Shelby Falls now made sense.

"Knowing I only had months to live gave me the courage to act. I'm looking for peace, Vince," she said. "I don't think I'm going to find it until I see my daughter. I know she may not want to see me, but I'd at least like the chance."

"You're not concerned with the trouble you might be in for stealing another's identity?"

She gave Vince a wry smile before looking down at her clenched hands. "I figure I'll be dead long before any legal action could be brought against me."

Vince nodded in agreement.

"I know Kozy. Not well, but I've met her," he admitted. "I'm friends with some people who know her much better than I do and who care very much about her."

Her eyes reflected relief and a glimmer of hope. "Do you think they would help me, Vince? I realize that finding out that I'm alive will come as a shock to her. She's not likely to welcome the news. But I'd really like to try."

Vince tapped his fingers on his desk as he thought. Elizabeth Hanner, alias Joni Farnsworth, may not be concerned about legal actions, but Vince wondered just what his own responsibilities were in this situation. He wondered how soon he should talk with a lawyer. He looked over at the woman who gazed back at him with utmost trust in her eyes. He decided to let God lead him. For now, she was a member of his small flock. He would do all he could to help her find peace and closure before her death.

***

Vince asked both Tom and Nolan to come to his house so he could explain the situation in privacy. Tom was now Vince's pastor, so who better to advise him? Nolan knew Kozy better than either of them, so Vince thought it important for him to be involved. Nolan listened carefully as Vince explained the bizarre story that Elizabeth Hanner had shared with him. Both Calderon men sat in stunned silence.

Vince gave them a moment to absorb his words and then continued. "In the weeks I have known her, Joni has given me no reason to doubt the sincerity of her faith. My impression of her from the start has been nothing but positive. I have racked my brain trying to find any motive for her making her secret known beyond simply wanting to make amends with her daughter before she dies."

"Could she be trying to extort money from Kozy?" Nolan asked.

Vince shook his head. "What would be the point? She's dying."

Nolan shrugged, still unconvinced.

"I won't go into it all, but she did tell me where she's been for the past eighteen years. She's lived in a women's rescue mission in California. I've already checked it out. It's legit. I was able to talk with a woman who had been there since the nineties. She verified what Joni had told me and went into more detail. While she was working at overcoming her addiction, Joni began to do menial work at the shelter. Cleaning the toilets, washing floors, and things like that. Later, they trained her to counsel new residents. She had a natural gift for it and eventually received formal training, all the while remaining in residence at the mission. She worked all those years for only a small stipend plus room and board up until a couple months ago. That's when the heart damage from her past drug use started to take its toll. The church that runs the mission paid for Joni's airfare and is sponsoring her during her time here at Hospice House." He stopped to let the information sink in.

"And she's been able to stay clean since then? No relapses?" Tom asked.

"Not according to the nun I talked with. She seemed to think that Joni's greatest fear was of being tempted back into her old lifestyle. She felt safe at the mission and felt she had a purpose there in helping others fight their addictions. Of course, knowing what we do now, perhaps she also feared her true identity being found out."

Nolan paced the floor of Vince's den, trying to make sense of what he was hearing. "They had no clue at this place that she wasn't who she said she was?" he asked.

Vince tapped his fingers lightly on the arm of his chair. "I got the impression from Sister Aquinas that if she did have any suspicions in the beginning, she wasn't about to let them cloud her opinion of the person she knew as Joni. In fact, her exact words were, 'God has her name written in the Lamb's book. If it doesn't match the one I know, does it really matter?'"

Nolan sighed deeply and closed his eyes. *Can this be the answer to my prayers? Is this God's way of bringing healing to Kozy, or will meeting her mother only serve to reinforce her fears? Please guide us here, Lord.* After another twenty minutes of discussion and prayer, the three men unanimously agreed that if this woman was indeed telling the truth, Kozy must have the opportunity to reunite with her.

"But I have to meet her first," Nolan insisted. "If this turns out to be some cruel joke or outright fraud, it would be traumatic for Kozy. It's not that I don't trust your judgment, Vince, but I need to know firsthand what kind of person she is. I don't want Kozy hurt."

"Agreed." Vince walked to his desk and retrieved a photograph from a file folder. It was faded and cracked with age and was a picture of a little girl about three years old. He handed the picture to Nolan. "She wanted you to see this." Nolan took the picture and looked into the brown eyes that unmistakably belonged to Kozy Hanner. "It took her all this time to have the courage to face her past, but I think we have to believe that her daughter was always on her mind."

Vince arranged for Nolan to come to Hospice House after work on Friday evening to meet the woman who claimed to be Kozy's mother. When Nolan finally saw her face to face, he was convinced she was who she claimed to be. In spite of the age difference and the obvious physical frailty, the family resemblance was beyond question. Even her voice and gentle mannerisms reminded him of Kozy. They talked for a half hour. She explained her reasons for wanting to meet her daughter, and Nolan expressed his concern and commitment to Kozy's well-being. By the time he got up to leave, he found that his initial distrust had vanished. He had to agree with Vince that Elizabeth Hanner, whatever her past may be, was now a changed woman.

"You deserve a chance at making amends," he told her. "I'm not sure of the best way to break this to Kozy, but I plan to have her here first thing tomorrow."

Please God, let this be a good thing for both of them.

Chapter 23

He wrestled with his doubts for much of Friday evening. He could see the potential for healing for both mother and daughter, but what if they found it impossible to reconcile? What if the relationship just reinforced Kozy's fears about having children? He forced himself to be optimistic. *It was painful for me to find out about my mom's past, but God turned that into something good. Kozy's a solid Christian. It'll be a joyful revelation for her, I just know it!*

By the time he was ready for bed, Nolan still hadn't come up with a script in his mind of how to break the news. He decided to text her:

Missed being with u this week! Pick u up at 9 am and spend the day together?

Sounds great. Casual clothes?

Casual is good. C u then.

As he promised, Nolan arrived at Kozy's place at nine the next morning. He rang her doorbell, feeling a bit nervous, but strangely at peace. A moment later she stood in front of him looking relaxed and exceptionally attractive in her powder blue sweatshirt and jeans.

Kozy greeted him with a smile. "Where to?" She asked while slipping on a light jacket.

"Well, it's kind of a surprise," he hedged as he opened the car door for Kozy. "I'll explain once we get there. It's not far." She accepted his explanation with a good-natured shrug and a slight lift of her eyebrows. He started the car and turned on the radio. A familiar worship song was playing, and they contented themselves with singing along. He asked her a few questions about her past week at school, and she chattered lightly, telling him of a humorous incident in the classroom.

He had decided to take her directly to Hospice House. Once there, he would break the news to her before going inside. Vince Mateo would be waiting there to introduce the two women. Nolan had had a hard time falling asleep the night before, anticipating the joy the reunion could bring. Kozy had such a loving heart, and he knew she would be thrilled with the opportunity to be reunited with her own mother. Still, he wondered if he should have come up with a better plan.

Once they had pulled into the parking lot, Nolan's anxiety heightened. How to begin? All the rehearsed speeches he had gone over in his mind this morning vanished. He breathed a quick prayer for guidance, and began telling the story of the woman known as Joni Farnsworth.

Kozy listened to Nolan's jumbled explanation and began wondering if he was going to ask her to give her testimony to the woman or that they might volunteer to help in some way. Puzzled, she tried to make sense of what Nolan was saying.

Then she heard the name Elizabeth Hanner and heard Nolan's voice saying, "Kozy, I'm trying to tell you that your mother is alive!"

Kozy heard the words but struggled to comprehend the meaning. "What are you saying, Nolan? I don't understand. What are you talking about?" She shook her head, trying to push back the mental fog. Her heart began to pound. Nolan struggled once again to explain, and she had to remind herself to breath. She tried in vain to draw sanity from the words. *This can't be happening! No!* Then she responded in a weak whisper, "Are you telling me, Nolan, that my mother is here, that she only pretended to be dead for the past eighteen years? And now that she is dying for real, she wants to meet me? Is that what you're telling me?"

It sounded so cruel to hear it put that way. It felt nothing like it did when he had talked it over with Vince and his father. Nolan's heart sank as Kozy's face became masked in bitterness. *I should have let Vince handle this. But I wanted to be the one to deliver the great news, to be the hero. And now I've botched it.* He opened his mouth to protest but the words caught in his throat. Kozy watched him with smoldering eyes as he gave a single nod of his head.

"Who are you to speak for me, Nolan Calderon?" she said harshly. "That woman abandoned me. She chose her drugs over her own child!"

Her voice was strong now and full of fury. "Take me home, Nolan." As Nolan opened his mouth to speak, she cut him short with a wave of her hand. "I don't want to hear anything more, and I don't want to talk. Just take me home!"

She bristled when he reached out to touch her. So instead he started the car, his hand fumbling with the keys. On the drive back he made himself concentrate on all of his surroundings, taking careful note of each vehicle he passed, every tree, building, and intersection. Anything to avoid looking at Kozy, who sat stone-faced and staring straight ahead. When he finally pulled into her driveway, he had barely put on the brakes before she was out with a firm slam of the door and had vanished into her front door. Nolan moved the gear lever to park, leaned forward, and rested his head on the steering wheel. He stayed that way for several minutes before finally backing out of the driveway. He pulled into the street, gave one last glance at Kozy's closed front door, and headed back to Hope Hospice House.

Kozy stormed into her house, slammed the door and locked it. Memories, long suppressed, assaulted her without mercy. She remembered the day the bad men came, the police raid when her father was led away in handcuffs, and the succession of foster homes. Once again, she felt the dread and panic she had experienced each time her caseworker, Mrs. Gonzales, had appeared with a shopping bag of new clothes and carried her off to a new family. There was never any warning or explanation. She experienced, all over again, the heart-crushing fear of not knowing what was going to happen to her.

Her memory was assailed by the image of her grandmother, gazing at the photograph of her only child in her graduation cap and gown. How often had she watched Maria's fingers touch the bright face in the photo, as though in benediction, eyes filling with tears? In those first months, it had deeply upset Kozy to see her grandmother's anguish, so Maria had removed the picture from the living room and kept it hidden in her own bedroom. Kozy and her Gramma had been close, but Betsy Hanner had been one subject that Kozy refused to talk about. Still, even after her grandmother's death, Kozy could not bring herself to destroy the picture of her mother.

Kozy powered off her phone and threw it onto the couch so hard that it bounced to the floor. Pacing the room, she tried to force the barrage of memories from her mind. At one point she got out the vacuum cleaner and furiously ran it over the already clean carpet. She put the vacuum away but later started the process over again. And then again. She knew she should pray, tried to even, but the words evaporated before they could form in her mind.

By early afternoon her fuming had taken a toll on her body. Shivering and drained of energy, she escaped to her bedroom and crawled fully clothed into her bed. Wrapping herself tightly in a blanket, she shut her eyes and eventually fell into a fitful sleep. Strange scenes ran rampant through her dreams. She dreamed she was with her grandma in Hungary, fleeing over the frozen fields at night. Maria was urging her to hurry. "Run, Kozy, the sun will be coming up! We must find a place to hide!" Kozy tried to run, but her legs were paralyzed. The scene changed, and she was alone in a barn, hiding under a pile of straw. She heard the sound of soldiers' heavy boots outside the door and the cocking of a gun. Her heart pounded in her chest and then nearly stopped as she heard the sound of Maria's voice calling, "Kozy! Where are you? Come home!" Kozy, terrified that the soldier would hear her, willed her grandma to be quiet. She could see her grandma's face in the distance; then the face morphed into that of Auntie Em from *The Wizard of Oz*. Then Kozy saw herself dressed in a blue jumper and white blouse, just like Dorothy wore in the film. Kozy's blond curls were in pigtails. Instead of ruby slippers, she wore two mismatched powder blue shoes. She tapped her heels together and repeated the mantra: "There's no place like home! There's no place like home!"

A sudden shrill bark startled her awake, rescuing her from the frenzy of her dreams. Without a glance at the clock, she knew it must be close to four o'clock. Her mail carrier rarely varied his timing by more than a few minutes. To CoCo, the little dog next door, the mailman was not an intruder to be reckoned with. Instead, he appeared to be the object of a girlish crush. Confined behind her short chain-linked fence, the miniature poodle/terrier mix seemed to instinctively know the time and started her ritual each day, the moment the mailman came into view. Once she heard the distinctive plunk of the mailbox lid across the street, the dog would start in earnest with a series of straight-up jumps and lunges at the fence that resulted in a couple of rolls and somersaults. When CoCo heard the sound of the footsteps across her own porch and heard the mailbox close, she would stand stretched as far as her stubby legs would allow, barking, panting, quivering, and wagging her tail furiously until the man walked over to the fence. Once he delivered a couple of pats to the head and crooned a few words of endearment, the little dog was appeased. One short "yip" as the man continued his rounds to step onto Kozy's porch and the ritual would be complete. The now-satisfied CoCo would quietly resume exploring and sniffing her backyard domain.

Normally Kozy was delighted to be a witness to the humorous antics next door. Today she only watched furtively out her bedroom window, hiding behind the drapes, still unwilling to be seen and be forced to talk with anyone. Seeking a distraction, she stood at the front door and waited until she was sure the mail carrier was well on his way. Only then did she slink out and retrieve the contents of her mailbox. In the safety of her living room, she dejectedly sorted through the advertisements and solicitation letters that typically comprised her mail. Her heart warmed just a little when her eyes lit upon a familiar postmark and spidery handwriting.

Dear old Mrs. Dobos. You always remember me, don't you?

Kozy sat down to read the cheerful card from the woman whom her Gram had considered her closest friend; the one she had chosen to be Kozy's godmother, her *keresztanya*.

"It's a little early for your birthday, Kozy, but I wanted to be sure to get the card to you while I remember. Ha! At my age I'm lucky I don't forget my own name. How have you been? I think of you so often, honey. Why don't you give me a ring sometime? I would love to hear your voice once more. Here's my number …."

Tears clouded Kozy's vision for a moment. *And I would love to hear your voice as well.* Mrs. Dobos had a thick Hungarian accent that Kozy would love to hear again. It always made her feel connected to Gram. She knew that she herself would barely have to do any talking, as Mrs. Dobos was known for her longwinded, one-sided conversations. She would merely listen to the voice and let the lady ramble on.

Kozy picked up her phone and tapped out the number. Rose Dobos was elated when she answered her phone and heard Kozy's warm greeting. True to form, with just a little prompting from Kozy, the woman began to reminisce about her cherished friendship with Maria Kozma. Kozy shut her eyes and rested her head against the back of her sofa, concentrating on the familiar cadence of the monologue and paying scant attention to the words. Each time Mrs. Dobos paused to catch her breath, Kozy murmured a few words to acknowledge and encourage her. Kozy was just beginning to relax when Mrs. Dobos's memories wandered back to the years prior to Kozy's birth. Kozy was about to give an excuse to end the call, but when she tried to speak the words stuck in her throat. Mrs. Dobos was recounting how lovingly Maria had cared for her husband, Kozy's grandfather, as he lay dying. John Kozma had died a few years before Kozy was born. In her mind he was no more than the faded image in Maria's wedding photograph. Maria had never spoken much to Kozy about her loss, believing that Kozy had already suffered enough of her own losses.

"Betsy took it pretty hard when she lost her daddy," Mrs. Dobos was saying. "Maria always felt bad that she didn't keep a better eye on her while John was ill. But life is hard. She did what she had to do at the time. And things were changing in the neighborhood. Not like the old days. Betsy got restless and ran off to the other side of the country. What a sad time for Maria. Our prayer group spent many hours on our knees for Betsy."

Kozy was listening now, trying to put herself in her grandma's place, imagining how she had felt. Mrs. Dobos rambled on. Then eventually she came to her recollection of the call Maria had received from the authorities in San Diego. It was as though she had forgotten Kozy was on the other end of the phone; she was so caught up in her memories.

"I asked Maria if I should go with her, but she said, 'No, this is something I must do alone.' We took up a collection for her. When she got back home, she told me what had happened there in the police station. They told her that Betsy's roommate had found her after she had overdosed on her drugs. They had Betsy's things, what little there was. They wanted Maria to see the body. But when she got in that cold room and they opened the drawer, she could barely make herself look. Just one peek and she had to shut her eyes, poor woman. She thought she must have fainted. And she worried that they might not think she was able to take care of little Kozy."

"I'm here Mrs. Dobos," Kozy reminded her.

"Oh, is that you Kozy? I forgot. What was I talking about? Oh, I remember. Yes, Maria wondered sometimes if it was all a mistake, and maybe it wasn't Betsy at all. Maybe it was just somebody that looked a little like her. With something that horrible, you know, the mind plays tricks. Then she would think, no, they had her papers, the roommate had identified her. She had to accept it. But I was her best friend. Sometimes she would tell me her doubts. She knew I wouldn't think less of her. If I were her, I would always hold on to hope. So we prayed sometimes about it. You know how the Bible says, 'if two of you agree on earth concerning anything that they ask, it will be done for them'. We thought it couldn't hurt. You know, Kozy honey, life is funny. Years ago I used to worry about who would miss me when I'm gone. Now I spend my time thinking about who will be there to greet me when my time comes. After Jesus and my husband, the first person I'm going to look for is my friend Maria Kozma!"

Ten minutes later, Kozy said goodbye to Mrs. Dobos with the promise that she would keep in touch more often. She wandered back into her bedroom. Her whirling emotions began to settle one by one like leaves falling to the ground. She could see her anger now for what it was. It was less about the indignation over how her grandmother had been hurt than her own feelings of abandonment. She was surprised by the revelation from Mrs. Dobos that her grandmother had always suspected, or at least hoped, that the woman in the morgue was not her daughter.

Kozy had accepted the news of her mother's death and never doubted what she was told, but she was only eight years old at the time. She was four or five years old when she last saw her mother. She tried to form an image of the woman who had abandoned her, but she could not. She walked to her dresser, opened the top drawer and carefully unfolded the linen cloth that lay inside. She tried to remember her mother's face compared to the one that looked back at her in the framed photograph: fresh, pretty, with clear blue eyes and wavy blond hair. But the only image she possessed was the one in the photograph: flat, faded, devoid of life.

Kozy set the picture on top of her dresser. She picked up the linen cloth to fold it but instead decided to spread it open on her bed. It was actually a wall hanging and was one of the few items Kozy's grandmother had carried with her from Hungary. Maria's mother had carefully sewn the hand-embroidered linen into the lining of her coat before Maria and Miklos had fled the country. Kozy could picture her Gram's old-fashioned kitchen. She remembered how the linen had hung on the wall above the stove. There had been a clear sheet of plastic tacked over it to keep it clean. Kozy ran her fingertips over the silky embroidery on the cream colored linen cloth. She traced the vibrant yellow, lavender, and red tulips interwoven with green vines, which formed a border around a short poem, *Hazi Aldas*. She remembered Gramma calling it the House Blessing. She vaguely remembered her grandma translating it for her, but as a young teen, she hadn't paid much attention. Kozy went to her computer and googled "traditional Hungarian house blessing." Several sites popped up with pictures of wall hangings, plaques, and various other objects featuring the poem. She found one that showed an English translation:

Hungarian House Blessing

With faith comes love.

With love, peace.

With peace, blessings.

With blessings, God is present.

With God present,

There is no need.

She printed a copy of the poem and took it with her to the kitchen table. She sat down and alternated studying the poem and gazing out the window. *What a picture of Gram's faith! I have faith because of her. It may be just a small faith sometimes, but my Abba, you are a big God. Will you please accept my weak faith and make it stronger? And I have love. You've filled my life with people to love and who love me. Peace!* She shook her head. *My peace was shattered today. I need your peace. I want your peace.* She wished her Gramma were here to comfort her. Or that she could pick up the phone and talk with Carrieanne who had always given her encouragement. But Carrieanne had been called to her heavenly home shortly after her Gram had passed on.

Kozy stood up, walked over to the window, and stared out at the back yard. She recognized the faint signs of spring in the drab landscape. There were hints of red on the tips of the maple branches and fat green leaves of the hyacinths starting to poke from the brown earth. She looked at these symbols of hope and newness and shook her head sadly. *What must Nolan think of me?* She tried to recall the words of his fumbling explanation when he realized she wasn't thrilled with his news.

She remembered Nolan saying, "She's not the person you think, Kozy. She conquered her drug addiction years and years ago."

Then why did she wait until now to come back? And the answer was clear. *Because she is dying.*

The mother she had thought was long dead was actually alive. *A less callous person would have reacted to the news with joy.* She flushed now to think that her first reaction had not been joy. Far from it. She had instead felt a sense of betrayal. Betrayal by her mother and yes, by God. She looked up and called out, "I suffered!"

An image of Christ on the cross came unbidden to her mind. Shame burned in her heart as she remembered the one who had voluntarily suffered more horrendous pain than she could even make herself imagine. And who had allowed himself to be separated from his loving father. *To cover my sins and,* she admitted reluctantly, *my mother's sins as well.*

Kozy thought back to the times in the hospital when her conversations with Carrieanne had led her to examine her faith. She could picture the young woman's slight, broken body and her smile glowing as she talked about the need to surrender to Christ. And to surrender to the God who may not necessarily give you what you want, but was always ready to give you what you need. She could hear the voice in her mind, rasping and weak, yet strangely strong in spirit. "He will always be there, to walk with you through your trials. You may not feel it all the time, but his arms are around you now. And he loves you so much."

Carrieanne had embraced Christ with such abandon. Ordinary people had considered her handicapped. But Carrieanne, for all her limitations, had only considered herself blessed. If she were in the room with her at that moment, Kozy knew exactly what Carrieanne would say to her. "Every day is a gift, not to be taken lightly. Use each one to praise, to serve, to love, to forgive."

Kozy took in a deep breath and released it slowly. A blessing was being offered to her. She could see that now. It might not feel that way yet, but it was true nonetheless. A gift. Perhaps a time to forgive, to love, and even to heal.

In her heart Kozy knew what Gram would do. She had prayed for this very thing, that her Betsy might be alive and that there had been a mistake. Gram would have run uninhibited to Betsy like the father did after his prodigal son in the gospel of Luke.

Kozy's face contorted with shame. *I have been such a hypocrite. There I was telling Nolan to try to look at others in the way God looks at us, yet I've refused to give my own mother a chance. I've known all along the right thing to do, but I chose to wallow in self-pity. I lived a good life with Gramma. But what must my mother have gone through, living with her guilt and being without Gram and me for all these years? She missed out on far more than I did.* Kozy sat back down at the table, covering her face with her hands. *I have imagined all the worst things about her ever since this morning, but I am surrendering all that to you now, Abba. I choose to forgive, if you will only give me the strength to do it. Help me to forgive.*

She was up before dawn the next morning. It was Sunday, and she went to her closet and picked out what she would wear. She took a long hot shower, feeling as though the water was cleansing her of yesterday's pain. When she had finished, she stood in front of her mirror and watched the golden glow of her curls as she combed and dried her hair. "No barrettes today," she decided as she finished. She sat at her kitchen table and waited nervously until 7:00, then turned on her phone and punched Nolan's name. He picked up at the second ring.

Her voice was soft and contrite. "Nolan, I'm sorry for how I acted. Will you come now and take me to Hospice House?"

Chapter 24

Kurt had finished reading through the gospels on Saturday evening. He'd taken the suggestion of Tom Calderon and started with the book of John and then plowed on through Matthew, Mark, and Luke. Once he had finished with Luke, Kurt found himself drawn back to John once more. If he was honest with himself, he had to agree that some kind of intelligence must have brought the world into existence. It made no sense that the complexity seen in the human body just happened by chance. It was laughable, really. No one would dare to claim that a car or a watch had come about without an intelligent maker. According to Pastor Calderon, the Bible revealed exactly what, or rather who, this intelligence was. If God was actually who the Bible claimed him to be, then Kurt had a sinking feeling that he fell far short of what God considered good.

Several times in the past weeks he had called to ask Tom about some of the things that were confusing to him. "If God is so powerful and so good why does he allow so much suffering? Why does he allow evil at all?" The pastor had patiently explained the concepts of free will and grace to Kurt, and Kurt could understand to a degree. He had seen enough of life to realize that the predominant trait of the human race was selfishness. Still, why did everything have to be so hard? For some of the more difficult questions Kurt had posed, the pastor admitted he didn't have a pat answer.

"The Bible doesn't give us the answer to every single thing we want to know," he had told Kurt. "But I'm convinced that it does tell us everything we need to know. Some things have to remain a matter of faith."

Then Tom asked Kurt a question. "If you had a potentially fatal health issue and a doctor offered to save your life with an operation, would you reject that operation just because you didn't have the same skills and understanding as that doctor? Of course not! You would put your trust in the doctor's good intentions and have faith that his years of training and experience qualify him to save your life.

"Truth is, Kurt, we all have a fatal condition. It's called sin. But we have proof in the Great Physician's qualifications. He created us and everything we know. We also have proof in his good intentions and his overwhelming love for us. He sent his own son to take our punishment on himself."

Kurt had been thinking about his past, and his future, more than he ever had before. Tom had made it clear that a nondecision was virtually a rejection of Christ. Something in him wanted to trust what the pastor said. He thought it ironic that he used to be so quick to gamble on what any fool should know were near-impossible odds. Yet, here he was dragging his feet on what looked to be a sure bet. He thought so long that his head began to ache. Groaning in frustration, he got ready for bed, but it took him a long time to get to sleep.

***

Early on Sunday morning, Kurt got a text from Nolan. He and Kozy had other obligations, so they would be unable to pick him up. Kurt could have used that as an excuse to skip that day, but he found that he looked forward to the friendly atmosphere at Grace Church. The service was about to begin when Kurt walked into the church and slipped into a seat.

He knew something was happening to him, though he wasn't exactly sure what. He listened to the voices lifted in praise around him. He didn't open his mouth to try to sing along, but he was aware that somewhere inside of himself he was participating in a deeper way. When Pastor Tom got up to preach, Kurt kept his eyes focused on the man, but his mind wandered back to the words he had been pondering the night before.

I am the bread of life. I am the living water. Kurt felt the words rather than heard them. *How long will you allow yourself to remain hungry and thirsty?*

Before he ended the service, Pastor Tom announced, "The family altar is open to any who would like to stay over for prayer." Several people headed for the front of the sanctuary and knelt at the altar. Kurt stood to leave. He took two steps toward the exit before making an about-face. With his eyes focused on the cross that hung on the back wall of the sanctuary he slowly worked his way through the crowd. As he reached the altar he hesitated. Before he could turn back, he felt a firm grip on his arm. Startled, his gaze shifted from the slender blue-veined hand to the confident smile on the wrinkled face.

"He's calling you," Ruby said as she motioned for him to kneel. "He loves you, Kurt. It will be the wisest decision you've ever made." As Kurt sank to his knees, she set down her cane and painfully knelt next to him. Pastor Tom had just finished praying with a middle-aged woman when he spotted Kurt. Walking over, he laid a hand on Kurt's shoulder. After a moment Kurt looked up with tear-stained face and nodded. Tom smiled. "Welcome home, Kurt," he said softly. "Welcome home."

⁕⁕⁕

"It was so awkward," Kozy said at last. She was sitting in Cathy Dawson's kitchen on Sunday evening, sharing with her the news that had shaken her life over the weekend. She pushed back the tears that threatened to overtake her as she recalled the first encounter with her mother earlier that morning at the Hospice House.

Cathy listened in silence, and then sat back in her chair, shaking her head. "Who would ever imagine?"

"Crazy, isn't it?" Kozy responded with a sigh.

Cathy watched her friend with sympathy and waited for her to continue.

Kozy took a moment to analyze her thoughts. "Nolan was so kind. I had disappointed and embarrassed him with my reaction on Saturday. But he went back and faced my mother. He wanted to assure her that she had done the right thing in giving me the chance to meet her. He was surprised and hurt by my initial reaction, but he was also pretty sure that I would come around eventually and realize that if I did not go and see her, I would regret it the rest of my life."

She sniffed, and Cathy handed her a tissue. "I just don't think I could have faced her without Nolan."

"So, what did you talk about?"

Kozy's face twisted. "Talk?" she answered. "Let me tell you, it doesn't get much stranger than to have to be introduced to your own mother. I tried to speak, but the words got stuck in my throat. She must have thought that I would bolt for the door and never come back, so she launched right into an apology. She admitted that her bad decisions had hurt so many. And said she was very sorry for the pain she'd caused and that she hoped someday I'd be able to forgive her."

She gave a nervous laugh. "I expected any moment that Nolan would give me a prod with his elbow like Gram used to do when I needed correcting. But he didn't. He just touched me lightly on the back, like he was reminding me that he was there for me. I managed to nod my head then. Then Vince Mateo pulled up chairs and left the three of us to ourselves. You'd think Nolan had known her for years the way he managed to make things seem almost normal. He just eased the conversation along, prompting me to talk about safe things like my job and our work with the teens."

"You've got a good man there, Kozy. I think he's a keeper."

Kozy gave a sad smile.

"So, did you recognize your mother when you first saw her? You were quite young the last time you were together, weren't you?"

"So much of that first year after we were separated is a blur to me. If we had any supervised visits, I really don't remember. Yesterday I couldn't really recall her face in real life, only the image from the pictures I have. Of course she looks older, as well as being very sick and frail. I couldn't help but feel compassion for her. But what bothers me is that I didn't feel anything beyond that. Nothing really personal, I mean. Can you understand what I'm saying, Cathy?"

"You were thinking you'd feel strong emotions toward her just because she's your mother. Is that it? You feel like she's a stranger and it doesn't seem right to you."

Kozy nodded. "Exactly! This person is my mother! My first reaction to the revelation of what she had done was anger. But once I gave that anger to God, I guess I expected that he would reward me by restoring our relationship to, well, whatever it was before."

"So what now?" Cathy asked. "What do you plan to do next?"

Kozy responded in the way Cathy hoped that she would. "She's my mother. I have to believe God brought her back into my life for a reason. Feelings or not, I'm in this to the end. Who am I to refuse an obvious gift from God, even if I didn't ask for it? If there's a chance to form a relationship I want to try. I just don't know exactly how I'm going to do it. I doubt that we have anything in common. We don't exactly have time to squeeze a lifetime of experiences into the time she has left."

Cathy waited awhile before responding. "Kozy dear, it seems that you're missing the obvious here."

Kozy lifted a brow. "I don't understand."

"The same woman raised both of you! There has to be common ground there. You have a gift for storytelling. You've entertained me with so many delightful stories about your grandma that I feel that I know her. Use your wonderful gift with your mother. Tell her the stories you've told me, complete with the Hungarian accents! Share your memories, your happiest memories, with your mother. I think you can bring her some peace in her final weeks if she sees the good life you had with your grandma. And if you do this for her, I think it's going to make you feel a whole lot better, too."

Kozy sat with elbows on the table and her hands covering her face as she listened. When she finally looked up, her eyes glistened, but there was a hint of hope in her expression.

***

Shortly after returning home from Cathy's house she received a call from Nolan.

"No. I really appreciate your offer Nolan, but I don't want you to miss work on my account. I'm so thankful that you were with me yesterday; I couldn't have faced this without you. But I need to see her on my own. I've rarely had to take a personal day ever since I started teaching. Now is the time."

Nolan knew she was right. "If you're sure, then. But would you like me to stop by Hospice House after work?"

He could hear the soft intake of her breath and pictured her smile as she spoke. "I'd like that very much, Nolan."

"Tomorrow after five, then," he promised.

***

Nolan and Kurt had begun to bring their lunches from home on Mondays and Thursdays, part of the money saving budget Nolan had devised for Kurt. During cold weather they stayed in the office to eat, but today the sun was shining, and the temperature was a comfortable sixty-five degrees. They sat outside on the bench facing the employee parking lot. Nolan took a peek into his brown paper bag. "I've got peanut butter and jelly," he said.

"You always bring peanut butter and jelly, Calderon."

"And when was the last time you made something besides bologna on a bun, Mr. Culinary Skills?" Nolan grinned. "So, wanna trade or not?"

"What flavor jelly this time?"

"Blackberry."

Kurt shrugged and tossed his sandwich to Nolan.

"Thanks." Nolan pulled the sandwich from the plastic. Before taking a bite, he tried to sound casual, "So, how was church yesterday?"

"Your dad told you I went to the altar?"

Nolan nodded.

"I finally realized that I just can't do it myself."

"None of us can," Nolan said.

Kurt focused his eyes on a blossoming magnolia tree across the parking lot. "It was like I felt him urging me and I just had to obey. And when I did, it felt right." He tossed the peanut butter sandwich up in the air and caught it before removing it from the plastic bag. "There's so much I don't understand yet, but I'm not too old to learn, right?"

"Of course not, Kurt," Nolan assured him. "I've been a Christian most of my life and I'm still learning new stuff all the time. I'm sorry I wasn't able to be there for you, though, when you went forward."

"Yeah! What happened? I'll bet you don't miss church very often. Everything's okay between you and Kozy, I hope."

"Now it is," he said grimly. "But things did get pretty tense over the weekend." Without going into great detail, he explained how Kozy's mother had suddenly popped back into her life after an eighteen-year absence.

"I was sure it would be a good thing for Kozy to reconcile with her mother. Kozy seems so well adjusted most of the time, but I underestimated how much pain she's carried from her childhood. I saw myself as her knight in shining armor helping to bring about the reunion." The remembrance made him grimace. "Didn't work out the way I'd pictured it."

Kurt nodded his understanding. "Was it a 'shoot the messenger' situation?"

"It sure was. Kozy was so furious with me. Worse thing was I had to go back and explain to a very fragile, dying woman that her daughter refused to speak to her."

"That just doesn't sound like Kozy," Kurt said.

"It's not like Kozy at all. But I can't blame her. She went through a lot when her mom abandoned her. She struggled with her emotions all day Saturday and finally surrendered. By Sunday morning she was ready to face her mother."

"How'd the reunion go?"

Nolan shrugged. "Awkward. Uncomfortable. I found myself doing most of the talking, but at least it was a start. I sympathize with both of them. It's going to take time for them to bond. I just hope there's enough time for that to happen."

"Kozy's going to see her again?"

"Yep. Should be there as we speak."

**

Kozy entered the front door of Hospice House and trudged slowly down the center corridor. She paused outside of the door to her mother's room. *Help me out here, Lord. Give me the words to say.* She knocked timidly at the half open door. Vince Mateo popped his head around the doorway and greeted her with a wide smile.

"Why, it's Kozy!" He sounded pleased. "I was just chatting with your mother about how much she enjoyed your visit yesterday. We didn't expect to see you this early since it's a school day, but it's great you're here!"

Kozy took a tentative step into the room. "I have personal time built up at school. I thought this would be a good time to use it."

"Then come on in and sit." Vince pointed to the chair beside the bed. "Since I still have rounds to make I'll leave you two alone." With a reassuring glance at both of the women, he walked out of the room.

As Kozy settled into the chair, she let her eyes travel around the room, her foot nervously tapping the floor. *Alone.* Finally, she let her eyes stray to her mother's face and she gave her a timid smile. The woman smiled back and lifted her eyebrows slightly. At the gesture a giggle escaped from Kozy's throat. Covering her face with both hands she peeked out. "I thought it would be easier the second day," she confessed, "but I'm still feeling a little backward."

Elizabeth Hanner's smile widened. "It's better to laugh than to cry," she said softly.

"Oh!" Kozy's mouth dropped open. "So many times I heard Gram say that!"

"I suppose that did come from my mother," she said finally.

"Except Gram would have said it like this, "Is better to laugh than to cry, huh?"

"That was beautiful, Kozy! You captured the perfect accent and intonation." She looked at her daughter for a moment before speaking. "So, you called her Gram?"

Kozy nodded. "That or 'Gramma.'"

She bit her lip and looked hesitantly at Kozy. "I realize it's got to be hard for you to think of me as 'Mom', but perhaps you would be comfortable calling me Betsy?"

"That's what Gram called you," Kozy said flatly. She swallowed the wave of resentment that threatened to rear its head and averted her eyes. "I guess I could try."

She lifted the tote she carried with her. "I brought something to show you," she said as she lifted a photo album from the bag. Betsy's eyes lit with interest. Kozy decided she would begin with the first day she met her grandmother.

"When Mrs. Gonzales, my caseworker, came that day with a backpack, I knew I would be changing homes again. I guess you could say I was skeptical when she told me that this time would be different. She told me that my real grandmother would be getting me and that I would live with her permanently."

Kozy avoided looking at Betsy's face, fearing what she might see. She didn't want to cause her pain, but she felt this needed to be said. "She told me that my real mother had died and that my grandmother wanted to take care of me." Her eyes clouded just a little, but she went on. "I didn't know how I should feel or respond to that news."

She sat in silence a moment until Betsy responded in a hushed voice, "I understand. I was a stranger to you by then."

Kozy nodded and went on. "I met Gramma for the first time in a motel room. We shared some food she had brought, and she let me watch the television until I fell asleep. The next morning we went to the bus station. The oddest thing happened. While we were sitting there, Gram struck up a conversation with a Hungarian couple who had walked in. The three talked together in a jumble of English and Hungarian. I was pretty intrigued by it, but I didn't let on. I just kept pretending to read the book she had bought me. Gram and the lady talked nonstop. When it came time to get on the bus, we sat in the back with Gram's new friends.

Mr. Szabo told jokes, and we shared our snacks. Gram and Mrs. Szabo never stopped talking. To make a long story short, they invited us to go with them and their son on a trip through some national parks."

She opened the album and scooted her chair closer to Betsy. "Here we are in front of the camper we traveled in. I was so excited! Our first stop was Hoover Dam." Kozy was surprised at the delight Betsy showed as she explained each picture. The time seemed to pass quickly, and Kozy made a mental note to thank Cathy for her wise advice.

When they had finished looking at the pictures Kozy tucked the album back into her tote.

"Thank you for sharing that," Betsy said. She shook her head in wonder. "I never knew my mother to travel more than a few miles outside of the Cleveland area. She always said that she had traveled enough for a lifetime when she escaped from Hungary. It must have been a real sacrifice for her to venture that far alone to get you."

"I guess I never thought about it that way," Kozy responded. "She certainly seemed to enjoy the time we spent together with the Szabo family. She always spoke as though God arranged for us to meet them as a special blessing. She cherished that memory for the rest of her life."

Betsy smiled weakly and turned her gaze to the floor. "Still, what I did to her, and to you, was inexcusable. I know I said this yesterday, but I am truly sorry. I wasn't thinking rationally in those days. I didn't even know for sure that Mom was still alive or able to take you. Her lips trembled and Kozy was sure she was about to burst into tears.

Kozy stifled a sarcastic thought. *Help me, God.* She waited a moment before trusting herself to speak. "I admit that I hate what happened to our family, for all of our sakes, but God has given us this chance to be together. Let's just use the time we have to get to know one another." Kozy had questions—lots of them—but she didn't feel ready yet to face the answers. She noticed how pale and tired the woman suddenly looked. "I'm going to let you rest now," she said. "I'll take a walk and come back. If you happen to be sleeping, I'll just sit here and work on my lesson plans until Nolan stops by after work."

Betsy shut her eyes and within minutes she had fallen asleep. Kozy gazed a moment at her face before standing up and leaving the room. As she passed Vince's office he motioned for her to come in.

"I just wanted to tell you how happy I am that you've come to spend time with your mother, Kozy. It's meant so much to her!"

"Frankly, the whole situation has been so bizarre that I'm still trying to take it all in. It felt super weird yesterday, but I'm counting on every day getting a little easier. I'm figuring each step forward is progress, right?"

"I'm glad you've decided to stick it out, Kozy. I think you're doing the right thing."

She looked soberly at him and nodded.

She was at Betsy's bedside, quietly working on her lesson plans, when she caught movement out of the corner of her eye. It was Nolan. She smiled and gave him a nod to indicate that the day had gone well.

Nolan turned to Betsy, "Good afternoon."

She greeted Nolan with a warm smile. "Please, have a seat."

Kozy was still amazed at Nolan's ability to put her mother at ease. Later, as they were walking out together, she mentioned it to him.

Nolan shook his head and dismissed her compliment. "I don't think I can really take credit for that, Kozy. I've never had the gift my father has with people. But God has been working on me these last few months. The fire at my apartment, finding that letter from my mom and discovering Kurt's gambling problem—God managed to work all of those things for good. He's been teaching me lessons all along. I think he's helping me to find the compassion that had been eluding me lately. I believe that part of the reason for that was so I'd be able to help you get back into a relationship with your mother." He took her hand as their eyes locked. "Your friendship is very important to me, Kozy. I care about your mother because she's part of what makes you who you are. I want you to get the most out of this opportunity to reconcile with her. I want you to know that I'm going to walk with you through this, as long as you need me."

She blinked back tears as she enfolded him in a fierce hug. "You're the best, Nolan Calderon," she whispered in his ear. "Thank you."

"Hey," he said when she let him go. "How about if I pick up some kind of carry-out and we can eat together? I'd like to hear more about your day."

"Did I mention that you're the best, Nolan?" she beamed. "I've been so nervous the last two days that I could hardly eat a thing. I could use a good meal. How about Chinese?"

"Chinese it is," he agreed.

Chapter 25

"You're killing me," Kurt huffed as he rounded the bend for what he felt must be the hundredth time.

Nolan glanced over his shoulder and slowed his pace until the two ran side by side. "Don't go wimpy on me now. Come on! Give it everything you've got for the home stretch!"

Kurt let out a growl, but sprinted to keep up. Nolan crossed the finish line a yard ahead. Kurt gave an exaggerated stumble and fell to the track, rolling onto his back with a loud groan. Once his breathing slowed, he eyed Nolan. "Are we done with the torture yet?"

Nolan chuckled at the theatrics. "Couple more laps to cool down is all," he said as he took off at a stroll. Kurt got up with a sigh and shuffled to catch up.

They walked in silence until a group from the high school track team jogged past them. "I wish Lila would notice how buff I'm getting," Kurt said wryly.

Nolan grinned. "Oh, I'll bet she's noticed, even if she hasn't said anything. How much have you lost so far?"

"Just shy of twenty. My goal was thirty, so I'm more than halfway there."

"Still attending your support meetings?"

"About the extent of my social life," Kurt admitted ruefully. "In the beginning, I was determined just to sit out the meetings and stay mum. I guess I was afraid of appearing, well …"

"Vulnerable?"

"I was going to say 'weak' but maybe 'vulnerable' is the better word."

"'Vulnerable' is sort of like 'weak' but with hope and trust attached."

He mulled over the thought and nodded. "Yeah. Anyway, now I can't seem to get through a meeting without blurting out something. I never would have imagined how much it helps to just get everything out there in the open and to admit my failures. It feels good to realize that I'm not alone and that I still am accepted."

"I'm glad for you, Kurt." *It does help to get things out in the open. I'm learning that myself.*

"Yeah," Kurt continued. "I'm sticking with both groups as long as I need to. I don't want to get too confident. I can't let myself forget that it's God who gives me the strength to resist temptation. Your dad has really been helpful in keeping me on track, too. You're so fortunate to have him in your life."

They reached the stands where they had left their jackets. Nolan lifted a foot onto the seat and stretched his opposite leg. "I know. I guess I should tell him that more often." Switching legs he asked, "So, how about Lila? Think she'll ever go out with you?"

Kurt frowned. "It's just that Lila is really hesitant about starting any relationship, let alone one with somebody with a past similar to her own. The thing is, when we talk on the phone, we really click. I've shared so much about my past, and she understands and cares. So far, she's nixed the idea of us actually dating. The only time she allows us to spend together in person is the AA meetings. But I'd love to have a relationship with her like you have with Kozy."

Nolan cringed. "Watch what you wish for," he said flatly. Then he reluctantly explained the recent roadblock to their relationship.

"Say it ain't so," Kurt cried. "When squeaky-clean Nolan Calderon gets demoted to 'just friends' status, what chance can a guy like me ever have? Man, I feel for you!"

"I haven't given up hope. Neither should you, Kurt." He pulled his jacket over his shoulders and zipped it. "Let me ask you this: what are you looking for in a relationship with Lila?"

Kurt chewed on his lip as he thought. "I watched my mom go through a succession of men who either abused her or strung her along and then left when she most needed them. After getting to know your family, I realize that the toxic situations I got used to growing up aren't the way things are intended to be. What I want is something I never dreamed possible when I was younger. I want a relationship that's going to last. I want to have someone who'll love me and stick with me even when things get tough. And Lila—well, I think she has the potential to be that kind of woman."

"That's what I want too, Kurt. I treasure Kozy's friendship, but I want more. I desperately want her for my wife, but she's got some issues to work through. It's not easy waiting; I'm no eunuch. But I want what we have to be forever, so I need to be man enough to wait."

***

"Gram's enthusiasm for berry picking was certainly unrivaled," Kozy chuckled. "She used to start scanning the newspaper for berry farm ads at the first sign of spring."

Betsy laughed and nodded her head in agreement. "She had this favorite place to pick strawberries out in Lake County back in the seventies. She was devastated when they sold out to developers and she had to find a different farm. But then she found out there were also places that she could pick blueberries, blackberries, and red and black raspberries. There was no stopping her after that!"

Kozy had asked Cathy Dawson to come with her this Saturday morning to meet Betsy. Cathy was enjoying the exchanges between mother and daughter as they discussed some of the things they had done during summer vacations while growing up in Cleveland.

"I must have picked gallons and gallons of berries throughout the summer, but I'll admit that I probably ate more than my fair share. I think Gram enjoyed the whole process every bit as much as the actual eating. She was always philosophical about picking berries. If I whined when a particularly large raspberry slipped through my fingers, she would say, 'The rabbits, they need to eat as well, you know.' Or 'Next year a new plant will grow from your lost berry.'"

Betsy added to their reminiscing. "When she took me to pick berries she liked to talk about how you could learn a lot about life from picking berries. 'Look from both directions, Betsy,' she would say. 'You will find more berries if you look back from the way you just came. Life is like that, too. Look back carefully so you don't miss any blessings. God likes to give us second chances.' I feel like I'm finally doing that now," Betsy said with a sigh. "The chance to spend this time with you, Kozy, to get to know you as an adult, has been a blessing beyond anything I imagined."

Kozy had brought another picture album today. She opened it now. "These are pictures from our time at Hocking Hills for the youth group retreat. I was going into seventh grade that year. Gram knew how badly I wanted to go, but she made me work to earn the money. And she worked just as hard as I did. That spring we made hundreds of poppy seed and nut rolls for church bake sales. And Gram was in charge of making the dumplings for the soup-and-sandwich fund raisers the church held for the youth."

"Mmm," Betsy interrupted. "I loved Mom's nut rolls."

Kozy nodded before continuing. "But Gram was also reluctant to let me go that far without her, so she volunteered to be a chaperone. Horrors! It was bad enough for a parent to tag along, but a grandma? I was convinced that she would cramp my style and be an embarrassment. I told her she'd never be able to keep up with all the kids. But I underestimated my grandma. She started hiking that spring at the Metro Parks while I was at school. And in the summer, she hiked early in the mornings while I was still sleeping." Kozy laughed as she remembered. "She was going on sixty-five, but by the time we left for our week of hiking at Hocking Hills, she was in better shape than me."

Kozy flipped the page and showed them pictures of the dramatic rock formations, waterfalls, and caves in the southern Ohio state park. She turned another page to show a picture of Kozy and her grandmother posing by a marker for one of the trails. Kozy pointed her finger at the picture as she began her story.

"Gram had cut two sturdy branches from a shrub in our back yard. She sanded them carefully and gave them three coats of spar varnish. Well, I scoffed at the very idea of using a walking stick, but she took them along anyway, saying she'd just use both of them herself. They would help her steady herself on the steps and hills. Everything went great that first day. But there was a storm in the night. The trails the next day were treacherous. A girl walking ahead of us slipped on the wet leaves and went down on her bottom in the slimy mud. Her shorts were a mess. Gram hiked the distance over to where the girl sat in the mud, and she helped her to stand. She offered the girl one of her sticks, and the girl accepted it with thanks. I slipped a few times and fortunately caught myself, but I was too proud to say anything. Then we came to a swollen stream that had to be navigated by stepping on wet, slippery rocks. I knew I'd never make it across without embarrassing myself. Gram wordlessly handed me her remaining stick and I was glad to accept it. Then she looked around until she found another stick for herself. She spotted a rough and dirty one that she used for the rest of the trip. I opened my mouth to apologize, but she stopped me with her fingers touching my mouth. 'You will learn my little *majom*.' Then she looked to make sure no one else was watching and she gave me a quick hug."

Cathy, who had been smiling throughout the narrative asked, "So, what exactly is a *majom*?"

"A monkey!" said Kozy and Betsy in unison. Then they looked at each other and burst out laughing.

***

"Tell me about my grandfather." Kozy had never asked her grandma much about him, and now she was curious. "You named me after him, right? He must have been a good dad for you to do that."

Betsy was feeling stronger and was sitting at the table with Kozy, sipping tea. She folded her hands under her chin before answering. "Yes," she said decisively. "He was a good dad. His close friends called him 'Kozy.' At the time, he seemed ancient to me. He was forty-four when I was born and was just an ordinary guy by the world's standards. He went to work at the factory, came home, ate supper, and then spent the evening reading the paper or playing cards with Mom. On the weekends he fiddled around in the garage or the yard, depending on the season, and went to church on Sunday. Aside from an occasional evening out with friends, he seemed to lead a pretty boring life." Her eyes drifted to the dining room window which faced a courtyard. Kozy glanced to see what had distracted her but realized that Betsy wasn't really looking at the courtyard. She stirred her tea while she waited for her mother's thoughts to return to the present.

"I'm sorry," Betsy shook her head. "He was kind, very kind, and funny too. He had a dry sense of humor. But more than anything, John Kozma was a gentle man."

"How old was he when he …?" The word caught in her throat. *Maybe I shouldn't talk about that.*

"He was barely into his sixties." Betsy answered quickly, sensing her daughter's discomfort. "Too young."

Kozy did the mental math. Betsy had just finished high school when she became pregnant. Early sixties was young for John Kozma to die, but Betsy was only forty-five, maybe forty-six. Kozy's stomach dropped.

Betsy's mind was not on her own mortality. "Before he came to America," she explained, "Dad had contracted rheumatic fever. Living conditions during the war were very bad. Malnutrition, overcrowding, and lack of antibiotics. He recovered from the fever, but his heart valves had been damaged. He had a relapse when he was sixty, which caused even more damage. After that, he grew weaker and weaker. Within a year or two his heart just gave out."

Betsy wiped away a tear with her frail hand. Kozy said nothing but reached over and covered her mother's hand with her own. She tried to wrap her mind around the fact that she and her mother were now living out the same scenario. She was just beginning to get to know her, and they had so little time. Betsy was growing weaker by the day, and soon she would die.

Am I ready to face this? Is she?

Later that evening, at home, Kozy curled up in her bed with her prayer journal.

My Abba, Thank you for giving us the healing words to speak to one another. Whenever we talk about Gram, it seems to draw us closer. I feel like Betsy could be an older sister that has just come back into my life. There is no one else who has experienced my grandma in quite the same way. I still have questions, but I'm not sure I'm ready to hear the answers. Please help me to get over my fears and resentments before it's too late. I need you to help me!

***

Kozy was daily coming up with new memories to share with Betsy. Each hour spent together brought subtle progress in their relationship. Still, there were subjects Kozy was reluctant to broach. "I'll understand if you don't want to talk about it," Betsy asked one afternoon, "but I was wondering what you remembered about the day you were taken away."

Kozy rubbed a hand nervously over her face before meeting her mother's gaze. Things had been going so well between them. Was it worth risking what they had built thus far to revisit that traumatic day? Was it necessary to bring this out in the open in order to purge the remnants of bitterness she still harbored in her heart?

Reluctantly, Kozy recounted the events she could remember from that fateful day. She recalled being awakened by shouting. Then, bullets started flying, and there was an earsplitting shotgun blast and the door being kicked in by the police.

"I'm not certain what I actually remember, and what I imagine remembering," Kozy admitted. "Gramma kept all of the papers she was given by Children's Services. I read them after she died, so that's how I know what happened. We never talked about any of it when I was a child." *Because I refused to even think about it.*

Betsy had been sitting up in her bed. Her hands had swept restlessly back and forth over the sheets as she listened. Now she pulled her legs up and clasped her hands over her knees as she looked full into her daughter's eyes. "That was a pretty accurate account of what happened," she said. She took a deep breath, and after a moment she spoke hesitantly, "Kozy, I never took drugs while I was pregnant with you. That stuff all took place later, not that it excuses what I did in any way, but I just wanted you to know that."

"Okay," Kozy responded weakly.

"It was later on. Things started getting tough. Your dad didn't have the advantage of having a good family life like I did. It was hard for him to find work that could support us. He wanted it to be easier. The temptation to make easy money was strong. We didn't stop and think about how many people he would be hurting when he took that first job."

"And then you started using drugs." Kozy was just stating the fact, not intending to accuse.

Betsy spoke stiffly. "Everybody we knew was into drugs. Your dad was able to stop with marijuana, but I was not. It was when he realized how hooked I'd become that he tried to run from the cartel. When we made our escape, it wasn't because Ted knew too much that they came after us, at least that wasn't the only reason," Betsy confessed. "I had stolen drugs from them. Such a small package to be worth so much money! When the police found it hidden in the house, your dad took the blame for what I had done. I believe he thought that you would at least have one parent to take care of you. He didn't realize that I'd have so hard a time getting clean."

Kozy felt a claw of bitterness rake her heart. *She makes him sound like he had some good qualities. But I know better. I know.* I don't want to talk about that man," she broke in. "If you mention him again I'll have to leave." She watched as Betsy seemed to shrink into herself. She wanted to show mercy, but her question formed before she could stop herself.

"Why didn't you try to get me back while I spent all that time in foster care?"

Betsy's face took on a look of confusion. "But I did, Kozy, don't you remember?" Then the realization hit her. *She was so young. Could she have shut out the memory completely?*

"You didn't." Kozy felt a sudden sense of resentment. "There was nothing in the records. Just four long years in one foster home after another. Gram would have helped. You know she would have. Why didn't you just ask her if you could come home?"

Betsy looked at her with sad eyes. "A question I've asked myself a thousand times. A decision I've regretted every day. I just don't know. Pride? Stupidity? Shame? I didn't want my mother to see how far I'd fallen. I couldn't keep a job, and the drugs had me in such a grip. Eventually I started selling my body to get them. When I reached that point …." She stopped, unable to continue.

Kozy concentrated on breathing in and out, willing herself to not process the words yet. She stood and silently helped her mother lie back on the bed. "Rest now," she said with trembling lips. "I promise I'll come back tomorrow." Betsy wordlessly nodded as she turned her face to the wall. Kozy tried to block the sound of the quiet sobs that racked her mother's fragile body.

She walked out to the hallway and sank to the floor outside of Betsy's room. She was still sitting there, back against the wall and eyes closed when Nolan arrived a half hour later. She looked so forlorn that he glanced with alarm at the bed. He breathed a sigh of relief when he saw a slight movement of Betsy's shoulder.

Nolan knelt beside Kozy. "Hey. You look like you've lost your best friend."

She opened her eyes and smiled. "My best friend just arrived, so I guess I haven't."

"Rough day?"

Her smile twisted and she looked down at her hands.

"Wanna talk about it?"

"Not here," she whispered.

Nolan stood, took Kozy's hand and helped her to her feet. She kept her grip on his hand and pulled him down the hallway to the nearest exit. Once they had reached the parking lot, she let down her guard.

"Just hold me, Nolan," she said as hot tears filled her eyes. "Just hold me."

Nolan wrapped his arms around her, gripping her tight. He didn't try to talk. *Help her, Lord. Please give her peace.* Eventually, her sobs subsided.

"Nolan," she sniffled, wiping at her face with her hand. "Could you find some tissues in my purse?"

He searched through her small handbag but came up empty-handed, so he unlocked his car and helped her inside, quickly running around to the driver's side. He handed her the box of tissues that he kept in the back seat, and waited as she blew her nose loudly. When she was finished she looked at him.

"Oh, Nolan," she wailed. "Now I've ruined your shirt!" Her tears began anew as she took some fresh tissues and attempted to pat at his soggy chest. Nolan looked down. He had to admit to himself, it did look pretty disgusting.

He stopped her hand with one of his and lifted her chin with the other. "Kozy." He looked deep into her eyes. "It's just a shirt. You have to know that you are much more important to me than a piece of fabric. You know that, don't you?"

She nodded, wiping furiously at her eyes.

"Okay then," he said firmly. "Tell me what happened."

He listened in silence as she recalled the conversation she had with her mother. When she finished, she looked down in shame. "What kind of heartless person am I to make a dying woman cry?"

"You're not heartless, Kozy Hanner. You're one of the kindest people I know." He gave her a sad smile. "I wish it didn't hurt, but you need to talk it out."

Chapter 26

Vince tapped lightly on the door to Betsy's room before popping his head in. "Hi," he said softly. "I've got someone here who'd like to meet you. May we come in?"

Betsy gave a nod as Vince entered the room. "Betsy, this is my wife Wendy. She's going to be filling in occasionally while Nurse Jamie is on maternity leave."

Warmth flooded Betsy's eyes. "That's so wonderful! I've been hoping I'd get to meet you, Wendy. I've loved hearing Vince's stories about your adventures serving together overseas."

Wendy flashed her dimpled smile. "Vince has spoken highly of you. I'm glad for the chance to take care of you," she said as she clasped Betsy's hand. "Say, you've sure got yourself a sweet daughter, Betsy. She and Nolan make such a cute couple, don't you think?"

Vince walked out as the two chatted, thankful for his wife's gift of ministry to the hurting. He was confident that Betsy would be in good hands in her final days.

"Is there anything I can do for you, Betsy, while I'm here?"

"No. I'm fine," Betsy said. But when she saw the sincere look of concern on Wendy's face, she reconsidered. "How are you at typing, Wendy? Do you think you could get a hold of a laptop?"

An hour later, Wendy stopped by her husband's office and handed him a sealed envelope. "For Betsy's file," she said. "And Hon, do you think you could get the hospice attorney to stop over? It won't take long, but I think it had better be soon, this afternoon if possible."

***

It was early the next morning that Kozy got the call that Betsy's condition had worsened. "I don't want you to take off work," she insisted when she talked afterward with Nolan. "I'm going over as soon as my substitute arrives. Just pray, please. And tell your dad so we can be put on the church prayer list. And Nolan, I would like it if you'd come over on your lunchtime. Thanks."

As soon as Nolan had ended the call, Kurt stepped around the corner and stood at Nolan's desk. "I couldn't help but hear. I take it that Kozy's mother has taken a turn for the worse?"

Nolan nodded grimly.

"It's got to be tough on her. What's it been, a month that she's known about her? Not very long to make up for so many lost years."

"Going on five weeks," Nolan agreed. "It's going to be hard on her. But it's still a good thing that they've had this time, even if it has been short."

"Look," Kurt said after a moment. "I'm pretty new to this, but would you tell Kozy that I've been praying for her and Betsy?"

"I'll tell her, my friend," he said. "And I know she'll appreciate that you care."

***

When Kozy arrived at Hospice House, Betsy was awake. She brightened when she saw Kozy but soon grew listless. Her voice was weak and it seemed to take all her effort to keep her eyes open. "I'm here now," Kozy assured her. "You can rest. Don't talk unless you want to. I'll just sit here with you, okay?"

At Betsy's nod, Kozy drew a chair up next to the bed. She sat and watched as her mother smiled and then shut her eyes. Wendy came in to check on Betsy. "She'll likely keep drifting in and out of sleep for the time being. She doesn't seem to be in any distress. We expect her to eventually slip into a coma and then—into eternity." She patted Kozy on the shoulder. "There are lots worse ways to go."

"I don't want her to be alone when the time comes."

"You can gather whatever you might need, and we'll set up a cot for you in the small adjoining room," Wendy assured her. "You can be here round the clock if you wish. I hear Nolan and his folks have volunteered to help you keep watch."

"It means a lot to me to have friends around who understand what I'm going through." Once Wendy went off to check on her other patients, Kozy tried to stifle the slight panic she felt by making a mental list of the things she would need to get from home.

***

When Nolan stepped into the room early Sunday afternoon, Kozy was sitting slumped beside the bed, but she straightened when she saw him. She tried to produce a brave smile. "How was church today, Nolan?"

"So many people sent their love," he answered. "Look, I made a list for you of all the names." He handed her a card. "Dad's coming over shortly, and then I'm taking you to the dining room. You've not been eating much lately, and you're due for a decent meal."

She frowned. "I just don't feel like eating." She glanced over at her sleeping mother. "Have you noticed how thin she is? I was looking at the picture you took of us that first day. She must have lost twenty pounds since then."

He enveloped her with his arms. He had been there with her when Wendy explained how Betsy's body was slowly shutting down. He knew Kozy understood the process in her head, but it was taking more time for her heart to accept the inevitable.

"I'm sure there's still some homemade Hungarian vegetable soup in my freezer. I could run home and find that; maybe she'd be tempted to eat."

He held her tighter and whispered in her ear, "No, Kozy."

213

She moaned and squeezed her eyes shut. Finally she relaxed and sighed. "I know. I know that's not going to happen, but I'm not sure I'm ready for this, Nolan."

"It won't be easy, but you won't be alone. Neither will your mother."

***

Monday came and Betsy was still hanging on. Kurt was taking a turn at her side while Kozy took a much-needed nap on the cot in the next room. Betsy appeared to be sleeping soundly, and he was surprised when he looked up and saw her watching him.

"You're here, Kurt." Her voice was labored and weak, but calm. He had to draw closer to hear. "God is so good," she said slowly. "I've been talking with God. I asked him to bring you and he did. So wonderful."

"Shall I wake Kozy?" he asked.

"No, let her rest." He waited as she took several shaky breaths. "Kurt, when you make your trip home," she said at last, "I'd like you to do something for me."

***

They stood in the Marley's parking lot on Tuesday morning as Kurt explained to Nolan. "A month ago, the first time I met Betsy, I told her about my being from Nevada. Betsy was very interested when I told her the name of my hometown which, as it turns out, is just a few miles from the federal prison where Kozy's father died. I mentioned to her that I was acquainted with a man who had retired as a prison guard from there. Until last night, the subject had not come up again."

Kurt told Nolan how Betsy had made him promise to contact the retired guard when he went to Nevada. She seemed adamant that the man would have firsthand information about the prison riot that had taken Ted Hanner's life.

Nolan rubbed his hand nervously over his face and huffed out a deep breath. "I just don't know, Kurt, if that's a good idea."

"I didn't feel as though I could refuse a request from a dying woman, Nolan."

"But Betsy's not expected to live out the end of the week. What will it matter after she's gone?"

"That's just it, Nolan. She didn't want to want to know for herself. She wants me to find out for Kozy's sake."

"How much more pain does she think Kozy can stand?" Nolan sputtered. "The man died a violent death. Why dwell on the details?"

Kurt bent over to pick up a chunk of bark from the sidewalk and tossed it back into the mulch surrounding the building. "I think there's more going on here than we realize." He hesitated before adding, "Were you aware that I was taking a trip to Nevada, Nolan?"

"No," he said crossly. "I've been a little distracted lately."

"Well, guess what? I didn't know myself until yesterday. Lila and I have been talking about the eighth step in the Twelve Step Program: making amends with those you have harmed. It was just yesterday afternoon when I made the decision to go to see my mom. I found a super deal on an airline ticket for the middle of June. I never told a soul, but Betsy knew. She even mentioned the date! How could she have known I was planning that trip, Nolan?"

Nolan's eyebrows lifted in surprise.

"Right. Sounds like *The Twilight Zone* doesn't it? Well, when I go out to see my mom, I will do my best to keep my promise to Betsy. If I can find out anything about her husband's death, one way or another, I'll let you decide then whether it's in Kozy's best interest to know."

***

Betsy slipped into a coma late Wednesday morning. Wendy Mateo rubbed Kozy's back soothingly as she explained once again what was happening. "Your mom's body is shutting down, Kozy. But she doesn't appear to be in any pain. Her passing will likely be very peaceful. You can be thankful for that."

"But I'm not ready, Wendy," she cried plaintively. "There's so much more we should have talked about." *And I wouldn't let her talk. Now I'll never have the chance.* She laid her hand over Betsy's. *Her hand feels so cold.*

"Go ahead and talk to her, Hon. Even if she's not able to respond, your mom may still hear you." Wendy walked to the doorway and turned. "You ring for me if you need me, okay?"

Kozy stood at the bedside watching each shallow breath from the woman who had so recently re-entered her life. After a few minutes she stepped out of her shoes, lifted the blanket, and lowered herself onto the narrow bed. She gently scooted until she was cuddled next to her mother, willing her own body heat into the thin form. With her mouth next to her mother's ear, she began her narrative.

"When I heard Gram talking to Mr. and Mrs. Szabo that first day, I almost giggled. They sounded so funny …" She talked of anything and everything, the silly and the serious, holding nothing back. She spilled out her fears, her sorrows, and her insecurities. She shared her joys and her triumphs. She revealed her feelings for Nolan and talked of her faith in God. She had a burning desire to redeem every moment of the years she had missed sharing with her mother. Kozy continued on, stopping only to take a sip of water now and then when her mouth went dry and her voice grew hoarse. Her eyes lit with gratitude when Nolan stepped into the room later that afternoon. He knelt beside the bed and she clutched his hand as he prayed silently. Twenty minutes later, Betsy opened her eyes, reached an arm into the air, and gave one short gasp. As Kozy saw the light fade from Betsy's eyes, she cried out in anguish, "Mama!" Then she turned to Nolan and sobbed.

Chapter 27

Doug Dugan, the attorney who did much of the pro bono work for Hospice House, was talking to Vince when his secretary ushered Kozy and Nolan into his office the next day. The tall gray-haired man stepped from behind his desk and offered his hand to Kozy.

"Miss Hanner, first let me say that I am sorry for your loss," he said. "It has to have been tough for you these last few weeks."

"Thanks," Kozy responded in a quiet voice.

"And Mr. Calderon," he said as he reached to shake Nolan's hand. "Still working for Fred Marley, I hear. I take it you're here in a personal capacity today?"

"Yes, sir," Nolan nodded, putting a protective arm around Kozy.

"Very well," he smiled as he motioned for the three of them to sit. He returned to his desk and eased himself into his own chair. He cleared his throat. "We have a rather unusual situation here. Ever since Chaplain Mateo conferred with me a few weeks ago, I started doing some research to help answer some of his questions. The foremost thing the chaplain was concerned with was whether he, as a representative of Hospice House, was under any obligation to reveal to the authorities what the person known as Joni Farnsworth, told him about her true identity."

The lawyer, elbows on the desk, clasped his hands and rested his chin upon his thumbs. His eyes settled on Vince, who now scooted forward in his seat. The lawyer tapped his foot on the floor before continuing.

"Now as I was told, the woman who entered hospice care as Ms. Farnsworth confessed to her chaplain that her real name was Elizabeth Hanner." He looked with sympathy to Kozy. "And after meeting the woman, you, Miss Hanner, have found that to be the truth. Your mother, after failing in her attempts to regain custody of you, made the unfortunate and rash decision to switch her dead friend's identity with her own, a decision that, for better or worse, affected the lives of many people.

"However, I've done some checking into the woman known as Joni Farnsworth. For the eighteen years prior to when she entered Hospice House this winter, she had lived a quiet, law-abiding, and productive life at a mission house in California. I found no sign of criminal activity. In fact, several of those who knew her and worked with her during those years have written to me, giving me details about her self-sacrificing nature as a drug counselor. You can be proud of her, Miss Hanner," he said. Kozy took the folder he handed her and clasped it to her chest.

"Now, as to the touchy part," he continued. "You know who your mother is, as do a handful of others in this town. But, we have no written documentation to prove anything. As far as the State of California is concerned, Elizabeth Hanner died eighteen years ago of an accidental drug overdose. Aside from the original switching of identities, I found no indication of any other crime committed. My advice to Hospice House and to you, Miss Hanner, is to let sleeping dogs lie. I see little point in taxing our already overworked courts over a moot point. After all, both parties are deceased." He waved a hand, indicating that he welcomed the opinions of the others.

"Kozy?" Vince asked.

She swallowed at the lump in her throat. "At least my mother died knowing she was loved by God, Gram, me, and the people she helped."

Attorney Dugan nodded. "Your mother, that is, Joni Farnsworth, left a simple will," he told her. "No estate to speak of. Virtually everything she earned over the years was donated back to the sisters at the mission, who by the way, have prepaid for her cremation. Ms. Farnsworth requested there be no public calling hours or funeral service. Kozy, you are to receive her ashes to do with as you see fit." He handed her two thin manila envelopes. "Her personal effects," he explained.

Kozy's eyes clouded. "I can accept that she wanted it this way, but it just feels so unfinished."

"I understand your need for closure," Dugan said. He rose from his seat and moved to stand before her. "You know, Miss Hanner, as long as we don't slander anyone, we are free to put anything we want on a tombstone. Think on it," he suggested as he guided them to the door.

***

"*It is well; it is well with my soul.*" The voices of the dozen mourners faded into the stillness at the cemetery. People wandered away from the gravestone to chat quietly in small groups.

"I can't begin to tell you how much this means to me, Vince," Kozy said with a quivering voice. "To have these few people see that her life wasn't wasted and that God redeemed it. To have someone know about all the lives she impacted for the better in her years of counseling. Sure, I wish things could have been different, but I am grateful for what time we had together. To think that I might never have had the chance to know her and love her."

Vince put a fatherly arm around her shoulder as they stepped around to the back of the granite memorial that marked the final resting place of John and Maria Kozma. "It's hard to fathom all the mysteries of life, Kozy. Maybe someday we'll get the answers."

"It's funny how I never even realized that Gram hadn't added the date of death when she had the ashes buried," she mused. "Only the date of birth." She straightened the spray of red roses that saddled the stone. "I never wanted to visit the cemetery when I was growing up, and Gram didn't force me. When Gram died, I don't remember even looking back here for my mother's name."

"And now the information is accurate," Vince said as they studied the carvings on the headstone. Elizabeth Kozma Hanner's date of death had been newly etched in the granite. Also recorded were the dates of birth and death of Joni Farnsworth, whose ashes had rested there in Betsy's place for nearly two decades.

"My heart aches for the real Joni; no one to care, no one to miss her all these years. I'd like to think she mattered to someone."

"Your mother must have cared, Kozy. She called Joni a friend. And she spent eighteen years working to give dignity and meaning to the name she borrowed. We'll probably never learn Joni's whole story; we can only trust in God's mercy."

Nolan broke away from a tiny group of elderly women. "The ladies are heading back to the church now to get the food ready to serve. I'll wait here with you as long as you need." To Vince he said, "Wendy wants to know if you have the address in your GPS; otherwise you can follow Dad and Marcy over."

"I hardly need a GPS. I'll be able to instinctively hone in on the place if there's a hint of stuffed cabbage in the air. If you want some time to yourself, Kozy, I'll head on over with my wife."

"Thanks again, Vince. Nolan and I will be along shortly," she said with a wave. She turned to Nolan and stroked the sleeve of his coat. "I'm glad you suggested telling the paprika ladies. They deserved to know what really happened, and that their prayers all those years ago were answered."

He took her by the hand, and they strolled through the winding gravel path, reading the names recorded on the monuments and plaques, taking in the quiet for a few minutes before going back to Nolan's car. "I'm glad you decided to have a service, no matter how small," he said as he opened her door.

She glanced back at the gravestone one more time and nodded. "It was the right thing to do," she said. "I think they all would be pleased."

***

Wendy stood to gather the plates and help clear the table. "The ladies did a wonderful job feeding us, Kozy. You can tell they loved you and your family very much." She hesitated as she held the stack of dishes. She cocked her head and looked back at Kozy. "Maybe I have no business asking, dear, but I was just wondering about the letter your mother wrote. Was it helpful?"

Kozy stared down at the table before venturing a peek at Wendy. "I'm afraid I haven't been able to bring myself to open it yet," she admitted. "How did you know?"

Wendy set down the pile of plates and laid her hand on Kozy's arm. "Betsy was too weak to sit up to type, so she dictated the letter to me. She put her whole heart into it, dear. It was stuff she wanted you to know. Once she had her say, it was like she was ready to go."

"I intend to read it eventually," Kozy said defensively. "It's just been such a painful time."

Wendy's eyes showed sympathy. "I know, Hon. And I hope I'm not offending you by putting in my two cents worth, but I hope you don't put it off too long."

Chapter 28

"Anybody for another hot dog?" Nolan asked. He, Kozy, Kurt, and Lila were seated around the small fire pit in Kozy's backyard, helping her to celebrate the end of the school year. She loved her job, but the stress of the last few months had her looking forward to the summer break.

"None for me, Nolan," Kurt answered. "I think two is my limit these days. I've worked hard to take off these extra pounds and I don't want to backslide." He smiled at Lila who had been the driving force in convincing him to trim down.

"No more for me," she said. "However, you could maybe talk me into a couple of toasted marshmallows."

"Yes!" Kozy agreed with enthusiasm. "Let's make s'mores! I have graham crackers inside. And one of my kids gave me a giant chocolate bar the last day of school. We can split it four ways."

"Okay, so long as we limit ourselves I won't feel too guilty," Lila conceded. "Let's take the other stuff inside, and I'll help you clean up your kitchen first."

As the two went chattering into the house, Nolan stood to pick up another small log and added it to the fire. "I spoke with Mr. Marley today," he said quietly. "He told me that you've paid off the last of your debt to him." He glanced over at Kurt whose eyes were still focused on the flames.

Kurt nodded. "I tweaked my budget even more so I could pay it off a little faster than the agreement. I wanted to get squared away with Mr. Marley before I make the trip to see my mom."

Nolan reached into the back pocket of his jeans and pulled out his wallet. He took out the tattered paper and handed it to Kurt. "Here," he said. "You might as well 'burn the mortgage' while the girls are still inside."

Kurt unfolded the check and stared at the proof of his indiscretion. He looked soberly at Nolan. "Thank you. Not just for this," he said indicating the paper that Nolan had used to force him off the disastrous course he had almost taken. "For everything. I gave you no reason to trust me, but you were willing to stick your neck out to give me a chance. It sure changed my life for the better." He stooped and carefully dropped the check into the orange glow of the fire. They watched as it momentarily flared and curled and then was finally reduced to ashes. Kurt stared into the flames, chewing on his lip as he recalled how differently he had approached life only six months earlier. Nolan nudged Kurt's shoulder and smiled.

"Come on, my friend," he laughed. "Let's go in and make sure the girls aren't in there eating our portion of that chocolate bar."

***

"Traffic's not bad," Nolan noted as he eyed the dashboard clock. "We should get there with time to spare."

"Thanks for offering the ride," Kurt said. "I wasn't that keen on leaving my car at the airport all week. It sure relieves a lot of stress to know it'll be safely parked in my driveway."

"Glad to help out." Nolan glanced over at his friend with concern in his eyes. "You sure you're prepared for this?"

Kurt's eyes held steady as he answered. "I hope so." He sighed and set his gaze on the road as Nolan made the exit to the airport. "Mr. Marley knows what I'll be up against. Where I come from, it's hard to even make a trip to the john without seeing a slot machine staring you in the face. Add to that the possibility of things going sour between my mom's new husband and me. I only hope the picture she's painted of how things are is the truth. Marley thinks this is an important step for me."

Nolan agreed. *Still, lots of things could go wrong.* "I hope it goes well for you," he said, deciding to keep his worries to himself. They rode in silence and pulled into the short-term parking minutes later.

Nolan turned off the ignition and popped the trunk, but Kurt remained seated, his doubts suddenly multiplied. "I don't want to blow it—I just can't go back to my old way of life. What if I'm not strong enough for this, Nolan?"

"You may not be strong enough, Kurt, but God is. How about if we pray right now before you leave?"

Kurt nodded and shut his eyes as Nolan began. "Father," he said, "You know how Kurt longs to make amends with his mother. I pray that you will continue to pave the way to peace and forgiveness with his mom and stepdad. Help him to face any temptation that comes his way during his time at home. Help him to remember that since he belongs to you, he no longer has to rely upon his own strength, but that you are a there, always, to relieve his burden. Keep him faithful and ever mindful of your love for him. We're asking this in Jesus' name. Amen."

There was a moment of awkward silence before Kurt said in a hoarse whisper. "Please, God, help me to resist the pull. I don't want to disappoint my friends, or Lila, or you. If you get me through this, I'll just be so grateful. Amen."

He stepped out and retrieved his luggage from the trunk. After shouldering his backpack and grabbing the handle of his suitcase, he punched Nolan's arm lightly. "I guess I'm good to go. Thanks again."

"Stay in touch, Kurt. I'll pick you up next week."

As he watched Kurt disappear into the terminal, he pondered once more what Kurt might find out from the retired prison guard he planned to meet while in Nevada. He shut his eyes and tried to think how to pray. Words didn't form. "Please," he finally whispered, "Please, let it not bring more pain for Kozy."

***

Kurt checked in with him midweek. "My mom's okay," he said before Nolan had a chance to ask. "She's changed, and her husband is way nicer than I expected."

"So it's good you decided to go."

"I shouldn't have waited so long," he said with regret. "All those years when I was little, never being able to keep those creeps from hurting her, I had felt so frustrated, so powerless. Then when I graduated and got my first real job, I was finally in a position to protect her. I thought she'd jump at the chance for me to take her away. My pride really took a hit when she refused. 'I don't want to leave Charlie,' she'd told me. Well, I'd heard stories like that before. So, I left. I couldn't bring myself to watch her destroy herself anymore."

Nolan had heard this part of the story before, but he was glad that Kurt was talking it out. "So her life really has changed?"

Kurt's voice thickened. "She's been sober for three years. He was the one that got her to go to AA. And they really did get married. Mom showed me the certificate. Charlie's not perfect; he has quite a past, but then so does Mom. So do I, for that matter."

"But you're not the man you used to be," he reminded Kurt.

"And I thank God that I'm not." The seconds ticked by as Nolan waited for him to continue. Finally Kurt sighed. "I've had a lot of time to think. If I had talked Mom into leaving with me back then, what might have happened? I had thought that having enough money would be Mom's salvation. But I wasn't in any shape to give her what she really needed. I was just as lost as she was."

Nolan thought of the verse from Proverbs that he had read that morning. *A man's heart plans his way, but the Lord directs his steps.*

"I guess Charlie was who she needed. He understood her weaknesses and loved her in spite of them. They started going to the little church where their AA meetings are held. The people there reached out to them where they were and showed them the love of Jesus. You'll never believe it Nolan, but my mom had people out there praying for *me*."

Nolan smiled. *How awesome you are, God!*

226

"I'll have to fill you in on the details when I get home. They're waiting for me to go to a Wednesday night prayer meeting. Can you believe it? And I've talked with the guy I told you about, the retired guard from the prison." He quickly gave Nolan the details of what he had learned. "I said I'd leave it up to you to decide, but if you think it's good for Kozy to hear I've got the go-ahead to set up a video conference with him tomorrow night."

"Go ahead and set it up, Kurt," he said. "I'll do all I can to get Kozy to agree to it." *Even if I have to fall on my knees and beg her.*

***

Nolan was surprised at her lack of resistance when he told her that, at Betsy's request, Kurt had met with Bill Waltz, a retired prison guard who had witnessed the prison riot that Ted Hanner had been involved in. It was as though Kozy were summoning courage for a final blow. He hated the pain he saw in her eyes, and the quiet resignation was enough to make him consider calling off the video conference. However, that wouldn't be right, and Kozy's mother had somehow known that it was in her daughter's best interest to learn what had really happened. Painful as it might be, Nolan knew that this story was one more step Kozy needed in order to be free of the fears that haunted her.

She had felt jumpy and embarrassed as she waited for Nolan to set up the computer for the Skype session. She sat clutching Nolan's hand when the man appeared on the screen. He looked ordinary: a round faced, balding man dressed in a black t-shirt. He had a crooked smile and kind looking blue eyes. Not scary at all, but what had she expected a former prison guard to look like?

After the awkward introductions, the man began his narrative.

"I didn't know your father personally, Miss Hanner. But I was on duty during the short-lived riot that took his life." The man shut his eyes at the memory. "Sorry," he said after a moment. "Even after twenty years it still affects me to recall."

Kozy bit her lip. "I'm sorry to put you through this," she whispered.

He shook his head and continued. "One guard, who was a friend of mine, and two inmates were killed that day. Lots of injuries, too. I won't go into details, but somehow several of the more violent inmates managed to get a hold of enough pilfered metal to fashion some sharp instruments. Couple of them managed to jump my buddy, slit his throat, grabbed his weapon, and went to wreak havoc wherever they could. The instigator was a big guy, strong as an ox, always with an extra ugly attitude. They called him 'Spike.' By the time the alarm went out, he had got into an area where the prison chaplain worked. In a crazed frenzy he went after the chaplain who was in the middle of counseling two inmates. When the inmates saw Spike going for the chaplain, they threw themselves onto the chaplain, shielding him with their own bodies. One of those inmates was your father, Miss Hanner. He took a shot in the gut right before Spike was cut down by a guard. By the time things were settled down enough to get medics inside, your father had bled out."

Kozy's face turned white. Her hands shook even though Nolan held them tight. In spite of the succinct telling, the story impressed itself indelibly on her mind. She could picture the chaos and terror in living color. It made her stomach churn.

"I wish there were more I could tell you," Mr. Waltz apologized. "As I said, I didn't know Ted Hanner personally. But I was well acquainted with the chaplain, Father Al. He was middle aged at the time and passed on years later of natural causes. He thought it was a shame that Ted was ever put into our facility. He was a young kid who got himself into things he shouldn't have, but he wasn't a violent man. Father Al always considered your father a tragic hero, and had he known where to find your mother, he would surely have shared the story with her."

Kozy tried to voice her appreciation to the man for taking the time with her, but her throat was tight and dry. In the end, it was Nolan who thanked him and Kurt for bringing the truth to light.

Chapter 29

The manila envelopes had sat undisturbed on Kozy's coffee table for weeks. She had immersed herself in her teaching duties and the myriad activities involved in wrapping up the school year. Her final reports were turned in, and her classroom clean. She had even given herself a week of rest. Still she hadn't summoned the courage to open them. *This is the last correspondence I will ever have from my mother. I should welcome it.* She sank onto the couch, grim faced, and ran her fingers nervously through her hair. Last night's report from Bill Waltz had taken her by surprise. That her father would have acted heroically was something she had never considered. Trying to reconcile the new information had just added more confusion to her already muddled thoughts. *What am I to think?* She thought she wanted the truth. *Is that what I want?* Well, if truth was the goal, she wasn't going to find it on her own. She had no more excuses to avoid reading the letter her mother left for her. Her hands trembled as she broke the seal on the thinnest envelope. *Help me, Lord.*

She pulled out the typewritten pages and began to read.

Dear Kozy,

I'm so grateful for having had the chance to get to know you. Thank you. Your grandmother did a wonderful job raising you; I can take no credit. But I'm proud of the woman you have become. I wish you would have let me talk about your father. With so little time left, I don't want to ruin what progress we've made by forcing you to listen if you aren't comfortable. Maybe once I'm gone (if you are reading this, then I am) you might be willing to hear me out. It's not what you think. I understand now.

Kozy paused in her reading, heartsick that she had refused to listen to her mother when doing so might have brought her a degree of comfort. She was truly grateful for having been given the time to reconcile with Betsy. God had given her a precious gift, yet she had still resisted surrendering all of her pain. *I'm sorry I didn't trust you enough, Lord.* Her confession gave her the courage to continue. She read the remainder of the letter quickly. Then she went over it again slowly, digesting every word, trying to summon what she'd long suppressed.

Images from her recent nightmares melded with bits of memories that tried to surface. What was real and what wasn't? She had to believe her mother. But it was still so confusing. Then in a moment of clarity she saw him. His hair was long, stringy, and blond. She could see a tattoo of a snake on one of his pale arms. His breath was stale with tobacco, and she gagged at the heavy odor emanating from under his arms. "Come on. Come with Daddy." He was grinning with long crooked teeth, laughing at her confusion, touching her in a way that scared her. She heard her own ineffective squeal. Felt the effort of her fighting, kicking, pinching, anything to get him away. Then the taste of blood as she bit the soft flesh until she thought her teeth might break off.

He had yelled, cursed, and slapped. She knew now that it had been real. With more cursing and a little whimpering, he had shoved her into the little bedroom she shared with her mommy. He turned the key in the lock and she heard the retreating sound of footsteps. A door slammed hard. She was glad, until the minutes had turned into hours. She had to go to the bathroom, but was afraid to make a sound. Where was Mommy? She held it in until it hurt too much and then she cried in silent shame when she felt the warm liquid roll down her legs and onto the beige carpet.

***

Kozy didn't know how long she had sat there, her mother's letter still clutched in her hands. Long enough that her legs were stiff and made her move clumsily as she walked to her bedroom. She opened the top drawer of her dresser and retrieved the old and yellowed folders. Skimming through the records from San Diego Children's Services, she realized that she hadn't paid enough attention before to notice the discrepancy in the numbered pages. *Oh Gram, I wonder what compelled you to destroy those pages? Were you trying to protect me? Or was it Betsy's memory you protected?*

She plopped herself on her bed and stared blankly at the wall. Yes, unraveling and reliving the memory had hurt. Yet somehow, facing it head on had diminished its sting. It was in the past, after all. How had things gotten so mixed up? How could she have been so mistaken? She had held onto her anger like a hard-won prize. Her little girl instinct had been to forget and suppress the pain of betrayal and shame. Gram's love and acceptance had nurtured and sustained her until the time came that she had surrendered to the unconditional love of Christ. She thought her surrender had been complete, but she was wrong. *I wanted to hold on to my anger. I didn't want to forgive everything. I must have sensed you'd ask me to.*

She sighed and lifted the remaining manila envelope. She gave it a shake and guessed at the contents. In anticipation she sat cross-legged on the bed and emptied the envelope. Photographs. Eagerly, she spread the snapshots across the bed. The only photos she ever had from her earliest years had been those two that Betsy had included with her identification papers when she made the rash choice to change her identity. Now, Kozy stared at dozens of images ranging from the day of her birth until she was about four. Betsy had penciled the dates on the back of each picture. She smiled as she arranged the pictures in order.

The largest photograph still lay face down. Kozy read the date scribbled on the back. It was the date of her third birthday. Her heart pounded as she turned the picture over. It was a picture of her at the beach, in the arms of a young man. A younger version of Betsy stood grinning beside them. Kozy studied the image of the slender man. He was handsome, with tanned skin, short brown hair, and a gentle smile.

She was mesmerized by the scene in the photograph. The ocean was in the background, and a tiny sailboat was visible in the distance.

I remember this.

She allowed her mind to carry her back in time. She felt the rhythm of the waves hitting the shore, the warmth of the sun on her skin, and her hand in the hand of her father. She felt the wet sand between her toes and smelled the salty air. She could hear the raucous call of a seagull and her own giggle. Then, a familiar voice calling her name.

"Kozy, bring your daddy back! He's hungry! Come see what we have to eat."

Spread out on the sand was a red and white striped blanket. She could see her mother laying out fruit, sandwiches, and a small round cake. The cake had three candles on top, their dancing flames awaiting her wish. Kozy let the memories wash over her and felt their comfort. She traced her finger lightly on the face in the picture.

"I'm so sorry, Daddy," she whispered. "I didn't know."

***

Later that afternoon, she was awakened from her reverie by a phone call from Nolan.

"You doing all right?" Nolan inquired.

The concern in his voice was clear, and it warmed her heart

"I'm fine, Nolan." She realized, after saying it, that she meant it. She still had some thinking to do, but she felt more at peace than she had for weeks.

"I can come over, or we could go out if you feel like it." Nolan tried hard to not sound desperate. He wondered if he had done the right thing, encouraging Kozy to face so much about her past. The thing with her father seemed positive, or at least he thought so. He thought that it would certainly be a relief to Kozy to know the kind of man her father was, that he died saving someone's life.

During the Skype session the night before, she had listened in silence while Mr. Waltz shared his story. Nolan was not sure what he expected Kozy's reaction would be, but it definitely was not the quiet confusion she had shown. His motivation had been to bring her healing.

"Trust me," he had told her. Had he forced her to face a trauma she wasn't yet ready to face? She was preoccupied and introspective when she sent him home as soon as the interview had ended. She had not seemed angry with him, just quiet and distant. She had wanted to be alone so she could try to process what she had learned. He did not want to leave her, but he did as he was asked. He barely slept during the night, and now he ached to see her. He wanted to know she was all right. He waited anxiously for her response.

Kozy wanted to be with Nolan, and experience the comfort his presence was sure to bring. She longed to share with him what she had learned from her mother's letter. But the revelation was too fresh, her understanding, too tenuous. Another evening alone would give her a better grasp on her feelings. She looked in the dresser mirror at her disheveled hair, the dark circles under her eyes, and her stained sweatshirt. *I look awful.* She allowed a huge yawn to overtake her.

"I just can't tonight, Nolan," she said. "I'm too exhausted. I need to go to bed soon."

But it's only six o'clock! Nolan kept his thoughts to himself. He loved her too much to push her.

"How about tomorrow?" Kozy offered. "We could talk in the morning."

Nolan threw away caution. "Have you ever watched the sunrise over the park pond?"

"The sunrise?" she asked with a hint of humor that renewed his hope. "Surely you're not asking me to get up in the dark?"

"Well, if you're going to bed early anyway. I've heard it's an awesome sight, and I would love to watch a beautiful sunrise with the most beautiful woman in town." He wasn't too proud to use flattery.

"How does a girl resist that kind of talk?" She closed her eyes and smiled. "What time?"

***

The weatherman had promised a perfect Saturday, and he was true to his word. Kozy, a little bleary-eyed, was dressed in jeans and t-shirt and ready to go when Nolan's headlights appeared in her driveway early the next morning.

233

They drove the short distance to the park in a comfortable silence.

Wisely, Nolan gave her the space she needed. *She'll talk when she's ready. We'll just enjoy the moment.*

In the rosy half-light of early dawn, Nolan led them to a bench in front of the small pond. He pulled a paper towel from his pocket and wiped the morning dew off the seat. Kozy smiled at his thoughtfulness. They sat shoulder to shoulder and watched as the new day unfolded, bathing the sky in vibrant swaths of magenta, gold, and purple. The colors were mirrored beautifully on the water. A lone white duck made a swath that rippled the glassy surface. Birds began to call to one another in the surrounding trees, their songs combined to create a symphony of sound that expanded to a crescendo. The birdsong gradually faded away to silence.

"It almost feels like we're on holy ground," she murmured.

He turned to her with a smile before shifting his gaze back to the sunrise. They sat silently, each lost in their own thoughts. And then, as suddenly as it began, it was over. Only baby blue sky remained, dotted here and there with cotton candy clouds. He took her hand and pulled her to her feet. They strolled together until they came to the crest of a long, gentle slope.

The idea struck both of them at the same moment.

"How long has it been since you rolled down a hill?" Nolan asked, smiling from ear to ear.

"Ages and ages," she answered with eyes wide. "Let's do it!" She hesitated as a woman passed by them with two dogs in tow. "But Nolan," she giggled, "what if there's some—you know—the dogs?"

"Ah. Gotcha!" Nolan skittered to the bottom of the hill, and slowly worked his way up, scanning the surface for anything suspicious. "Looks good!" he announced as he reached the top of the hill.

"I'll push," she volunteered as Nolan lowered himself to the ground. She gave him a shove and watched him roll. He gained more and more speed as he went until the terrain leveled out and he slowed to a gradual stop. He looked up with a wide grin and motioned for her.

"Here goes," she said to herself when she pushed off. "Catch me, Nolan!" she squealed as she began her lightning descent. He scrambled to his knees and waited with arms extended and caught her as she reached the bottom, nearly bowling him over. They laughed until tears streamed down their faces.

"Why, Mr. Calderon," she teased once she had gained some control over her laughter, "your hair is all mussed!"

He looked her over and said evenly, "Well, Miss Hanner, you look a little disheveled yourself." He stood then, pulling her to her feet, and flicked grass clippings from her shoulder. "So there!"

She tried hard to suppress a giggle, but it escaped from her throat. She sobered then, her brown eyes carefully searching his gray ones. His heart thumped in his chest as she drew closer. He reached out, and she stepped into his arms. Her mouth was next to his ear as she spoke in the quietest whisper.

"If you ask me now, I'll say 'yes.'"

"What?" He jerked his head back and searched her face. "Did you say—do you mean it, Kozy? Are you saying you'll marry me?"

She stood chewing her trembling lip. "If you still want to marry me, I mean, unless you've changed your mind."

"No chance of that," he said breathlessly. "I love you so much." She melted into his embrace as his lips met hers. Sounds of laughter reached them as a group of teenagers assembled for a game of Ultimate Frisbee in the field next to them. Reluctantly, he reined in his feelings. He stepped away but didn't release her hand. They circled the edge of the pond and settled onto a bench in a more secluded area. The questions were in his eyes as he waited for her to speak.

"After talking with Mr. Waltz about my father's death, I forced myself read my mother's letter." She pulled her legs up on the bench and hugged her knees. "She had tried over and over to talk about him, but I stopped her each time. The nightmares made me think of him as a monster. I refused to listen. I feel so bad about that now," she confessed in a whisper. "It turned out that the person in my nightmares wasn't my dad at all."

"I don't understand. How could you not know who your dad was?"

She shook her head. "I guess I had worked so hard to forget all the stuff that happened when I was put into foster care." She stared down at her feet as she gave him some details from her mother's letter. "My mother did manage to stay clean long enough to regain custody sometime that first year. I had completely shut out the memory. We lived in an apartment building, and one of the neighbors befriended us. He seemed nice. He paid extra attention to me. He offered to watch me while she worked extra hours at her waitressing job."

"Oh, Kozy." Nolan searched her face. "Don't. You don't need to tell me if it hurts too much."

"No, Nolan. I need to say it out loud. Once I read what my mom had to say, I started remembering. He tried to molest me but I think I hurt him worse than he hurt me," she said with a grim smile. "I fought back with everything I had. When I bit him, he whimpered like the cowardly lion. It's no wonder I always hated that part of *The Wizard of Oz*. He looked like that too, with his long reddish hair and pasty skin." She shuddered but after a moment continued.

"When Betsy got home from work late that night, she found me locked in our room. He had gone off on a drinking binge and forgot all about me. But she could see how I had been slapped hard, and when he came back she confronted him. She saw where I had bit and scratched him. She felt devastated by her failure to protect me. She took me back to Children's Services the next day, voluntarily giving back custody. She was convinced that she wasn't fit to care for me. Maybe she gave up too easily. Who knows? I always looked on those years in foster care in a negative way, but now I can see that maybe she wouldn't have been able to keep me safe. After being given the chance to know her, I now know she loved me and she did what she thought was best at the time. I realize that it was wrong of me to act as though God had abandoned Shaina when she was put into foster care. Sure, I wish things were different for her, but I need to trust Shaina to him as well."

She pulled him up from the bench and, hands entwined, they continued on the path around the pond. "Oh!" Kozy exclaimed. "And Betsy left me a photo of my dad! He doesn't look anything like the other man, and now that I saw him, I've been getting bits and pieces of memories coming back to me. I think our times together were good."

"It sounds like you've forgiven him."

"How could I not, Nolan? My mother loved him. And he was so young, years younger than I am now. He made some stupid mistakes, but in the end he did a great thing. He gave his own life to save another."

"I wish you could know for sure if …." He stopped himself, unable to utter the words.

She nodded, knowingly. "If he accepted Christ before he died? Yes, it would be nice to know, but I have peace with what I do know. Why would God have given me this chance to find out the truth if there was no hope? I've forgiven my real daddy, and as far as the other man, I realized last night that I had to let go of the hatred for him also. I am in no way excusing what he tried to do, but I'm praying for him to know forgiveness. I knew it was the only way to have the courage to overcome my fears. I thought of Gram, the courage it took for her to leave everything she knew just to have a chance of living free. She was alone and had to learn a different language, not to mention losing her husband and her only child. Yet, she still was able to face life with courage and faith."

"I remember my friend and faith mentor, Carrieanne. She faced limitations that would have embittered the average person. Yet every chance she got, she embraced life. She refused to let fear rob her of her joy."

"Yet there I was, afraid to face a memory. Afraid I might have to forgive. Afraid I might fail like my parents did if I dared to have children of my own. There I was, a girl with good health, friends, and a job I love, with the best boyfriend anyone could ask for."

He clasped her hand harder and stopped her on the path. He lifted her chin and kissed her.

Her face flushed. "Ahem. Where was I?" she asked, once her heart rate slowed.

Nolan grinned. "Uh, something about having the best boyfriend."

"Yes, this wonderful guy," she continued, placing her hands on his chest, "who declared his love to me, then proved it by being willing to be my best friend until I was able to come to my senses. I have always loved kids, Nolan. I guess I allowed my fears to cloud my thinking. No one is immune from making mistakes. Granted, my parents made some pretty big ones that had terrible consequences. But you were right. I'm not them." She clenched her fists. "Life is risky, but I'd be dishonoring to God to continue to live in fear that I might not do everything perfectly, as though he weren't a loving enough God to forgive."

"*1 John 4:18: 'There is no fear in love, but perfect love casts out fear ….'*"

"Why, yes," she said with lifted brow.

"Years of Bible quizzing," Nolan explained with a shrug. "It sticks with a person."

She grinned. "Anyway, I'm not afraid anymore, Nolan. I do want children."

"I would have married you anyway, Kozy. I love you. But I am glad you changed your mind."

"I love you, too, Nolan." Her eyes glistened.

His thumb caught the single tear that trailed down her cheek. "Happy tears, I hope?"

She nodded. "Yes. Happy tears."

"Then it's settled. We're getting married! Whoopee!" He laughed as he grabbed her and twirled her around in a circle.

Their revelry was interrupted by a ping from Nolan's phone. Stopping, Nolan frowned as he pulled the phone from his pocket and checked.

"Text from Marcy," he told Kozy. "Hmm. It's an invite for breakfast. She says she's making a mountain of blueberry pancakes." He chuckled. "Shall we accept?"

"Are you kidding?" Kozy's eyes opened wide. "All of a sudden I feel like a bear that just came out of hibernation!"

With a grin he texted back, "make room for 2 - c u soon!"

***

Marcy could sense something was up as soon as Nolan and Kozy sauntered into the kitchen, both smiling from ear to ear. She added a final pancake to the stack and popped the roasting pan back into the warm oven. Tom and Zane were already seated at the table. The three looked questioningly at the couple who stood hand in hand.

Nolan looked at Kozy and took a deep breath. "We have something to announce," he began.

"Hold on a moment, please," Marcy interrupted. "I have a feeling that this is something Kelsey won't want to miss." She stepped out into the hallway and called urgently up the stairs, "Kelsey sweetheart, please stop whatever you are doing and get down here—quickly!"

It took only a minute for Kelsey to plod down the stairs, but the moments dragged on as they all listened to the ticking clock. "What?" she asked grumpily as she finally entered the kitchen.

"Shush, slow poke," said Zane. "Nolan has something he wants to tell us."

Kozy's cheeks flamed. Nolan stood grinning at the expectant faces. "We're getting married!" he announced.

Kelsey, all smiles now, squealed and rushed over to give Kozy a hug. "Finally! We'll have even numbers in the family—three boys and three girls!"

Marcy stepped up. "We're so happy for you, Kozy," she said. "You've felt like family from the first time we met you."

"So, what are your plans? Have you picked a date? What can we do to help? How many bridesmaids are you having?" Questions bombarded Kozy on all sides as she smiled nervously. Nolan came to her rescue then and called for quiet.

"I'm afraid we haven't had time to discuss any details yet. We just wanted to share our happiness with you all for now, so …." He sniffed the air. "It smells awfully good in here. Why don't we eat?"

Tom asked a short but heartfelt blessing for the food and for the news they had just received. Then Nolan lifted the roaster out of the oven. Kelsey and Zane descended on it with enthusiasm. Marcy set the milk carton on the table, then stepped behind her husband's chair and wrapped her arms around him in a happy embrace. Tom turned his head to meet her face and gave her a quick kiss.

"Mom! Dad! Yuk! Do you always have to act so mushy?" Zane complained as he sat back at his place with his loaded plate. "We're trying to eat!"

"Must you be so juvenile, little brother?" Kelsey countered with a dramatic roll of her eyes. "I, for one, think that a little romance is sweet!"

"I am not your little brother," he said defensively. "I'm taller than you. We're the same age. You're only two minutes older because you couldn't wait your turn!"

"Children!" Marcy's eyes narrowed with the warning look that told them that the bickering had gone on long enough. She gave Kozy a wink as the twins grinned sheepishly and then resumed their competition over the number of pancakes they could each devour.

Kozy sat down at the table and looked happily around at the Calderon family. *Abba, bless this dear family! Thank you that I will soon become an official part of it!*

***

Late that afternoon, Tom walked into the kitchen where Marcy was preparing a light supper of tossed Italian salad and tomato basil soup. "Have a nice nap?"

"Mm-hmm," he said, stifling a yawn. "I shouldn't have slept so long."

"You've had a busy week, and you needed that rest, so stop feeling guilty." She turned, kissing his unshaven cheek and running her hand over his rumpled hair. "The Lawsons will be dropping the twins off shortly."

"Now I really regret sleeping away the afternoon while we had the house to ourselves," he declared as he stretched his arms.

"Oh, we weren't alone, dear." She pointed a thumb toward the window facing the backyard.

He peeked out. "Nolan and Kozy are still here?"

She watched through the window to where the two sat cross-legged on the picnic table facing one another, smiling, laughing. "Deep into the wedding plans. They've already decided that they'd like to marry before the new school year begins—whichever weekend fits in with your schedule."

"Well then, we'll have to start right away on their prenuptial counseling."

"You're not concerned that they're moving too quickly?"

His brow wrinkled as he contemplated. "No, not at all. We've watched these last months while they each experienced some pretty extreme emotional upheaval. I have to say that they've both handled themselves well. They have been faithful and supportive with each other in a remarkable way. From what I know of our son, and Kozy, I'm convinced that Christ will be at the center of their marriage. They're ready."

Marcy smiled and lifted her chin. "I was thinking along those same lines, myself. While you were napping, they asked if we'd mind if they spent their free time here in the coming weeks. So we can chaperone."

"They said that?"

She nodded. "They intend to do things right. They want their wedding night to be special."

"Then Nolan really has taken my teaching to heart. I feel blessed."

"And he's learned by example," Marcy added.

He wrapped his arms around her. "Ah, Marcy," he said softly. "I well remember that exquisite torture while I counted down the days until our wedding."

"Mm-hmm," she murmured as she cuddled into his embrace.

"The rest of the summer will be pretty hectic, I suppose," he said with a sigh.

"I'm sure."

"I'm happy to take care of the ceremony, but I won't have to be involved in all the other rigmarole, will I?"

Marcy looked at him with narrowed eyes. "Rigmarole? Tom darling, this is family. We're all in this together. Of course you'll be involved, and you'll enjoy every moment. I promise."

He groaned. "If you say so."

She planted a loud kiss on his pouting lips. "I do say so," she laughed.

Chapter 30

"You Calderons are certainly miracle workers," Wendy said as she and Marcy watched the bride and groom make their rounds of greetings. "It's hard to believe you managed to pull this all together in four weeks."

Marcy beamed at the compliment. "It was a true joint effort," she admitted. "Kozy thought she had no family to help her plan a wedding. But she's seemed like family to us from the moment we realized how much Nolan loved her, and the church family adores her. Our ladies' hospitality group insisted on helping provide the potluck after the ceremony just as they did for mine and Tom's wedding."

"And your Nolan is so thoughtful. The happiness on Kozy's face as she saw her students sitting in the front rows with Cathy was a sight to behold. And when she realized Nolan had arranged for all of her grandmother's friends to come, it brought tears to my eyes."

"Like I said, it was a joint effort. We really appreciate Vince for volunteering to drive the rental van to pick them up."

Wendy let out a chortle. "Vince admitted he was practically swooning with the aroma of chicken paprika permeating the van all the way from Cleveland. He could hardly wait for the ceremony to be over so he could taste it. They may be old, but those little Hungarian ladies still know how to cook!"

Marcy sank onto a folding chair and discreetly wiggled out of her high heels. "Ouch. The price we women pay to look elegant!"

"Well, I'm sure it was well worth a blister or two," Wendy continued. "How I'd love to have those slender legs of yours. The twins looked so proud to be best man and maid of honor. It was sweet of Kozy and Nolan to ask them. It really made it a family affair, what with Tom performing the ceremony."

"Tom was elated. I could tell he was having a hard time keeping his emotions under control. He's so happy for Nolan." She smiled. "It really was a great wedding, wasn't it? Low-key, relaxed, and full of joy, the way it ought to be. Kozy was so beautiful in her simple white gown."

"Yeah," Wendy agreed with a giggle. "Nolan couldn't keep his eyes off of her."

"You know, Wendy, there are so many awful things happening in the world today, it makes you scared for your kids. But Nolan and Kozy, I think they're going to be fine. They've already faced an awful lot together, and they're committed to keeping God at the center of their relationship. It gives a person hope for the future."

***

Ben gave a wide sweep of his arm as he stood at the open back door of Nolan's car.

"What's this?" Nolan asked warily. "You are my best friend, but I don't remember inviting you to go along on my honeymoon!"

"Never fear, you two," Ben snickered. "Nikki and I are only here to see to it that you get safely to the lake cottage. It was your dad's idea. He told us that when he and Marcy left for their honeymoon, he stopped so many times to kiss Marcy that it took them twice as long to get there as it should have."

"Whoa, Ben! Too much information!" Nolan interrupted with a grimace. "My dad's honeymoon is not an image I want in my mind." His eyes honed in on the enticing smile of his bride. *Hmm … Maybe not a bad idea to have a chauffeur after all.* "But we'll want our vehicle to use."

"No worries," Ben assured. "Kurt and his girlfriend are following behind to take us home."

"Oh, Kurt and Lila are just friends," Nolan clarified.

Ben frowned. "Huh? Just friends? Oh, well, whatever."

Nolan looked back to where Kurt's vehicle sat idling. Kurt and Lila waved cheerfully.

"Meanwhile," Ben continued, "you and Kozy can do all the smooching you want for the next half hour. We'll barely even take notice."

Kozy squeezed his hand and looked at him with wide eyes. "Sounds like a great idea," she whispered.

"Okay, you talked us into it," Nolan agreed as he helped his bride into the back and scooted in next to her. He immediately took advantage of Ben's suggestion.

"We might have to open the window a mite so I can see to drive with all the steam coming from back there," he said in an exaggerated whisper to Nikki.

"Just shut up and drive, Ben," Nolan growled as he gave his bride one more leisurely kiss.

"Yes, Ben, for goodness sakes, don't be such a tease! Has it been so long that you've forgotten how they feel?" Nikki turned and gazed smugly at the newlyweds.

Nolan and Kozy exchanged a tender look, and then Nolan leaned forward to reach under the front seat. "Ah, here it is!" He handed over the gift bag with a flourish. "For you, Mrs. Calderon, from your loving husband. Guaranteed to please."

Kozy tilted her head, her curiosity piqued, then carefully broke the seal and looked inside. He relished the joyful look of surprise on her face as she realized what she was holding.

"Oh, Nolan. I had no idea they were publishing a new cookbook!" She ran her fingers over the glossy, paprika-colored cover. "Why, it's beautiful!"

"Very professionally done," Nolan agreed. "But it's much more than a cookbook. Mrs. Dobos says it also includes a history of the church and lots of vintage pictures."

"Oh my!" Kozy tried in vain to blink back tears as she flipped through the pages. "They've included Gram's best recipes, and look! Here's a photo of the group of refugees they sponsored back in 1957. There she is, Maria Hegedus. She looks so young!"

Nolan scrutinized the black and white image. "I can see the family resemblance," he said. "Looks like the shape of your eyes came from your grandmother. And I can see a touch of your mom's smile there, too."

Kozy clasped the book tenderly to her chest. "I'll cherish this book always. Not only for what it is, but because of your thoughtfulness in giving it to me on our wedding day. Thank you," she finished in a whisper as she cuddled close to him.

"Well, Mrs. Dobos was a good salesperson," he admitted. "The money was going for such a good cause that I bought a half dozen. I figured that you could always give them away as gifts."

She straightened in her seat and shook her head vigorously. "No way!" she cried. "This is a family heirloom, Nolan. We have to keep them to give to our children!"

"Just how many kids are we planning, my dear?" he asked with a grin.

"We don't know how many little ones God might bless us with," she said, her face turning a lovely shade of pink, "so we'd better keep them all just in case."

From the front seat Nikki whispered to Ben, "Oh, I hope they have a little boy first! Wouldn't it be fun if our Emmy and he—?"

Ben looked aghast at his wife until he saw the twinkle in her eyes.

"Just kidding," she said with a grin. She turned her attention to the scenery as they approached the entrance to the Lake District.

Naturally, little Emmy has decades to go before she's ready for marriage. But Kurt and Lila … now that's a different story. "Just friends" indeed!